# The Lace Makers

## Kate Ingersoll

*Acknowledgements*

I am indebted to the dedicated researchers and historians who paved the road for my own journey into writing this novel.  For those who endured slavery and the concentration camps, I am deeply grateful to have been led to their written and recorded memories, particularly Mendel Grossman, whose photographs profoundly illustrate why the innumerable stories of Holocaust need to stay alive through words, music, film, and pictures.

In the winter of 2014, I finally watched *Schindler's List*. The experience was heart-wrenching, but not as much as viewing the first-hand accounts of Holocaust survivors, liberators, and family members who were filmed through the Shoah Foundation program.  Sincere thanks to Steven Spielberg and his production company for their determination to provide such a valuable resource for future generations.

For everyone who has worked to create or maintain the Holocaust Museums in Washington D.C., and Farmington Hills, Michigan, and the historic residences in Mount Vernon, Williamsburg, Monticello, and Greenfield Village, I thank you all for providing tangible ways to learn about the sorrows of the past so that they might never be repeated.

To whomever shared the lovely cover photograph on Google and allowed it to be used for free digital download, I thank you kindly.

Heartfelt thanks to Michelle Thomas for discovering some hidden treasures within the shelves at Sanger Library...and to Allison Fiscus, Carole Malczewski, and the rest of the staff for their encouragement and support during the writing of this novel.

Joy and love to Clara Rona who shared her past with benevolence and clarity. Her story has been a treasure chest filled with endless gifts of grace. And to Nancy Hattner, Amber Hall, James Dickerson, and Lynda Dolgin-Duda for being gracious and honest every step of the way.

Many thanks to Richard Reese for his love, kindness, generosity of spirit, and incomparable encouragement. And to my sweet Aunt Karen for showing me how to begin at the end.

Love and gratitude to Tony Zimkowski for his stalwart presence as I found both my inner and outer voice through writing this novel.

Thanks once again to Joyce Yarnell, Zee Czerniak, and Becky Boyle for their incredible dedication to detail, to Barb Peters for her eternal optimism, and to Deb Macdonald for sharing heartfelt memories of her mother.

Vielen dank zu Edith Kippenhan fur ihr wunderbare Nachhilfe in alles Deutsche. Ihr sanfte Fuhrung immer half mir die richtigen Worte zu finden.

And as always, to the Source of all things, I am most grateful.

*for my grandfather*
*who helped to free my little caged bird*

*and for Tony*
*who taught her how to fly*

*A note to the reader*

THE LACE MAKERS is told in alternating chapters through the voices of Sapphire, an eight-year-old girl living as a slave in Lincoln County, Tennessee, and Karin, a nineteen-year-old German girl surviving the Holocaust in a Nazi concentration camp. I wrote their chapters in sequence as their narratives intertwine and often reflect each other; however, you may wish to read Sapphire's story first and then Karin's (or vice versa).

If you do read them separately, I suggest that you wait until you have finished them both before reading the epilogue.

This novel is a work of fiction. Names, characters, businesses, places, events, and incidents are either the products of the author's imagination or used in a fictitious manner. Any resemblance to actual persons, living or dead, or actual events is purely coincidental.

*No man can put a chain about the ankle of his fellow man*
*without at last finding the other end fastened about his own neck.*

Frederick Douglass

*The life of the dead is placed in the memories of the living.*
*The love you gave in life keeps people alive beyond their time.*
*Anyone who was given love will always live on in another's heart.*

Marcus Tillius Cicero

# Sapphire

The sun be peeping over the old barn where I hear the cow moaning to get milked. The air sharp like little pins and needles where my arms be peeking out from my shawl. I watch the sky turning the color a egg yolks Mama like to break jest to watch 'em get runny. She do that sometimes. Break them egg yolks for Massa and keep on frying 'em 'til they be hard as shoe leather.

He don't say nothing. Jest gobble 'em up like they be the best thing he ever et. Sometime Massa even say, "Lord, Ruby...these eggs are truly delicious."

He know to keep his mouth shut 'round Mama 'bout eggs and such. He be the Massa and all, but he owe my mama a lot. He owe her a husband. He owe me my daddy.

Massa done gambled Daddy away in a poker game two year ago. He told a mean old man that 'stead a paying him money, that man could take any one a his slaves. My sisters and me was scared out our minds...'fraid one a us gone be chained to his wagon and made to stumble 'hind like a dern mule as Mister Rotten drove back to his plantation.

They be older than me...my sisters, Pearl and Opal. When my daddy got taken away, I was only six. They was fourteen and twelve back then. Big girls. Now they has husbands and Pearl be having a baby a her own come summertime. Opal say a baby be coming over her dead body, but I don't know what that mean. She gone kill herself when the baby come? Or she not want any babies at all? I hear some slaves kill they own babies, but I cain't imagine my mama doing such a thing 'cause she loves me like a bird loves to fly.

I know *I* don't want no babies a my own 'cause I know they ain't gone be mine anyway. They be Massa's. Anything we gots, it be his first.

13

When I tell Opal that, she say, "Sapphire, you is smart! I be chewing my cotton root ever day since Hale and me jumped the broom and you ain't gone find no baby in my belly, no suh. Hale and me say that when we be free, we can has babies then."

I has no idea 'bout what it mean to be free 'cause I been a slave ever since I took my first breath. Since Mama put knitting needles in my hands when I was only three and say, "Play with 'em, Sapphire, and soon you be making hats for Massa's chil'ren." Mama say she done teach me how to sew and make lace and all them fancy things so I can stay with her in the big house, not like my sisters who gots to work in the fields and such. I's lucky 'cause I get to be with Mama always...and that jest the way I like it.

My sisters be called Pearl and Opal and I called Sapphire 'cause Daddy say he got him a bunch a precious jewels living under his roof, such as it be. I's born on a night when the sky be as blue as a sapphire. That how I got my name, even though my eyes be green.

Green jest like Massa's.

I figure I gone be his slave 'til the day I die...or 'til he do. But Opal say the war that be raging all over the country be 'bout setting us all free, that one day, they ain't gone be no more slaves.

What gone happen then? Will I get taken from Mama...or she from me? What from I already done seen, they ain't no telling.

Two year ago, Pearl and Opal was standing near the barn when that mean man, Mister Rotten, stumble toward the place where my daddy do his work. Mister Rotten not be his real name, but I's naughty and call him that under my breath whenever he come on Massa's land. His real name be Mister Birch like them trees growing in the back a our shack. But the only thing white 'bout Mister Rotten be his skin 'cause his words be black as tar and his soul be dark as the bottom of the well where I pull up buckets a water to tote to the big house.

When Mister Rotten went past the folks in the yard, I heard him yelling, "You niggers get back to work!" He and Maasa was drunk as skunks. I could tell by the way they was walking, and ain't nothing good ever come when Massa be drinking.

Daddy look up from the anvil where he been banging on a piece a iron. He be the best horseshoe maker in the county. Or least he was. Now he dead, so I 'magine him in heaven doing God's bidding.

Mama was in the house with me on that horrible day. She been cooking supper while I sat knitting at the table near the open window so I could hear what was going on outside. Mama always say I has a gift from the Father God Almighty. She tell me I make lace an angel be proud to wear. When she say that, I feel my chest puff up and my heart grow wings.

But not on the day Daddy got taken away from me.

Mister Rotten pointed his shaky finger toward the barn. "That buck's uglier than sin," he snarled. "But he'll do just fine."

Mama knew something bad gone happen, and she always been right 'bout things like that. "You has the gift a lace-making, Sapphire," she told me one time. "But you also has the gift a insight, jest like I has it and my mama and her mama 'fore her."

"What *insight*?" I asked.

"Knowing when things gone happen," Mama said. "Like a prophecy."

I looked at her like I still confuse.

"Don't worry, baby girl," Mama told me. "You gone learn how it feel soon enough."

And ain't it the truth if I do.

When Mama ran to the barn after Massa and Mister Rotten, I felt a little cornbread I jest et start to curl up in my stomach and fix to pop right back out. It didn't though, jest ride up my throat a little, but I swallowed it back down.

"Massa Sam!" Mama cried, running like her feet on fire. "Please Massa Sam...*please* don't let him take my babies!"

By the time she reached Massa, she was shaking 'cause she so upset. Angry and scared both, and I ain't never seen her like that 'fore. I stood in the doorway a the kitchen, my heart banging in my chest, but I couldn't move 'cause my feets felt like they was nailed to the floor.

Mama pulled on Massa's sleeve, crying, "Please Sam...don't give him my Pearl or Opal! I begging you! I do anything you want. *Please!*"

Massa looked at Mama and a strange look crossed his face. He ain't never hit none a us. Run a clean plantation where the slaves be happy to work -- or at least that how he tell it. He be the boss, the overseer, *and* the owner all in one. Not like some a them plantations we hear 'bout from Earle, the slave who sometime ride along with Mister Rotten when they make deliveries to the big house. Earle say some slaves get whipped. Some get hung 'til they nearly dead. Some get sold to places far away from Lincoln County, Tennessee.

But Massa ain't never been mean to none a us...least not that I seen. When he been drinking, it always be Missus he take his anger out on and I feel right sorry for her. But when Mama beg Massa, I knowed she done embarrass him in front a Mister Rotten.

*Maybe he gone hit her now*, I thought.

But I ain't never seen no whipping on Settler's Plantation. No hanging neither. There been slaves living here since Massa Settler's daddy built this place fifty year ago. Long 'fore I was born, and ain't nobody ever tell Massa what to do.

'Til now.

When Mama thought Pearl and Opal gone be taken away, she screeched like the devil and pulled on Massa's sleeve. She screamed. She cried. She begged something fierce.

"You got yerself one righteous nigger, Samuel," Mister Rotten said, his voice all mean-like. "But I do like a spitfire...maybe I'll change my mind about that buck."

It then I think Mister Rotton gone take my Mama, so I ran to her side and grabbed her skirt, holding on tight. "Mama," I cried. "Don't let them take you away!"

Massa looked at Mama and his eyes be wet with tears. "You and your girls aren't going anywhere, Ruby. You have my word."

Mama fell at his feet, taking me right on with her. "Thank You, *Jesus*," she wailed. "Thank you, Sam!"

But when she dried her eyes enough to look up, she see my daddy be talking to Massa and Mister Rotten. Daddy's eyes was filling up. He bit his lip. His shoulders shook.

"Mas-sa," I heard him say, the word sticking in his throat. "Massa...please don't do this...I do anything you want. I do *anything*. Work like a dog all winter long. You can hire me out to Massa Birch here...I go to his place to work and then come back and be with Ruby and my chil'ren."

Massa Settler shook his head, and I knowed this be the end, and I ain't never gone see my Daddy again. By the way Masa looked at Mama, I knowed he feel he gone owe us plenty for what he jest done.

Daddy didn't fight. He didn't do nothing but hug Mama. Hug Pearl. Hug Opal. Hug me.

He whispered in my ear, "Baby girl, you and I gone see each other 'gain. We is...I promise. I gone get free and we all going up north once this war be done. I gone come back for all ya."

I didn't say nothing, jest let my tears fall while I hugged my daddy like I was trying to memorize the way he feel. His face was covered in stubbly hair. His muscles was tight. His skin soaked in sweat. He been working hard, but I know this sweat was from fear. Back then, I was too young to know what of, but I learn right quick.

Daddy tried to get free too soon.

He run off once and get his back whipped something awful.

He run off again and get hung from a rope 'til his tongue turned black.

The third time he tried to run and come back to us, Mister Rotten said he done had enough a my daddy and hang him 'til he dead. Ever day since then, I's scared he gone come back and take Mama, too.

But Earle say now Daddy in heaven watching over us every day. "Him and Jesus both," he told me while he be drying my eyes. "They ain't gone let nothing bad happen to you or your sweet mama."

Poor Earle got whipped for crying when Mister Rotten kilt my daddy. I heard it right from the dern horse's mouth 'cause Mister Rotten brag 'bout it to Massa. He say any slave who spill a tear for another one deserve to suffer a little, too.

I know Mister Rotten be the devil right here on earth and he gone suffer plenty on the other side when hell be the only place wicked enough to hold him.

Now the sun rise higher over the barn and I hear a shrill train whistle in the distance. Shivering in my shawl, I head to the big house where Mama be waiting on me to help cook breakfast. It be early April, or so Missus Settler say. She oughta know. Got her nose stuck in books and calendars all day long.

Missus teach me all kinds a things. Like I know it be the day after Palm Sunday, and that be the celebration of Lord Jesus when He come to Jerusalem and all a them folks be waving palm branches and yelling stuff like, "Hosanna!" and "Blessed is He who come in the name of the Lord."

I read all 'bout that in Massa's big Bible.

I can read and write good as his kids, even though that against the law. Missus Settler could in get a heap a trouble if anyone find out, so I keep my mouth shut and my eyes busy whenever she hand me a book. Massa and Missus' kids, Little Sam and Marybelle, be 'round the same age as me, and we all learn together. Marybelle be better at learning figures, but Little Sam and me be quick as lightning with new words.

Missus nice to me and all, but I know my place in the order a things 'round here. Ever time I finish my lessons, Missus say, "Now Sapphire, please go fetch me a cup of tea."

She ain't never ask her kids to do nothing but put they books back on the shelf 'fore they go outside to play. It be then I come back to what Mama call *reality*. She say I may be Missus Settler's student, but I always gone be her slave first. No matter how smart I is, I still gone be colored 'til the day I die.

But then Mama say not to worry 'bout such things. "You cain't change nobody's mind but your own," she tell me. "So keep reading and learning so you can keep on changing for the better."

So I do.

Jest last night I finish the second McGuffey Reader. I read all 'bout Jimmy getting up in the morning. *The sun is just peeping up over the hills in the east*, it say. I memorize them words so I can repeat 'em back to myself while I knit or sew or dust or sweep. *Never forget, 'fore you leave your room, to thank God for His kindness. He is indeed kinder to us than any earthy parent.*

This morning as the sun be rising, I say my prayers and thank the Lord for all the things I love: Mama and my sisters. My lace making and reading and all the things I be learning. And like always, I thank Him for it being one day closer to when I gone see my daddy.

Then I walk to the kitchen where I know Mama gone be breaking Massa's egg yolks and he gone be eating 'em like they fit for God Hisself.

# Karin

At four o'clock in the morning Aufseherin Grese kicks my bunk. I struggle to get up quickly because when I don't wake fast enough, she hits the bottoms of my feet with her baton so bruises won't show on my body. Kapitan Dieter would beat *her* if she left a mark that he could see, but he doesn't seem to take notice when I hobble around for days with swollen feet.

"Number 811993, get *up!*" Grese growls. "Kapitan Dieter wants you! NOW!" She sharply pokes me in the ribs and shines a flashlight in my eyes. I hate her...everyone does...and not only because she smiles when she thrashes one of us for not moving faster. For not washing thoroughly.

For still being alive.

Kapitan Dieter always calls for me before Appellplatz where I must stand and be counted, sometimes waiting for hours to make sure all of the calculations are correct. The dead must be accounted for, the bodies hauled from the barracks by unlucky prisoners while I wait in agony. But this morning I'm not sure what will happen, if we will have to meet for roll call or not. There's been gunfire in the distance, and everything is different since the S.S. ordered most of the prisoners to be evacuated, since the officers started packing their belongings, rushing around the camp yelling, "Schnell! Schnell!"

*Faster, faster.*

Even the executions are done hastily, then the bodies piled up near open pits or stacked in wagons. For weeks the unholy flames of the crematorium never seem to stop and cannot keep up with the countless corpses littering the camp.

When Grese pokes me once more, I rub my eyes and rise to my feet, careful not to wake Simka, my friend who traveled with Mutti and me from Buchenwald a few months ago. We share the bunk, one of the better ones that's lined with straw, yet filled with bugs. Mutti says I'm lucky to have it. Lucky to be near the door where I can breathe better air, unlike so many others crammed into their bunks where the air is dank and rotten and heavy.

I don't sleep well anymore as I dream of steam whistles screaming in the distance that startle me awake. I dream of boxcars crammed with too many men, women, and children all crying out for water, for bread, for air. I have nightmares in which spruce and pine trees are set afire, their elongated branches bursting into flames so the endless piles of corpses can keep burning. I used to love the scent of the forest, but now the sweet smell of evergreen will be forever tangled with the odor of death.

Before Grese can stomp on my feet, I quickly shove them into a pair of worn-out wooden shoes and follow her out of the barracks. I don't say a word, don't make a sound as we pass the piles of corpses, left to rot in the open air. I pretend I'm walking past vegetables harvested from Mutti's vegetable garden, that the corpses rotting on the earth are piles of corn she will soon grind into flour.

The stench is unbearable. The sight, even more so. I no longer remember the smell of clean air as the cloying odor of burning flesh remains lodged in my throat, smothering me with a relentless warning. I know that with one swift decision, my life could also be snuffed out. Every night, I close my eyes and say to myself, *If God wills it, I will wake again tomorrow*. But I don't know what is the real nightmare...what I see in my dreams or what I experience upon waking.

As we pass the Appellplatz, corpses still hang in the gallows - a warning to us all about the dangers of escape. Leah's body swings from the rope and I remember what she had told me last week...that she would rather die trying to escape than die waiting for the war to end. But death is an every day occurrence here and my mind has become as tough as shoe leather so I can bear it.

21

When we reach the disinfection building, I strip, then stand in the scalding shower, my raw skin all but numb to the the hot water which feels like sharp pins and needles. I gag as Grese throws a cup of delousing powder on my head which stings my eyes and mouth.

"WASCH DU! SCHNELLER! *SCHNELLER!*" she shrieks.

*Wash...faster...faster!*

Frantically, I rinse my legs and arms, scrubbing harder at the tattoo on my left arm. It should have been six numbers long, but the S.S. officer took pity on me when my mother shouted, "Wir sind **Deutsch** Christen! **Deutsch** Frauen! Meine Schwester is **Deutsch!**""

*We are **German** Christians...**German** women. My sister is **German**!*

Mutti lied when we arrived at Auschwitz. She knew we would be separated if the S.S. thought she was my mother, so she told the guard we were sisters and he let her live, let her walk with me to a room where we were ordered to strip naked and shower, let her watch as a guard laughed while shaving my head and body, then endured the same humiliation herself before we were taken to be tattooed.

The S.S. who had a death grip on my arm put down the needle, then shoved me out the door, but I was left with *811* inked in bluish gray over the triangle of freckles near my wrist. Now I will never again be simply Karin Vogel, my mother's oldest child. Even if I do survive this war, there will always be a truncated number to remind me of what I've become.

There's no towel to dry myself, so I quickly throw a thin dress over my head, then tie a kerchief around my head, thankful for even that bit of warmth. The wooden shoes rub layers of blisters on my heels and toes. I can't walk properly in them, so trying to get from the barrack to the workhouse or the Appellplatz or Kapitan Dieter's room is hell on earth. It's been an uncommonly frigid winter, and even though I work making lace near a cast iron stove, I'm never warm enough. I'm never full enough, though I eat more than most because Kapitan Dieter is an important man and always gets what he wants. He doesn't want me to be skinny and dirty like so many of the poor girls in the camp left to rot and die in their own filth.

I don't speak in his presence, but I know his name - Herman. And I know I'm nothing more than his prostitute because he tells me, "Your payment is you get to live."

I'm supposed to feel grateful, but I don't know why I've survived for years while so many others have died. Perhaps now I won't live that much longer either.

Mutti says I have to. She says I have to do whatever the guards want. Whatever Kapitan Dieter wants. Whatever Kommandant Kramer wants. Whatever Grese wants. I have to do what they say in order to stay alive so I can bring more food to Simka.

"You're young and pretty, and that's what they all want," Mutti once told me.

So I lie in Herman's bed, a hollow shell, all the while staring at the wall or the ceiling or the knobs on the small glass cupboard that's filled with cans of evaporated milk and chocolates and creamy caramels...the one Herman said I must never touch. I know he wouldn't hesitate to shoot me with the pistol he keeps strapped to his leg. I've seen him use it more than once, and he's deadly when he's angry and drunk.

"You can take bread and cheese from the trunk," Herman told me the first time I was ordered to his room. "But if you touch that cabinet, you'll be dead before you can turn around."

Herman digusts me, yet I owe him for saving Mutti's life and my own. Often in the middle of what he does to me I think, *How can a man be both a sadist and a savior?*

This morning, Herman is quick about it, his tight, angry body all at once on top of me and then not. He doesn't make me sing before or after, neither does he mock me by calling me his *little songbird*. I stare at the calendar on the wall while Herman gets dressed and wonder why the compound is so busy at this hour. The living are made to carry corpses for burial or burning while the S.S. rush here and there, yelling at each other to be prepared for the end.

*The end of what?* I think. *The war? This camp? The end of our misery or the end of our lives?*

"I've been good to you, 811993...*Karin*," Herman says as he buttons his coat. "You will say how good I've been to you, yes?"

I frown. He's never called me by my name and I'm surprised he even knows it...or cares to.

"I've never beat you or hurt you," Herman insists. "I let you take extra food whenever you wanted it. I protected you from the other prisoners. I saved you and your sister from the gas."

I nod, my eyes swollen with shameful tears.

He knots his tie. "So if anyone asks, you will tell them I am a good man, won't you?"

*Why is he asking this?* I wonder. No one in power asks me anything. Not who I am. Not what I want.

When I say nothing, Herman comes to the bed where I sit pulling my dress over my head. He kneels, then gently strokes my face. "I've always been good to you." He kisses my forehead, then whispers my name.

I cringe and curl away from him, but Herman presses his warm, damp lips to my ear. "Remember what I said," he says. "If you tell anyone about what happens in this room, I can't be responsible for what happens to you."

I look at the floor and nod my head in compliance.

"Good girl," Herman says, rising. Then he struts out the door as if he has won the silent war between us.

A gray light gradually fills the room where I've been making lace for more than three hours...waiting for orders from the guards. For almost four months I've spent eight hours a day, six days a week knitting hats and mittens and scarves. I knit cable-knit sweaters and woolen socks. I knit yards and yards of lace that are sewn into curtains and sent to all corners of Germany where the S.S. live in luxury while those of us slaving in the camps can barely remember what our parents' faces look like.

I shiver in my threadbare dress and wonder, *How many girls wore this rag before me? Are they all dead? Will I be soon?* My shawl slips to the back of chair, and as I pull it up over my shoulders, I study the other women's faces as we endure the harsh silence of this cold, dank room, our knitting needles clicking and clacking while we do our duty for the Fuhrer. They've all become shadows of their former selves...and I know I have as well.

Simka sniffs and wipes her nose. Dark circles shadow her eyes as she pushes a curl behind her ear. Kapitan Dieter let all of us grow our hair back so we would look more presentable. He says women in his service are to look like women, and yet my breasts and curves aren't like Simka's. We've only been here since January, but the food her friend, Vitya, steals from the kitchen and the bread I bring from Kapitan Dieter's room keep her healthier than the rest of us. Even though I long to taste the sweet yams and mashed potatoes Vitya smuggles to her in little tin cans, I cannot ask Simka for even one bite.

The baby hidden inside of her needs it more than I do.

Still, my gnawing hunger never goes away. When we were in Auschwitz, my mother used to slip me her bread before the guards could see. Before any one else could grab it out of my hands and shove into their eager mouth. If there were a stray pea at the bottom of her soup bowl, Mutti would press it into my palm and beg me to swallow it. "Eat, Karin. *Survive*, Karin. Live one more day. Then live another. One day when we are liberated, we will remember what we saw here and tell others so that this madness will never happen again."

Now Simka winces, holding her stomach, and I'm afraid of what will happen when the pain gets worse. I've seen what the S.S. do to people who can't work, who show any type of weakness. I try to forget as I mindlessly work the yarn back and forth. My hands ache, but the bony knuckles and tissue-paper skin toil until I can no longer feel my joints. Instinctively, I work the needles back and forth in a rhythm that still has the power to calm me, even now when everything is so uncertain.

I think back to more than ten years ago when Mutti taught me how to knit. At that time, everyone was worried about the uprising of the Nazi Party. In 1935, work was scarce. Money even more so. It was cheaper to light the stove with the paper money my father had hidden in his fishing tackle box than to use it to buy kindling. Vati worked hard at the theater he owned with his friend, Herr Zweig, whom he had known since the Great War.

Herr and Frau Zweig had three boys of their own, Heinrich, who was my age, Georg, who was seven, and Fritz, who was only three. They usually visited on Sundays after we came home from church. The Zweigs went to Temple on Saturdays, so they arrived with a nice brisket or a basket of freshly baked apple dumplings while we were changing out of our good clothes.

My parents visted with Herr and Frau Zweig while I played tag in our backyard with Heinrich and Georg. Fritz preferred to hunt for worms, bugs, and other dirty things in Mutti's garden. She gave him a small trowel and a metal pail, saying, "Just make sure you don't harm my vegetables."

In the evening all of us went to the theater for an evening of Volkslieder...*folk songs*. Vati invited a host of people from the neighborhood and welcomed them warmly at the door. Mutti played the piano, Frau Zweig the violin, and I would lead everyone in song.

Vati especially loved to hear me sing "In stiller Nacht" to end the evening. Tears filled his eyes, and like Mutti who loves twilight, he was carried away into the imminent darkness of the words, the sorrow in the lyrics that foretold what our lives would soon become.

*In the quiet night, at the first watch,*
*a voice began to lament; sweetly, gently,*
*the night wind carried to me its sound.*
*And from such bitter sorrow and grief*
*my heart has melted.*
*The little flowers - with my pure tears -*
*I have watered them all.*

Back then, Mutti was expecting a baby. My brother, Jurgen, was tucked inside her belly and I loved to feel his little hands and feet kick and punch through Mutti's dress. I sang *Guten Abend, Gute Nacht* to him, leaning against our mother's side, rubbing the little knobs and bumps of his elbows and knees.

When Mutti saw how much I loved Jurgen, even before he was born, she gave me a ball of yarn and a pair of knitting needles, saying, "Karin, let's make something for our baby."

For years I had sat by Mutti, watching her create intricate pieces of lace which filled our modest home with lovely tablecloths, placemats, and doilies. Several delicate shawls hung on a peg near the door so Mutti and I could wrap one around our shoulders when we walked into the garden at sunset. My favorite was a Queen Anne's Lace pattern interwoven with open stitching that Mutti had created all by herself.

So I was overjoyed when she placed the polished rosewood needles in my hands. First she taught me how to cast on, then how to knit and purl. After that I learned how to make little hats and booties. Next came a simple sweater for Vati. Then a pair of socks for my baby brother. By the time

27

Jurgen was two, I asked Mutti to teach me how to make lace. Under her gentle guidance, I learned how to yarn over and knit two together. To pick up stitches and create tiny hearts and leaves and shells.

Mutti marveled at how quickly I garnered the skill. "Wie deine Gesangstalent, deines Stricken ist auch ein Geschenk," she said proudly.

*Like your singing talent, your knitting is also a gift.*

Now this gift is saving my life...and Mutti's as well...such as it is. But I know that without her, I won't survive either.

So I make lace like my mother taught me, and with every stitch, with every row, I weave in the memory of those who are gone forever. A stitch for Olga. One for Anne and Mary and Elisabet. A stitch for the woman who died of typhus in the bunk above me two days ago. A whole row for Frau Daiga and her daughter. Rows and rows for the Zweig family who perished long before I came to this place.

Countless stitches for my father and Jurgen.

And always...every stitch for Bruno.

# Sapphire

My feets are wet with morning dew as I walk into the kitchen where Mama already been for an hour. She wearing her hair tied up in a rag and her light brown skin shine with sweat. Sometime I think she look like the hot cocoa we make for the chil'ren at Christmas time. I's light like Mama, but Opal and Pearl be dark like our daddy. But I's the only one with green eyes, 'cause everone else gots brown. Mama say they be special. She say her Mama had a little bit a green in her eyes, too, and ain't it lucky I get to carry a little a my grandmama with me ever day?

I wipe my shoes on the rag rug Mama done made last summer, then hang my shawl on a peg by the door. The coffee already be made. The tea set be ready to serve Massa and Missus. Mama even polish up the silver forks and knives and spoons.

*Who coming to visit today?* I wonder.

Then I remember -- it be Mister Rotten's day to deliver the flour and oats and cornmeal from the general store. That make my stomach tie up in knots and want to stay close to Mama all the time. But he need to come 'cause we low on everthing with the war raging on and spring not coming on real good yet. Massa be one a the few plantation owners still left in our corner a Lincoln County 'cause done lost the hearing in one a his ears when we was a boy. The Rebs told him, "The heck with you," and Massa go back to farming.

Earle say when they was in town, he heard them Yanks done whupped up on the Rebs in Alabama and all over Virginia, 'cept I don't know where them places is. How can people I ain't never met be willing to give they lives for folks like me? I's always thinking on something and today that what I's wondering as I take down an apron from the peg by the stove. Then I remember Mama's story 'bout Jesus and how

He done give up His life for all a us poor folks here on earth. But Jesus done come back three days after He been hung on a cross, and I know as sure as the sun be shining that none a them Yanks gone rise up out they graves any time soon.

"Morning, Sapphire," Mama say, giving me a little peck on the cheek. "You sleep good last night?"

I shake my head. "No, ma'am."

Mama know I ain't sleeping good 'cause I lie in bed with her now that Daddy gone. Mama and I keep our shack neat as a pin. We even has some old chipped up china Missus say ain't no good to keep in the big house.

Mama's bed has a quilt my grandmama done made and a pillow and even a hay mattress, but that don't do no good to help me sleep. I lie there and hold my token -- a little chunk a stone on a leather strap that I got to wear 'round my neck. It has my letters on it. It say, *S.S.* for Sapphire Settler so in case I get it into my head to up and run off, anyone who catch me know who I belong to. That be so dumb! Even I know all I got to do is take it off and bury it in the forest somewheres and no one gone know who I is.

Mama give me the token that Earle stole when Mister Rotten made him bury my daddy, and I wears that, too. I rub Daddy's little chunk a stone and feel them letters. *J.S.* they say 'cause his name be Juniper Settler. One day when I big enough to use an awl, I gone scratch that dern "S" right off a both our tokens. Then we jest be Sapphire and Juniper...the way it oughta be.

I rub them tokens like Missus be rubbing her rosary. Ever time I see Missus fingering them beads, I think on when she say it stop her from worrying so much. It don't do nothing for me though. I still worry 'bout Mama and Opal and Pearl, how they might get taken away, 'cause no matter how much I rub Daddy's stone, I know I ain't never gone see him again.

"Baby girl, will you please get me some butter from the cooler?" Mama ask. She busy slicing bread for toast. Massa like it thick. Missus like it thin. And I like the end piece, which Mama always save for me even though Missus say give it to the sparrows and crows who be pecking at her little garden all the live long day.

Mama toast the end 'til it nice and crunchy, then coat it up with warm butter and sprinkle it with cinnamon, sugar, and a pinch a clove. "Here you go, *little bird*," she sing, giving me a wink.

"Tweet, tweet," I chirp.

That be the best thing I et all day long! Plus I get to set at the table in the kitchen and plop my behind on a real chair, not like how Mama and I has to sit on the bed or on an old stump when we eats at our place. Sometime I pretend I's not a slave, but a little girl setting in her own kitchen. And I pretend Mama ain't no slave neither, but jest my mama, making me breakfast like any other white chile in Lincoln County.

Now I go to the cooler and pull out the box a butter. "You want it all, Mama?"

"One little slice do jest fine," she say, stoking the fire. "I be making Massa's eggs early today. We's going into town later this morning to get the dry goods."

"That true, Mama?" I ask, lifting my brows.

I's so excited! First 'cause I ain't gone have to see Mister Rotten. Plus whenever Massa take me and Mama into town, I get to set and watch the chil'ren play outside in the school yard. *And* I get to go with Mama while she barter with Missus Snow, the lady who run the store. Mama sell her lace and quilts and even some a the vegetables from our own garden when we has too many, which ain't often.

Missus Snow be nice, but not too nice. She give Mama yarn ain't nobody want and old scraps a material, then say, "Let's see what miracles you can work with *that*, Ruby."

Mama always surprise Missus Snow. No matter how uneven the yarn be, no matter how nasty the material, my mama can always make something beautiful outta something ugly. Then she sell it for money that belong only to her...not to Massa.

She saving to buy our freedom. Her'n mine both. Mama once tell me, "I know they's some folks who be running off and such, but I ain't in they shoes, so I cain't fault 'em. But I want to be free legal. I ain't gone take the chance somebody snatch you away from me like they done your daddy if we got caught."

I ain't know how much Mama got saved so far, but I do know where she keep it and I ain't telling nobody no how. I's excited we get to go to town so Mama can earn more nickels and dimes and maybe even a dollar if she can sell Missus Snow that pretty baby quilt she done sewed with all a the clothes Little Sam and Marybelle growed out a this year.

"I gets to come, too." I say, handing her the butter. It not be a question. Mama know I do almost anything to get out the house for the day.

"Yes, chile," Mama chuckle. "That why I get the silver done now. Missus says she gone have company tomorrow and I's not sure I be able to get it done and put supper on the table tonight."

"You need me to make something for Missus and Little Sam and Marybelle for supper?" I ask.

"No, baby," Mama say. "But you can go pick some peas from the garden and start shelling 'em."

Mama crack Massa's eggs into the hot butter as I take a wooden bowl from the shelf. I wrap my shawl 'round my shoulders, then step outside to the small garden Missus and Mama tend nearly all year long. The spring peas be popping and in no time, I got enough for more than Missus and the chil'ren. Maybe Mama will let me has some for my supper, too. I love peas more than anything, and we don't get 'em much. Mostly we jest has hot cornbread and pork rind and whatever we can grow in our little patch by the shack. Massa done give us a bunch a seeds, but they never seem to grow as good as Missus' garden do.

Even so, my onions be the best on the plantation, but I don't know why. Whenever they be coming in strong, I always take a handful a 'em to Massa's kitchen 'cause Missus don't know how to tend 'em. Maybe she don't like to touch stuff that make her cry. I cry enough over my daddy so a little onion juice ain't gone hurt me none.

When I bring the peas into the kitchen, Mama already has another dish on the table ready for me. It be my favorite one 'cause it has Queen Anne's Lace painted on it with silver ink. It nearly match the lace Mama done stitch into the collar a my shirt she made for me last Christmas.

When I put it on, she told me, "Sapphire, I's gone teach you how to make different laces, but that be the most perfect kind on earth."

"How come?" I asked, running my fingers over the little knobs and bumps in the flowers.

Mama fixed my collar so it set jest right. "'Cause that be God's lace, honey...and ain't nobody nowhere can make lace like that. It bloom and die and bloom and die...over and over."

"That be a miracle, huh?"

"Yes, baby," Mama said, hugging me.

Now I set on the stool and, one by one, I shell them peas, feeling the hard little balls slide off a my finger as they go *plink, plink, plink* onto the little china dish. Some days I feel like dropping it on the hard, wooden floor so it might chip and Missus will say Mama can tote it home to our shack.

*But what if it break into pieces?* I wonder.

I decide to jest let it be. Maybe sometime it get chipped when Mama or Missus or even Marybelle be using it and I don't have to worry 'bout destroying something that be a picture a what God done made.

Mama clear her throat. I look up to see her gazing out the window. Then she look back at Massa's eggs in the pan. Jest like always, they be a mess a yellow and white, all mixed up together. Mama give 'em a little flip, then press hard with the spatula so they get nice and cooked on that side, too.

"Why you do that, Mama?" I ask, taking the peas to the sink where I gone rinse 'em good.

"Do what?"

"Why you always break Massa's eggs like that?" I pump the handle a the faucet as hard as I can. It be cold and stiff in the morning chill, but soon I get a trickle going.

Mama don't say nothing for a moment. I think she don't hear me, so I ask one more time.

As she slide them eggs on a plate, she say real quiet-like, "When I break Massa's eggs, I ain't no slave. I do it to send him a message."

"What message?"

Mama give me a gentle smile. "Sapphire, you need to listen with different ears."

I frown as I rinse the peas. "These be the only ears I got! I cain't be changing 'em like Marybelle change her hair ribbons."

"Don't sass me, baby girl," Mama snap. She mad 'cause I got a sharp tongue, but who she think I got it from if it weren't her?

"I ain't sassing," I say. "I's jest wondering how you send a message to Massa by messing with his eggs."

Mama sigh. "Sapphire...you may be a slave in your body, but you only a slave in your mind if you wants to be." She say it like it be fact. I know what that mean 'cause Missus done teach me fact from fiction jest last week.

Still, I don't understand 'bout wanting to be a slave in my mind. "What that mean?" I ask her.

"All them Yanks and folks up north be fighting for our freedom, but I done figured out long ago that I's already free...and you is too...you jest don't know it yet." She set Massa's plate on a tray with the toast and jam and the big, silver coffee pot. "Ever time I break Massa's eggs, I feel a little more free. I *choose* to do it, see? He ain't never said nothing 'bout it and I don't do it malicious-like."

"What malicious?"

"It mean to be nasty on purpose," she say. "I don't hate Massa no more. I hate what he done to your daddy, but he ain't never lay a finger on me or one a you girls. Still, I do it to show him I's a person who can do what she want sometime."

I nod.

"See, baby, I used to play with Massa Sam when I was a chile, jest like you play with Little Sam and Marybelle. My mama's milk be both his and mine. Mama say we held hands when we was nursing, and when we got bigger, we played together like we's kin. I know him like I knew my own sister, you 'member her?"

"Uh huh."

But I don't really 'cause Auntie Jasmine died when I was jest a bitty thing. She got kicked in the head by a horse when she working in the field and never got up.

Mama put her hands on her hips. "When I break Massa's eggs, it be like saying to him, 'I's still the same Ruby you played with when you was a boy. I's still the same person who seen your daddy whip your hide. I's still the same person your mama done hate like the devil. I's still the same even though you the massa now.'" Mama put a fork and knife by Massa's plate, then look at me directly. "It like I's telling him I be a *whole* person...and *that* how I be free."

I hear ever word she say, trying to listen with different ears. I wonder what it gone feel like when Little Sam be the massa and I be like mama. I's learned my place in the order a things 'round here. I know I ain't never gone have no say in what go on in the big house. I know I got to do whatever the white folks say.

But when Mama talk like she do right now, I feel like I ain't no slave neither.

I be a whole person, too.

I jest be Sapphire.

While Mama feed Massa and the chil'ren they breakfast, I take some cornbread and a pail a fresh water to the folks in the field. They's been up since 'fore dawn milking the cow, toting hay, scooping poop and such.

In the fresh morning breeze, I smell the spruce and pine trees growing tall and proud near the edge a the plantation. The green leaves jest be popping on the maple trees, but they ain't no whirlygigs coming on 'em yet. I like evergreens the best 'cause they be jest that - ever green all year long. I smell them clean, sharp spruce needles and it make me long for Christmas when we ain't got nothing to do but set on our behinds and gobble up the holiday cake Mama done made and think 'bout what old Santy Claus would bring us if we had a stocking to hang by the fireplace. If we even *had* a fireplace and not jest a fire pit outside our shack.

I see Opal in the henhouse poking 'round the nests, careful not to get pecked to death. She say she ain't never seen a bunch a chickens as feisty as the ones Massa got this year. But they lays a heap a eggs ever morning, and Opal always tell me to sneak a few into our shack so Mama can scramble up some for my supper.

"Missus ain't gone miss a few eggs now and again," she say real sassy-like.

Opal always be trying to pull the wool over Massa and Missus' eyes. Lies pour from her lips like milk from a pitcher and land like thick cream no matter what she be saying. I think it funny how Massa and any a the menfolk 'round here lap it up jest like little kittens. Opal has big, dark eyes that shine and snap when she telling a tall one. She got long legs and roundish breasts and hips, and I guess the mens jest hear what they wants to when she start spinning her web a lies.

Everyone working while they singing "Follow the Drinking Gourd" and I long for Mama to teach me the harmony part. She already done teached me how to sing "Swing Low, Sweet Chariot" and "Ezekiel Saw the Wheel."

"Swing Low" be my favorite, 'specially when we sing the part 'bout angels coming after me. I wonder if them angels be wearing lace wings like Mama say. Jest in case, ever time I sit down to knit, I start a humming and weave the words a the song into the stitches.

When I get to singing out loud, Mama say, "With that pretty little voice, someday you gone get to heaven riding on them angels' wings."

Now Opal stop singing and motion for me. "Sapphire, get your behind over here and tote these to the big house. She pop two small eggs into my apron pockets, then hand me a straw basket. "Old Bessie done outdid herself this morning. I counted five under her rump!"

"How 'bout Gertie?" I ask. That be my favorite hen 'cause she be brown and black and red, not all white and plain like the others.

"She still ain't got a one," Opal say, standing up and stretching her long arms over her head. "Someday soon she gone be stewing in the soup pot."

I frown and tears come to my eyes.

Opal chuck my shoulder. "I's kidding with you, Sapphire. She lay them two little bitty things in your pockets. I figure you want to have Gertie's 'cause she your favorite and all...'cept I don't know why. She ornery as sin."

I smile, fingering them little warm, brown eggs that come straight from Gertie's nest.

"What you got for our breakfast?" Opal ask.

Like she don't know.

"I brought you some *fancy* pancakes and *maple* syrup," I sass.

Opal roll her eyes. "Oh, what a *feast*! We's lucky today!"

"Mama and me's going to town with Massa," I tell her. "We gone get the dry goods and such. Maybe Mama make you oatmeal for supper."

Opal nod. "I has some leftover honey from last summer. That be a nice treat after working hard all day long."

I know how lucky I is to work in the big house with Mama, 'cause they ain't a day go by that I not with her morning, noon, and night. The only time I has to get outside is when I tend Missus' little garden. Opal and Pearl and they husbands all gots to tend to the animals and the fields. Now that she be big, Pearl doing more a the hoeing and less a the toting. When the baby come, I guess she gone strap it to her back and keep on working. Keen done take over as the blacksmith when Mister Rotten take my daddy, and sometime he work with Massa, planning where to plant the crops and how to rotate 'em and such.

Old Albert come to our place jest last winter when his Massa done die and he give Albert to Massa Settler in his will. He ain't too happy to be here, no suh. Old Albert say he too feeble to hoe and rake and pick cotton. Said he was jest getting used to overseeing and now look where he be. The mens say he do the best he can, but Old Albert be stiff and slow. He cain't do half the work Hale and Issac can. Maybe Massa take pity on Old Albert someday and let him come be a butler or something in the big house. Then Mama and me can has someone else to talk to 'sides ourselves.

I like Old Albert. He tell funny stories 'bout Brer Rabbit and Brer Fox and how they always be getting into some kind a fix. I like the one 'bout how Brer Rabbit be stuck in some tar and beg Brer Fox to throw him in a brier patch to put him out a his misery. That mean old Brer Fox think it be some kind a punishment, so he do jest that. But sly Brer Rabbit done been born and live his whole life in them prickly bushes and he be free in no time, laughing 'bout how he done fool Brer Fox for good measure.

I beg to hear Old Albert tell that tale over and over while we warms ourselves by the fire at night. Mama say I like it 'cause I need to learn how to stay away from sticky things that cause a heap a trouble.

But I say I like it 'cause what look like the end for that clever Brer Rabbit turn out to be only the beginning.

## Karin

It's past time for Appellplatz, but the loudspeakers are still silent.  I wonder if roll call will be held since half of the barracks have been emptied.  Thousands of half-dead men and women were lined up like cattle and surrounded by S.S. guards with rifles who threatened to shoot them if they couldn't keep up on the forced march.  If they complained about the cold.  If they stumbled or leaned on each other for support.

I've seen Nazis kill prisoners for less than that.

The loudspeakers hover over us like metal slave masters, barking orders from morning until night.  Yesterday morning, one of the guards angrily shouted, "Alle Untermenchen aufstehen!  Alle Schweine schnell zu marschieren oder du wirst erschossen!"

*All sub-human beings get up!  All pigs will march quickly or you will be shot!*

Simka and I ran from the barrack to the cookhouse where her friend, Vitya, shoved us into the pantry and hissed, "Make no noise!"

Simka and I crouched on the floor and held our breath, waiting for the sound of steam whistles in the distance to let us know the trains were finally leaving.

"We'll be killed if they find us," Simka whispered as I wrapped my arm protectively around her.

I shook my head.  Said nothing.

While the S.S. were storming the barracks, Mutti told me that I must hide, that I must help Simka.  I must do it because I am Henry Vogel's daughter and I must be brave like him.  But Mutti didn't have to feel her heart leaping wildly in her chest while she pressed her face to her friend's cheek, not knowing how long she had to live.  She didn't have to feel her bladder fill to overflowing and her mouth become as dry as dust.

We were discovered by an S.S. officer later that day, but our lives were spared because I'm Kapitan Dieter's concubine and on his direct orders, I am never to be harmed. Once more, he has saved my life and the life of someone I love.

But staying alive seems like a never-ending atonement for an innocent choice I made long ago, one which led to an accidental betrayal and the destruction of everything that followed.

***

November, 1938

It's a cold, clear night as I stand staring out the picture window in our living room while Vati and Mutti argue in the kitchen. Their hushed, angry voices twist into each other while smoke billows into the sky from the synagogue up the street. Orange and copper flames burst from the windows beneath the Star of David and I wonder, *Is Herr Zweig safe? He is still alive?*

Yesterday the S.S. arrested him at the theater while he and Vati were working in their office. They forced him, along with all the Jewish men from our neighborhood, to walk to the synagogue, all the while mocking them, calling them Jewish swine. The streets were lined with people shouting ugly things as well: "Faulen Juden! Untermenschen!"

*Rotten Jews! Sub-humans!*

Since then, we haven't seen or heard from Herr Zweig or any of the other men. Frau Zweig is locked in her home with her younger boys, but Heinrich, the oldest, ran over to our house just an hour ago to tell us that the synagogue was set on fire by the angry mob. While my parents quarrel in the next room, he slumps in a chair by the fire, cracking his knuckles and nervously bouncing his leg.

I don't know what to say when tears fall down Heinrich's cheeks. He tries to hide them, but it's too late. I've never seen a boy my age cry before and it frightens me. To spare Heinrich, I turn my head and watch the synagogue burn, watch the flames and smoke rise higher into the darkening sky.

As night falls, neither of us speaks, for we both know that when the morning comes, nothing will ever be the same.

"Henry, we can't!" Mutti cries. I hear her voice through the thin wall between our bedrooms. They've been arguing all night long and even though sunlight slowly filters into my room, nothing has been resolved.

Heinrich tosses and turns on the couch downstairs while my parents decide his fate. He didn't leave last night, as my parents knew it wasn't safe for him to walk home in the dark. Now I wonder why it's so difficult for my mother to ensure his future safety.

"You cannot ask me to put the children's lives at risk," Mutti insists.

"But what about Heinrich and Georg and Fritz?" Vati counters. "Don't their lives matter? And what about Sharon? What about hers? What do you think Leonard would do if he were in my place?"

Mutti is silent for once.

"I'm not asking you to hide them here," Vati continues. "There's space in the theater's dressing rooms. Heinrich and I can build a false wall. Sharon and the boys will be safe there until this madness is over."

"Why didn't they just leave when they had the chance?" Mutti sobs. "They could have gone to America to live with Sharon's sister."

"By the time Leonard applied for Visas last year, the immigration laws had changed...you know that." Vati's voice is calm and clear. "Leonard never believed the Germans would take it this far. He's always said that he's a German first, a Jew second...as loyal to his country as the next man."

"Well, the *next man* has been issuing warnings for years...," Mutti argues.

Vati interrupts her, "Leonard is a loyal friend and I would do anything for him...anything. He took a chance to open the theater when Karin was just a baby and we had next to nothing."

Mutti bursts into tears. "But what does that matter when you've put all of our lives in jeopardy?"

"Josephine...Josephine," Vati says softy. "I cannot let Sharon and the boys risk deportation. I've heard what happens when people are loaded onto cattlecars."

I've heard those gruesome stories passed around school like notes hidden behind the teacher's back. Listening to my father now, I know for certain that I'm just like him. I'm not a coward like my mother who wants to save our skins, who would let the Nazis take Heinrich and his family away. But then I hear something in her voice, a whimper followed by an agonizing cry that sounds like a wounded animal.

"But my Papa's mother," Mutti cries. "I'm a Mischling...mixed blood!"

"Josephine...don't worry," Vati replies. "There is no record...I made sure of that."

"Grossmutter was a Jew," Mutti wails. "And that means I'm part Jewish...and so is Karin and..."

"Hush now," Vati says soothingly. "No one will know. I will tell no one. You will tell no one. Because you are an only child, there are no brothers and sisters who can tell. Your Mutti and Papa are both dead, God rest their souls, and Karin doesn't know, so she can't tell either."

I'm not sure what it means to be a Mischling...am I Jewish or am I Christian? Frau Zweig would often invite me for the Shabbat, and one evening she told me that the Jewish line is in the soul, not the body. She explained that it is passed down through the mother because babies are conceived in them, born from them, and their little souls are shaped more by their mothers than their fathers.

I'm thankful there's no Jewish bloodline the Nazis can trace, and yet I feel utterly ashamed of myself as well. I love Herr and Frau Zweig. Their sons are like my brothers. But I don't want to be taken to a place from which no one returns. I don't want to be persecuted for simply being born as I am.

Perhaps I'm just like Mutti after all.

I hear her sniffle and blow her nose. "But what if...?"

"There is no 'what if,'" Vati says calmly. "There is only what *is*. And what is now will not change. Sooner or later the S.S. will come to Sharon's home and take her and the boys away. I cannot let that happen. If Leonard returns, I want him to find his family safe."

Mutti says nothing and I think the argument is over. But after a moment she snaps, "How do you know they won't find them in the theater, then come here to kill us all?"

My heart pounds when I hear the sharp edge in her voice.

"All I know is that I have to help my friend," Vati replies sadly. "I have to take care of his family."

"But what about *our* family?" Mutti cries. "What about *us*?"

"We are all family, Josephine," Vati says insistently. "We are all part of God's family."

Shortly before sunrise, Vati drives to the theater with Heinrich safely hidden in the trunk. Then he will go to Frau Zweig's home as soon as he can to bring her, Georg, and Fritz to the safety of the theater. They're going to sleep in the office until Vati can build the false wall that he says will only take a few days.

Mutti and I hurriedly pack a picnic basket filled with bread, fruit, and a few brats before I have to leave for school. I pour some milk into a thermos and fill another one with hot coffee. In a big, cardboard box Mutti and I stack clean sheets, some blankets, and a few hand towels. I tuck in a stuffed toy, a few of my old storybooks for Georg and Fritz, and a copy of my dog-eared *The Sword in the Stone* for Heinrich.

Mutti makes me promise to be silent about what Vati is doing. To stay away from the theater unless I am with my father. To attend Jungmadel meetings and be a good girl in school. She makes me promise that I will never call attention to myself and risk questioning of any kind.

Soon Jurgen wanders into the kitchen. His blue eyes are still sleepy and his soft, blonde hair sticks up all over his head like little tufts of fluff. Eyeing the basket, he asks, "Where are we going?"

"Nowhere," Mutti says.

"But I want to go on a picnic!" Jurgen whines.

Mutti shakes her head. "Not today, Liebling."

"But when?"

"Maybe tomorrow...now be a big boy and help your sister."

Jurgen rubs his eyes, grinning at me.

I tousle his hair. "You're *my* big boy, too, yes?"

"Ja! Naturlich!"

*Yes! Of course!*

"Well, big boy, help me carry this box to the carport."

"Why?"

"Because Vati needs it." I try to smile as I tuck a chocolate bar inside one of the towels to surprise Heinrich.

I cannot tell Jurgen about the Zweigs. He's too little to keep a secret and can't be sure that he won't tell the neighbors by mistake. Especially Frau Roth who pompously displays a Nazi flag in her front window and brags about how every one of her boys proudly wears the S.S. uniform.

Jurgen pulls on my sleeve. "What does Vati need it for?"

"For his friends."

"Are they going somewhere?"

"Ja...a great adventure!" I tell him.

"Can I come, too?"

I shake my head. "Nein, Jurgen...we'll have our own adventures, but not right now...you have to wait until you grow up a bit."

Jurgen pushes the hair from his eyes. "Karin, can I come to school with you?"

"Why?"

"Because I want to learn my letters so I can read about adventures until I'm big enough to have them myself."

I hand Jurgen a bright green sweater I had knitted for his birthday last spring. "If you help me take these things to the carport, I'll teach you your letters today when I come home."

As Jurgen pushes his arms into the sweater, his face pops through the neck. Then he looks up at me and grins. "Karin...Ich liebe dich einfach."

*Karin, I just love you.*

Tears fill my eyes as I begin to understand what my mother must be feeling. Jurgen is more than my brother. He's my wenig Schatten...*my little shadow*...and I cannot imagine my life without him.

***

Now as I gaze out the cloudy window that's coated with ashes, I see children mill around the yard nearby, their tiny bodies swimming in filthy, raggedy striped pajamas, clothes that were once worn by men who have died from starvation and typhus and dysentery. Barbed wire surrounds the children in a gruesome playpen only Nazis could invent. Several boys dig holes in the dirt with their bare hands. Two girls stand with their arms around each other and press their faces together, trying to stay warm. Many of them sit huddled on the cold, dank earth, hungry and hopeless.

Simka presses a fist to her stomach and winces in pain. The lace in her other hand quivers on the needles. She looks to me and I lift my brows as if to ask, *Are you alright?*

She nods and tries to smile, tries to be brave, but we're both terrified of what will happen once her labor begins. I know what happens to babies born in the camps...and to their mothers.

As my hands work mindlessly, my eyes scan the yard hoping to see Jurgen among the children. Then I remind myself that it's not wise to imagine the impossible because here I am...still alive while my little brother's ashes have long since floated like angel's wings high above the earth and through the gates of heaven.

# Sapphire

The dirt road done kick up a heap a dust on my best red jumper. I set by Mama on the wooden seat and keep brushing it off as we round the corner toward the town. When we gets real close, I fuss with the little rag ribbons I done tied to the ends a my braids, making sure they still tight. Mama say soap be cheap and water be free, so she ain't gone take no dirty girl to town. She know she ain't got to tell me. I like to get dirty, but more'n that, I like to get clean, 'specially when I get to dress up and go to the store.

Massa gently tap the horse's flank with the reigns and say, "Giddy-up, Pete!"

I think that be funny, him calling a horse a man's name, but that be Massa's way. He got a cow called Sue, a mule called Nat, a goat called Timothy, and two sheeps called Joan and Joanna. Make me wonder who named my great, great, great, great granddaddy who come over on a boat from Africa. I's sure as sugar he weren't called Homer where he come from.

By the time we gets to town, the sun be shining warm-like and I don't need my shawl no more. They's white folks milling all over the place like ants crawling all over the sugar bowl. Some a 'em has they slaves with them, toting this and that. I see the kids playing in the schoolyard. Must be what Marybelle call morning recess. I cain't see Little Sam, but they's a bunch a boys playing baseball and I hear the loud "crack" the wooden bat make when it hit the little white ball.

I also hear old Mister Hawkins, the white folks' preacher, yelling at his man to "tie up them horses right quick!" His voice sound like an old creaky barn door and I's glad Massa's voice be soft and low, 'cept when he been drinking. But even then, I only hear him yelling at Missus through they bedroom door. He don't yell like he mad, he yell like he got so much grief inside a him, it be pouring out from his mouth in words 'stead a tears from his eyes.

I cain't understand him, but Missus do. Even though she can get madder'n a wet hen at Massa, she always say stuff like, "It's alright, Sam...I understand. It won't be long now. Your father would understand, too."

But I don't know what Old Massa Settler be understanding when he dead. And from what I hear, he weren't the understanding type. Mama say he'd yell an order and whoever in his line a fire best jump quick or risk a whipping. And that include his son. Mama say Massa get beat twice as hard as a slave sometime.

Now I watch Old Mister Hawkins bark some more at his man, then I look at Massa. I ain't happy to be no slave, but I don't know no different neither. I know what it like to be called *tar baby*. I know what it like to be asked when I go to town with Mama, "Whose nigger you be?" like I ain't got no name, like I ain't a person. I know that some white folks gone hate us all they lives 'cause they don't know no different...jest like I don't know no different than living like I do.

Even so, I know the difference 'tween belonging to a nice man and a nasty one. Massa may tell Mama to do this and that. He tell Pearl and Ruby and Hale and all a them slaves in the field how long to work and what they gots to do all day long. But he ain't mean. Sometime in the summer he even let 'em have the afternoon off if it be so hot they gone melt like brown butter in the boiling sun. They nap in they shacks 'til twilight, then heads back to the fields 'til it get real dark with Massa toiling right next to 'em.

I think sometime Massa feel guilty 'bout a lot a things. Guilty 'bout my daddy. Guilty 'bout his daddy. Guilty 'bout being who he be. Mama say Massa Sam ain't a lick like Old Massa...and that be both a blessing and a curse.

"Ruby, take all the time you need with Mrs. Snow," Massa say as he steer the horse toward a hitching post by the store. "I need to go to the telegraph office and the bank, so I'll ask Mr. Snow to help me load the staples into wagon if you're still inside."

Mama nod as she tie the ends a her shawl so it don't fall off. "Thank you, Massa Sam," she say, making sure his good ear be facing her. I keep forgetting which one it be, but Mama *always* know. She say nice and clear, "You think there gone be any news 'bout the war?"

"I hope so," Massa nod. "But you know what the preacher says about those darn reporters who hear a scrap of rumor and print it like it's the gospel truth."

"What he say?" Mama ask, shielding her eyes from the rising sun.

Massa smile. "He said that all of the reporters could be killed in the crossfire one day and dispatches from hell would arrive by sunrise the next morning."

"Oh, Lord!" Mama laugh. "He ain't got no use for them newpapermens."

"Well, let's hope for some good news anyway," Massa say. He get down from the wagon. "Have you made a lot of things to sell?"

Mama shrug. "I ain't had time to make but a few things, but Missus Snow say last time she gone look 'round for some more wool yarn. I's gone make you some new socks to wear to church."

"That's fine," Massa nod. I can tell he not really listening. His mind elsewhere, but that where it be most days since folks 'round here be talking 'bout how the war gone be ending soon.

"Can I learn how to make socks, too?" I ask Mama when I see Massa ain't gone say no more.

She nod. "Yes...jest as soon as you learn how to use them double-pointy needles I done give you last week."

"Them's hard to figure, Mama," I frown. "They flip and flop *all over* the place."

"Practice, baby girl," Mama smile. "You gots to *practice*."

"I'd rather practice my *reading*," I whisper. I know I ain't s'posed talk 'bout such things when we away from Massa's plantation, but ain't no one looking at us, so I figure I can sneak it in.

"*Hush it*, Sapphire," Mama hiss and squeeze my leg hard with her strong fingers. She don't want to get nobody in trouble, 'specially Missus.

So I hush it.

Massa hobble Pete, then reach up and help Mama down. He hold out his arms and grab me 'round my ribs, then set me on the ground. "There you go, Miss Sapphire," he wink. "Have fun with your mama at the store." He slip a shiny penny into my hand. "Why don't you get some stick candy...if Ruby doesn't mind."

Mama give Massa a look that say, *You spoil my chile, but that be jest fine with me.* "What you say, Sapphire?" Mama chide.

"Thank you, Massa," I say, staring at the penny in my palm. "I know jest what kind I's gone get."

"What's that?" he ask.

"Peppermint," I smile. "Like at Christmas time when Santy Claus done brung Little Sam and Marybelle a mess a candy."

"Well, you can pretend it's Christmas today if you want," Massa say, pulling a satchel from the wagon. "I expect that'll buy you a couple a pieces at least." Then he look at Mama. "Tell Mrs. Snow to give you the best calico they have...enough for new Easter dresses for you and your girls. She can put it on my monthly bill."

Mama wrinkle her brow. "Why you do that?"

Massa look at my shabby jumper and shake his head. "I can't believe how much Sapphire is growing like a weed."

I nod. "Yes, sir, I *is*."

It embarrassing to wear this old thing both Opal and Pearl done had when they was little. It be held together by threads and the seams be popping open where my arm pits be stretching 'em. Plus it got stains from where they spilt all kind a things on it.

"Want me to get some for Missus and the chil'ren?" Mama ask.

Massa shake his head. "No, they're going to visit her mother in Cleveland soon and I'm sure Mrs. Hamilton will take them to her tailor."

Missus be from a rich family up north and I think that why she teach me how to read and write. She don't like keeping slaves, but she love Massa a whole bunch or so I hear her tell him when he be so sad sometime. She say she ain't gone leave him, no matter how poorly the farm be producing. No matter how mean he treat her. She say she gone be with him 'til death do they part and she mean to keep her promise.

Missus don't make us work on Sunday 'cause that be the Lord's day. Mama and I does all our work on Saturday, and then we gets to spend the whole next day praying and singing hymns and knitting on our lace. Opal and Pearl come over to our shack and we get to talking sometime 'til I nearly bust a gut with them funny things they say 'bout they husbands...how they be farting and burping and scratching they behinds all the time. Last week Opal pretend she be Hale and rub her hind end while she sniff and snort and walk 'round the shack like she got a stick up her butt.

"The shine already done worn offa him," Mama smile, looking up from her lace. "That cain't be the same boy you done fell in *love* with last summer."

"He be the same boy," Opal say, wrinkling her nose. "He jest be more a hisself now that we be married."

It a wonder I even think 'bout jumping the broom someday.

Now Mama take my hand and we walk to the store. It be Monday, so Massa stop at the post office to mail some letters. I see him over my shoulder and notice he walking funny, like he ain't got no bones in his legs. Mister Toomey

52

work the telegraph at the post office and I know Massa gone ask him if they's news 'bout the war. He worry 'bout that all the time, 'specially when Mister Rotten come over and rant and rave 'bout what gone happen "when all the niggers get freed." They all know the Rebs is gone get they behinds whipped and then what they gone do? Make me wonder what me and Mama and everone who work Massa's farm gone do, too.

Where we gone live? Will I get to be with Mama always?

It make my mind spin to think a such things, so I watch the kids running in the school yard. Marybelle be swinging on a tire and her dress be flyin' up so I can see her underthings. Her mama would have a fit to know she be showing her business, but I won't tell. Marybelle and me is friends, even though I know I ain't s'posed to talk to her when we in town.

"Sapphire, you want to set on the porch and watch the kids while I talk to Missus Snow?" Mama ask.

"Yes'm."

"Fine...I come get you when I's done so you can spend that pretty penny."

I rub it 'tween my fingers and think a all the hours Mama done spent knitting and sewing and making things Missus Snow want to sell at the store. I know Mama only make a little bit a money and Missus Snow raise the price a heap so she can make what Missus teach me called a profit.

*That don't make no sense*, I think. *Why cain't Mama jest make all the money herself*? But ain't nobody gone buy nothing from no slave, so Missus Snow doing her a favor passing her pennies and nickels and dimes if Mama be lucky.

"You want my penny?" I ask her, holding it out. "You can put it with the money you saving for our freedom."

Mama pat my hand, then curl my fingers 'round the copper coin. "We gone be free soon enough. You ain't never had no money 'fore and today's a very special day. It be time you learn how to use it."

"Thank you, Mama," I say, thankful she let me keep it. I was thinking the same thing...that I ain't never had no penny. I ain't never had nothing that weren't somebody else's 'fore me...'cept my pretty shirt with the Queen Anne's Lace.

I set on a barrel near the door a the store and watch the kids while Mama go inside. I hear Missus Snow say, "Be right with you, Ruby. Lord, it's been a busy morning!" My legs itch and my feet hurt 'cause my toes be poking out the holes in my shoes. The socks I's wearing has holes, too, and the soles a my shoes be flap, flap, flapping all the time. Mama say she gone get Hale to tar 'em up sometime when he ain't too busy scratching his behind and burping and farting and such.

My mama a card or so Old Albert say. I think that mean she be pretty funny.

Now I look at all a them clean white kids and know how truly dirty I be. My hands. My feets. Even my being colored don't hide the filth I live in ever day. Mama done give me a bath ever Sunday, but still, I see them kids and I know what they is.

And I know what I is.

Still, I get to set out here and listen to songbirds singing while all a them kids soon gone be back setting on they behinds in that schoolroom doing all kind a work. But that not be work to me. It be more like playing. I see a boy who got a McGuffey Reader...the very same one I done read last night. I think 'bout that story a the little boy who like to play and when he done, then he like to work. To help me remember all them words in order, I take little steps 'round the wooden porch, one word for each step.

*He used to say, "One thing at a time."*
*When he had done with work, he would play;*
*but he did not try to play and to work at the same time.*

Over and over 'gain I whisper them words, but pretty soon that story 'bout mixing work and play get all mixed up in my head. It seem like them birds twittering in the trees and the horses clomping on the street and the folks walking by all be singing that story to me even though they ain't paying no mind to a little colored girl waiting on her Mama.

The birds be tweeting, "Work can be play, Sapphire...you know it can."

"I sure *do*," I sing to the birds. "'Cause knitting ain't no work, 'cept when Mama put them double-pointy needles in my hands."

"Oh, Sapphire," one a them red birds chirp. "You is a *card*!"

All the sudden I see the teacher, Miss Vincent, come to the door a the schoolhouse and ring a big, gold bell. *Clang, clang, clang*! Them kids stop what they doing right quick and hightail it to they teacher. I think they be like little slaves, too. Miss Vincent be they massa with her bell and when she ring it like she doing now, they all come running. 'Cept I know at the end a the day, they get the freedom a going home to they mamas and daddies.

Miss Vincent be strict, too. One time when Mama brung me to town, I seen her grab a boy by the ear and drag him into the school all the while screeching, "Don't you let me catch you doing that ever again, Douglas Pritchard!"

Later that day when I was washing dishes in the big house, Marybelle come in for a glass a milk. I ask her what Douglas done to get in trouble and she say he peed in the bushes in front a all the girls.

"That ain't no big thing," I shrug. "All the slaves in the fields do they business wherever they is 'cause they ain't no privy when you got to go."

"But there's an *outhouse* behind the school," Marybelle tell me. "And Miss Vincent says we're never, ever go to the bathroom outside because it's unsanitary."

"What that mean?" I ask, wiping a bowl free a mashed potato bits.

"I think it means *not private*."

"*Private* mean you does your business all by yourself?"

"Uh huh," Marybelle nod.

Now I think on all them times Mama say to jest piddle behind a bush at night 'stead a hightailing it to the privy. She say it keep raccoons and skunks and such away from our shack and that make me giggle jest to think on it.

"What you got to laugh 'bout, Sapphire Settler?" I hear a nasty voice say. It be coming from the mouth a the loudest woman I know. Whenever Queeny come near me, I want to run the other way. Fast. But I cain't now 'cause she right on top a me, her shadow covering me from the top a my rag ribbons to the tips a my ratty shoes.

"Morning Miss Queeny," I say real polite.

Mama say I got to be nice to all a the mayor's slaves, even a big, old witch like Queeny. She live in a little room the mayor's wife had built right next to they kitchen so Queeny can be at her beck and call day and night. All Missus Mayor got to do is ring a little bell and up Queeny jump to fetch a cup a tea or empty her bedpan or bring a little more honey for her biscuits.

Earle, Mister Rotten's man, say Queeny don't live in no tar-paper shack. When he bring dry goods to they house, he see that she sleep on a little feather bed *and* has her very own sink and privy. Plus Queeny get to eat a bit a whatever she making for the Mayor no matter what it be.

One time Earle say, "Even when that girl eat the fancy teacakes from her Massa's dinner parties, she still find a way to make it sound like she's made to lick a slop jar."

Queeny got nothing nice to say 'bout nothing. Ever time Mama and I see her in town, she be complaing like she Job. Maybe Queeny need to see what it feel like to have to do her business outside and sleep in a drafty shack and eat nothing but cornbread and pork rind. I ain't got no boils like

56

Job, but I know what it feel like to never be warm enough or full enough...not like I wants to be.

"What you got to be laughing 'bout?" Queeny ask one more time. Her sourpuss face be like the prunes Mama put on Little Sam's oatmeal.

"I's jest watching the kids," I tell her. I ain't gone tell her I's thinking 'bout piddling by the shack to ward off varmints. She jest say I's being fresh and threaten to tell my mama.

"Ain't you lucky to *set there* and do *nothing*," Queeny sigh. "I got so many things to get done today and Missus want me to come all the way across town to go to the store!"

I roll my eyes 'cause "all the way across town" for Queeny mean she got to walk past three houses and the bank 'fore she get to the store. She don't know nothing 'bout walking...not like poor old Earle do. He walk everwhere for Mister Rotten. I bet he done walked enough to go halfway 'round the world by now.

"How you?" I ask. As if I really want to know. I ain't got nothing nice to say 'bout Queeny, so most a the time I do like Mama tell me and don't say nothing at all.

"Missus gots me hopping today," Queeny sigh.

Mama poke her head out the door. "You wants to come in now, Sapphire?" She see Queeny and smile. "'Morning."

Queeny nod. "Ruby."

Mama pull on my sleeve. "Come on, baby girl."

*Thank you, Jesus,* I think. *Thank You for sending my mama to rescue me from that nasty woman.* "'Bye, Miss Queeny," I say, grinning. But in my mind I's thinking, *And good riddance.*

When we inside the store, Missus Snow be rolling out a big bolt a calico. Mama say I get to choose the color for our new dresses. Now it *really* be like Christmas! There be red and purple and blue. The one Missus Snow show me be green with little white flowers all over the place. They looks like the ones Missus and Mama done planted last year near the back door by the garden...the ones that smell sweet and clean.

I point to the bolt. "I like that one, Mama...if it be alright with you."

"That be fine, Sapphire," Mama nod. "A good choice, too. Don't you think that look jest like the sweet alyssum from our garden?"

"Yes'm." I love how we both think the same things sometime, like Mama and I be one person.

"Massa Settler say to put the calico on his monthly bill," Mama tell Missus Snow.

She fold it into a nice pile, then, jest like she do for the white folks, Missus Snow wrap it in brown paper.

"Thank you kindly, Missus," Mama say.

"I know how dusty the roads can be when we don't get much rain," Missus Snow say. "Now, Sapphire, your mama says you want to do some business with me."

I swallow hard and don't say nothing, jest nod at the floor and hold out my penny.

Missus Snow act like she do business with a little colored girl ever day. She not like her husband who yell at us to hurry up and be on our way. Mister Snow say we's bad for business and if white folks see us malingering, they won't come into the store. I wonder what *malingering* mean and plan to look up that big old word in Missus Settler's dictionary when I learn how to spell better.

"What would you like?" Missus Snow asks me. "Your mama says you might want some candy."

I steal a look up at her and when I do, I see a little corn cob doll on the shelf over her head. It be a little bitty thing, maybe only as big as my hand, but I think I want to see if I can use my penny to trade for her. I bite my lip and look at Mama.

"What you want, Sapphire?" she ask. "C'mon...we gots to meet Massa at the wagon."

I point to the doll on the shelf. She got curly paper hair and a dress that come down to her little knobby feet.

"You want that doll?" Missus Snow ask me.

"Yes'm," I whisper. "Can I trade my penny for it?"

Missus Snow pull it from the shelf and look at the little white tag 'round its neck. "It's three cents."

"I only got one penny," I tell her.

Mama open her coin purse and give me two more pennies. "Sapphire, you done helped me knit some a them doilies," she say. "I's happy to give you a little a the money we earn'd. You go on and get that dolly. It'll last longer than peppermint candy, won't it?"

My smile stretches big. "Yes'm." Carefully I put the three pennies on the counter and Missus Snow hand me the doll. The husk crackle when I stroke the dress and touch her hair. Her black dot eyes shine up at me like she know she be mine now.

Mama tell me to thank Missus Snow and I do, then we heads out the door to where the wagon still be hitched. They ain't no sign a Massa, so we take our time. I cradle my doll in my arms and wonder what I gone name her.

We see Queeny hurrying up the street toward the Mayor's house and Mama shake her head. "That girl gone be a victim all her life," she say. "When we's set free, Queeny still gone be stuck in them invisible chains."

I know what *invisible* is...that mean you cain't see it. It be like a ghost or a spook or something. Missus read me a book called *A Christmas Carol* last year and it have a ghost man who has to drag a heap a heavy chains 'round in the afterlife 'cause he been stingy when he was alive. Queeny ain't wearing no chains that I can see, but she drag 'round her complaints like she toting a heavy pail a water, spilling a little a her bellyaching on everone she meet. And she always seem to be able to go back to the well to pull up some more.

But Mama done seen Queeny's mama die in childbirth. She spoke to Massa, who be friends with the Mayor, and made sure Queeny was brought up by the house slaves so she'd never have to work on the Mayor's farm or get sold to a plantation. Jest like Mama made sure I work in Massa and Missus' house cleaning and helping with the cooking, knitting and such. She say everone done been born for some purpose and right now that be mine...to be her helper and to knit up pretty things for the white folks.

I wonder what my purpose gone be when I ain't a slave no more.

But I do know I ain't a victim a nothing. Like Mama say, I only a slave by what you see on the outside. I ain't got no invisible chains 'cause I got my freedom with Mama at night when she sing to me and tell me she love me. Queeny ain't never know her mama, and she probably ain't got nobody to say they loves her. Maybe that why she so mean all the time, and I got to find it in my heart to pray for her poor soul, not wanting to run like a jackrabbit whenever she cross my path.

Mama help me climb up on the wagon seat, then she get up right next to me. I hold my doll in my lap so I can see her little black eyes and a dot for a nose. The curve a her mouth be red and her cheeks be painted with tiny circles a pink.

"That be a pretty dolly," Mama say. "I think she need a calico shawl to match the jumper I be making you soon."

"Then we all match, Mama!"

I look up and see Massa coming from the bank. His face be drawn and white. Look like he want to cry, but I know he ain't. He carrying a little bundle a papers under his arm and it be tied up with a piece a string all neat and tidy. When he get to the wagon, he slide 'em into his brown satchel and put it under the seat.

Massa don't say nothing as he unhitch the horse, but when he climb into the wagon, he ask Mama, "Did you get everything you need?"

"Yes, Massa Sam," she say.

'Fore he pull on Pete's reigns, Massa look 'round. He real quiet for a moment, then he say, "The next time you come to town, make sure to tell Mrs. Snow I said, 'thank you' for her kindness."

Mama jest nod.

As we head back to the big house, I watch Massa from the corner a my eye. I know something ain't right 'cause I listened to what he done said with them different ears Mama told me 'bout. Now I figure maybe my ears need to perk up when they ain't no words to be heard.

It then I notice Massa ain't got the dry goods from the store. I wonder when he gone notice, too. Maybe not 'til we get home. Then Massa might send Hale to fetch Mister Rotten to tote the load to the big house.

I ain't liking that prospect...no suh...'cause that insight Mama say I has is jest starting to kick in.

# Karin

Renatta looks up from her lace and frowns. "None of us will get out of here alive," she murmurs, her face drawn and sallow. "Kramer will order this place burned to the ground before he'll ever let us have one breath of freedom."

I have sat with Renatta in this dank, gray room for weeks and every day she says different versions of the same thing. "We will never survive." "We will all die of typhus before this is over." "I will never see my family again." "I wish I would just die and end this senseless agony."

She feeds my fear with her incessant grumbling, but I focus on my hands, on their endless repetition of movement, and pray for strength. Being among all kinds of women has made me immune to their bickering, their anger and bitterness. I find that no matter where I am, the prisoners are all the same - some have hope, but the vast majority quickly sink like a stone into desperation.

Vati's words come back to me whenever I hear someone moan in grief and agony, whenever I hear someone call for their mother or plead for death to take them. When I feel like falling headlong into the dark abyss, I remember my father holding me close before we were separated at Auschwitz.

"Gute nacht, meine Liebling," he had whispered in my ear. "Du lebst...du lebst."

*Good night, my darling...you will live...you will live.*

Vati was right, I have survived, but for what? If the Nazis burn this camp as Renatta says they will, what is the purpose of suffering as I have? As we all have?

I look at Simka's face, curled up in concentration as she endures another wave of pain. I wonder what she's thinking, but cannot ask her. Cannot risk Grese or one of the other guards hearing my voice and charging into the room, demanding that we be silent and work harder. Or worse yet, taking one of us away to work in the yard, dragging corpses and digging trenches.

Simka knows what happens when someone dares to speak while in service to the Reich, what it costs those of us who are left behind. So she, too, remains silent.

But Renatta does not.

"For centuries, it's always been the same...the Jews must suffer under the boots of tyrants," she angrily hisses. "Hitler won't stop until every last one of us is wiped from the face of the earth."

The woman sitting across from Renatta drops a stitch and curses under her breath. "Scheisse!" Maria hisses. "Jetzt schauen was du mir gemacht!"

*Shit! Now look what you made me do!*

Renatta's eyes widen. "What *I* made you do?" she swats back. "I'm not holding that lace in my hands!"

"Please *stop* talking," Maria demands. "I cannot concentrate." She quickly slips the stitch back onto her needles and continues the intricate, yet delicate pattern.

"The truth is the truth," Renatta replies, pursing her lips sourly.

Maria glances up and lifts a brow. "And what truth is that?"

"We are suffering just because of our religious beliefs and nothing more."

I look from Renatta to Maria to Simka, knowing they are all Jewish, and I alone am not. I wonder what Renatta thinks of me...what she thinks I'm capable of doing.

Maria gently clears her throat, interrupting my thoughts. "That is true, yes...but Jews are not the only ones suffering here."

"But there are more Jews than anyone else, God help us," Renatta counters.

Maria sets her knitting in her lap and narrows her dark brown eyes. The lines on her face deepen into shadow, making her look much older than she is. "I no longer believe in God," she says plainly. "What kind of God would allow a place such as this to exist? What kind of God would take my husband and children away from me?"

"But your husband was a *Rabbi*," Renatta says, shaking her head. "He would be ashamed to hear you say this."

Maria's eyes fill with tears. "My husband would be ashamed if I didn't speak my mind clearly."

Renatta makes a tsk, tsk sound.

"The only shame I feel is in not helping others more when I could," Maria says, tears spilling down her face. She nods at me. "That girl right there is living proof of what the Germans will do to their own kind when one is willing to help a Jew. Her father died...her brothers...and even..." She chokes on her words.

Simka reaches over and gently touches Maria's hand. All of us had been imprisoned together at Buchenwald and were sent here by transport shortly after Christmas. Mutti and Maria had spent many hours talking together, so she knows the story of where I came from, what we endured at the hands of the S.S. Mutti has shared my childhood and the loss of it when we were sent to the camps and stripped of our belongings, our clothes, and our identities. Through Mutti's stories, Maria knows me as well as anyone.

And so does Simka.

Now Maria sniffles and darts her eyes to Renatta's. "Others are suffering just as much as you...all of us who are innocent or dare to defy the Fuhrer. My husband used to say that when we forget about the pain of others and only focus on our own suffering, we use our pain as a crutch that justifies our anger. We'll use it to live a life of superiority and separation...and in the end it only serves to add fuel to our misery." Maria looks at me and weeps openly. "Instead of seeing Karin as a person who has lost as much as we have, we see her as 'the other'...someone who cannot understand what we feel."

When Maria says my name, I feel ashamed. For years Mutti has told me to only answer to my number, to never call attention to myself. To never ask for anything, not even mercy. Hearing my name is both a comfort and a curse. I'm not just a number, but a human being, and yet, in order to survive, I cannot be the person I used to be.

"This is not only a tragedy for the Jews," Maria continues pointedly. "It's a *human* crisis first and foremost. You forget that human beings created the gas chambers, but other human beings walk into them saying the rosary and the Lord's Prayer and the Shema Yisrael. In the end, we're all human...we all choose what we do in this life, what we believe, and what we do with those beliefs."

"Oh, yes, I forget you attended University," Renatta snorts condescendingly. "Always the intellectual you are, Maria. But what about *reality*?!"

Maria shakes her head and goes back to her knitting. "You will never understand what I'm saying until you take off the shackles of your hatred. How are the Jews who wish to kill Germans any different in their hearts?" Her hands work furiously now. "We're taken down to the same level of survival here, and if you think a Jewish mother feels any differently than a Christian mother when witnessing the murder of her own child, then I feel sorry for you, because you will never understand what I am saying."

Tears stream down my face and I want to beg Maria to stop talking, but I cannot. Her words have torn open wounds that still fester deep inside my soul, wounds that will never heal no matter how many times I say the Twenty-Third Psalm or repeat the blessings Frau Zweig taught me. There is no prayer that can ever wash me clean again.

Simka's face is ashen as she tries to finish the row of lace. Still, she finds the strength to whisper, "Bitte, Maria, nicht mehr."

*Please, Maria, no more.*

Maria turns her face to mine. "I'm sorry, Karin. I am...please forgive me."

I nod and wipe my eyes, but there aren't enough tears to wipe away the memories of how my life had been before we came to this place. Before Vati and Jurgen died. Before Mutti and I were shipped from camp to camp like nameless, faceless chattel on a train.

Before a little one I loved more than my own life was taken from me in a moment I shall never forget.

***

October, 1941

Almost three years have passed since Vati bravely made the decision to hide Frau Zweig and her sons in the theater. Endless years of war, midnight raids, and the threat of the Gestapo and S.S. lurking everywhere. All of the Jews in our neighborhood have been stripped of their businesses, their homes, and their livelihood. Many of them have been deported to places unknown.

But Heinrich and Georg and Fritz remain locked with their mother behind closed doors, their lives ultimately contracted into one small room and a bath with only a sink and a toilet. Fritz cannot remember what it feels like to play on the grass. He cannot remember Mutti's vegetable garden or the wriggling worms he used to unearth with her trowel. Georg and Heinrich have grown sullen and dull, their bright personalities tarnished by remaining hidden in a building that, for now, is safe from the S.S..

Vati made sure of that.

He told everyone that Frau Zweig and her children disappeared into the night the day after Kristallnacht, and that he's still waiting to hear from Herr Zweig wherever he might be. In the meantime, the Nazis are satisfied that a Christian is keeping the theater open. Even though theatrical productions have been severly regulated and the Sunday Night Volkslieder has been permanently cancelled, Vati shows propaganda films to deflect S.S. attention, although he forbids Jurgen and me to attend.

"They are not for children," he tells me emphatically. "The only reason I show them is to keep the S.S. out of the theater."

I'm nearly sixteen now and Jurgen is six. He's old enough to suspect that there's something happening at the theater beyond the movies and the plays, but is still too young to stay quiet about the Zweig's hidden presence, so my parents and I continue to keep our closely guarded secret.

Gestapo thugs and Nazi S.S. have come to our house often enough during the past three years, as being the business partner of a Jew keeps Vati high on their list of potential criminals. The brownshirts bang on the front door and shout in their shrill voices, "Eroffnen, Vogel!! Alle ausserhalb!"

*Open up, Vogel! Everyone outside!*

Then they ransack every room until they're satisfied no one is hidden beneath the stairs or in the cellar or the attic.

The last time they barged through the door, Mutti scooped up Jurgen and held him close while I cradled eight-month-old Bruno in my arms, his chubby cheek warm against my own. He was born on Christmas Eve, a welcome miracle in the midst of the horror of everything we've lived through since the night Herr Zweig disappeared.

When Mutti told us that she had been given a great gift from God, I knew from the glow on her face that a baby was on the way. The next day I spent all of my money on some cream-colored yarn and began knitting a new layette for my little brother or sister. Little Jurgen didn't understand until Mutti's belly became swollen and he could no longer sit on her lap.

"Will our new baby be a boy or a girl?" he kept asking.

Mutti would pat her belly and say, "Warten und sehen...es wird eine Uberraschung sein."

*Wait and see...it will be a surprise.*

And it was a surprise to see Mutti sitting in a hospital bed a few days after her delivery with Bruno resting quietly in her lap. During delivery, her uterus ruptured and she had to have an emergency Cesarean and hysterectomy. Both she and my little brother survived...but just barely.

When I went to visit her, she looked pale and drawn. "I'm fine, Karin," she smiled. "I have my baby...that's all I prayed for."

Now that Bruno is here, I'm even more protective of both him and Jurgen. Alhough schoolwork keeps me busy, I don't mind changing Bruno's diapers or feeding him a bottle whenever Mutti is busy with Jurgen and the housework. I keep a close eye on them whenever we leave the house for a walk or to run an errand for our mother.

Whenever the Nazis pass our house or pound on the door, my heart leaps in my chest. I run and gather them into my arms. Bruno clings to me with wide eyes and watches while the S.S. men bark at our father, then hammer their way out of the house when they can do nothing more than order him to continue obeying the Nuremberg Laws.

Once one of them angrily grabbed Bruno's face and sneered, "Dieser Junge sieht aus wie ein Jude."

*This boy looks like a Jew.*

I cried that Bruno was my brother.

The S.S. looked angrily at my mother, then back to Bruno. "Es gibt judische Blut in die Mutter und das Kind," he spat. "Ich werde dass mich zu beweisen!"

*There's Jewish blood in the mother and the child. I will prove that myself!*

When they left, Mutti collapsed on the couch and sobbed while I put the boys to bed, all the while worrying that the S.S. would return that night and arrest us all. Nothing came of it, but still, every day I wonder what might happen if the Zweigs are discovered, if Mutti's secret about her grandmother comes to light.

Still, I know what I feel is nothing compared to what Mrs. Zweig must suffer. Over three years and no word from her husband. We all fear he's in a detention camp, not a prison. Vati hears through the underground about camps where men are starved and worked to death. Where many enter, but very few return.

Stefan Roth, the older boy who grew up next door, is now an important leader in the S.S.. When he visits his mother, Stefan loudly brags about how many Jews he's rounded up, how many of them have been sent to a place called Buchenwald. He hopes to soon become a member of the Schutzstaffel, Hitler's protection squad, and quotes Heinrich Himmler constantly saying, "We must stand firm and carry on the racial struggle without mercy."

"*Why*?" I long to ask when I'm hanging laundry on the line and overhear him talking in the backyard while he sips lemonade with Frau Roth. I cannot understand how they are ever going to carry out their plans to rid Germany of all of the Jews. *How can mass murder be legal?* I wonder. And then I realize that when a mad man creates the laws and gullible, fanatical men are easily harnessed to do the dirty work, the unthinkable becomes a reality.

Stephan's ruddy face curls into a scowl when he talks about the supremacy of the Fuhrer to make Germany the most powerful country in the world. "He has brought us back from the brink of destruction," he told his mother last summer. "And now we will carry out his plan to annihilate anyone who would stand in our way."

Now I'm standing in the kitchen making sandwiches for Vati to take to the theater. It's Saturday morning and he will be showing some new propaganda films later in the afternoon. Attendance has been uncommonly high, so business is good, but Vati says half of his profits have been stolen by the S.S., so any extra income he had been hoping to save for Herr Zweig is immediately diverted to the government.

He told Mutti, "They take whatever they think would rightly belong to Leonard and threaten to close the theater if I dare to raise any kind of resistance."

Our rations have been limited for years, but we are still able to share what we have with the Zweig's. Vati carries a basket with him to work every day and in the evening, returns with notes of thanks from Frau Zweig and tiny drawings and folded paper toys from the boys. Even little Fritz is now able to write simple words of gratitude.

Georg's birthday is tomorrow and Mutti has been saving our eggs so she can bake him a cake with chocolate frosting. I can't wait for Vati to bring it to him as we haven't been able to bake Kuchen or Streusel for ages and Georg has such a sweet tooth...just like I do.

I've wrapped my favorite book, *Grimm's Fairy Tales*, in newspaper and tied it with a red ribbon. I hope Georg likes it as much as I do, especially "The Elves and the Shoemaker." Sometimes it seems that Heinrich and Georg are like elves, making us little surprises and hiding them in the basket for Vati to deliver when he comes home from work. Every day there's something new and as I place several apples into a small paper bag, I wonder what magic Heinrich will be able to create with it. Perhaps a puppet or a boat or even a mask. Heinrich is a wonder with paints and charcoal. He wants to be an artist someday, but I think he already is and I tell him so whenever Vati allows me visit the theater.

I used to come every Friday and bring Frau Zweig the Shabbat meal, pretending that I was Little Red Riding Hood toting a warm supper to my father who was busy counting receipts from the week's treasury. But now Vati only allows me to visit once a month. Heinrich, Georg, and I play cards and chess and tell stories, but it's not the same as our special Sunday dinners and the evening Volkslieder with our friends.

Heinrich is moody and doesn't always like to talk, but Georg and Fritz are eager to hear what's happening on the outside.

"Is it raining today?" they ask.

"Can you bring more books from the library?"

"When can you bring Bruno to see us again?"

They love to hold little Bruno on their laps and play with his plump, dimpled hands. They rub his dusty brown hair and pull silly faces to make Bruno's dark eyes dance with delight. My little brother always rewards them with gurgles and chortles and hoots of laughter.

A few months ago when I had brought the Shabbat meal, Frau Zweig cradled Bruno in her arms and sang the Yiddish songs she used to sing to Fritz when he was a baby. Bruno cooed and nuzzled his head beneath her chin. Frau Zweig kissed my brother's temple and whispered something I had heard her say many times before but didn't understand.

"I'm blessing your little brother with a Shabbes prayer," she explained. "May God bless him and guard him. May God show your whole family favor and be gracious to you."

As I lit the small candles and said both the Baruch atah, Adonai, then the Lord's Prayer as Frau Zweig has taught me to do, she held Bruno close and rocked him. It was then that I understood what Vati meant when he said our baby is balm on her poor soul.

I'm remembering that Shabbat when Mutti walks into the kitchen with Bruno balanced on her hip. She looks frazzled, her hair wildly askew and her clothing rumpled. I know how difficult it's been since Bruno was born. He's a good baby, but there never seems to be enough time to cook and clean and do laundry. I try to help with my little brothers, but schoolwork has kept me uncommonly busy during the week and I'm still forced to attend Jungmadel meetings. Mutti says I must put on a front and go with my friends, even though I'd rather be home listening to records and knitting a new hat for Jurgen.

"Karin, will you take the baby for a walk?" she asks. "Jurgen is sick and I can't leave the house."

"It's such a nice day," I reply, nodding. "The leaves are just beginning to change...our favorite time of year."

She smiles and her dark eyes sparkle. "Ja...die Dammerung der Jahreszeiten."

*Yes, the twilight of the seasons.*

Mutti always takes a moment to step outside in the evenings to watch the sun set in the western sky, especially in autumn. She says the colors remind her of a Jules Breton painting, her favorite being "A Fisherman's Daughter" which she saw at the museum in Douai, France when she was a little girl.

"The German army stole it during World War I and no one knows where it is," she told me once. But then she intuitively described the lovely young girl who leans barefooted against a stone, knitting a fishnet for her father. Her head bowed, her face calm and stoic, the girl works diligently, yet peacefully as the long net cascades from her fingers down toward the earth.

Now I hold out my arms to Bruno as he shoves his fingers into his mouth, drool spilling onto his chin. He's teething and no matter how we try to soothe him, nothing seems to make him feel better...except going for a walk. I take him from Mutti and he babbles while I slip a light blue sweater over his head.

"What a good boy!" I exclaim, kissing Bruno's little nose. "Who's Karin's sweet little boy?"

He grabs a handful of my long, blonde hair and shoves it into his mouth.

"Hey! Give that back," I smile, gently pulling my hair out of his slobbery hands. Then I tuck Bruno into his pram while Mutti prepares a bottle for him.

Before we leave, I dart up to my room, passing Vati on the stairs. He's wearing his best tie and the dark blue cardigan Mutti made for him last Christmas.

"Good morning, Karin," he says, stopping to give me a kiss on the cheek.

"Morning," I reply. "How's Jurgen?"

"Mutti was up with him all night...he's got a fever, so don't get too close."

"I won't...I just need a warmer jacket. I'm taking Bruno out for a walk."

Vati adjusts the sleeves of his pullover. "I really appreciate all you do for your brothers, Karin. You'll be a wonderful mother someday."

I smile. "I hope so...the boys are good practice anyway."

"Especially when they're being naughty," Vati smiles.

"Yes...especially then."

My father heads down the stairs. "See you after work!"

I poke my head into Mutti's room where I find Jurgen tucked beneath the covers, his face ruddy, his eyes watery and swollen.

"What's wrong, little one?" I ask, walking to him.

"Sick," he says, glumly staring out the window.

I sit on the edge of the bed and smooth a wisp of blonde hair from his forehead. He looks just like Vati, as do I. Our straw-colored hair and light blue eyes are identical, although Jurgen inherited Mutti's sharp jaw line and high forehead while I have Vati's broader features. Bruno is the spitting image of our mother with his dark eyes and hair, and even darker skin.

"Do you want me to bring you some new books?" I ask. "Bruno and I are going for a walk and we can stop by the library."

Jurgen shakes his head.

"Hungry?"

He shakes his head again.

"Thirsty?"

"Mutti said she'll bring me a glass of water."

I nod. "Okay, well, I'll see you in a little bit. Maybe when Bruno and I get back, you'll feel better."

Jurgen shrugs drowsily. "Maybe...maybe not."

I kiss his temple and feel the moist heat of his skin on my lips. "I'm sorry you're sick."

"Will you sing something?" Jurgen asks, his eyes at half mast.

He yawns and snuggles more deeply beneath the covers while I hum the first verse from *Ihr Kinderlien Kommet*, his favorite song. Even though it's not Christmastime, I sing to him about the Christ child Who is more beautiful and beloved than angels are, and before I reach the end, Jurgen is fast asleep.

When I go into my room to get my jacket, I notice Georg's present sitting on my desk, its red ribbon tied neatly in a bow. Grabbing it, I dash down the stairs calling, "Did Vati leave yet?"

Mutti's sitting at the table with a cup of coffee, reading a book and absentmindedly pushing the pram back and forth to keep Bruno from crying. "Ja...he just left a moment ago."

"I forgot to give him Georg's book!" I say.

"Well, it's not his birthday today, so you're not late," Mutti says, sipping her coffee. "We'll put it in tomorrow's basket."

"But I want it to be a surprise," I tell her.

She turns a page. "It will be."

A moment of silence passes between us and I decide to slip the book into my pocket when Mutti isn't looking. I'll try to catch Vati in the carport, and if he's not there, Bruno and I will make a quick stop at the theater on our way to the park. Then the real surprise for Georg will be seeing Bruno and me for the first time in almost a month.

"Be careful and watch where you take him," Mutti says as if she can read my mind. She looks up at me and stops rocking the pram. "I mean it, Karin. *Stay away* from the

74

theater. It's Saturday and the S.S. will be watching to see how many people show up to watch that new film."

I nod, my chin stiff, my jaw tight. "I promise."

"Can you go to the store and get me some sugar, please?" she asks, getting up to find the ration booklet. "I think a pound will be plenty for Georg's kuchen and to make a little pie for Jurgen when he's feeling better."

"Do you need flour?" I ask, zipping my jacket.

"No...just sugar," Mutti replies. She folds the booklet and some money into my hand. "And tell Herr Wolff that Vati will need next week's rations a day early."

"Why?"

"Don't ask questions, Karin!" Mutti says severely. "Just do as I tell you!"

I'm used to my mother's changing moods, especially since Bruno was born. One moment she's amiable, the next she's angry about the slightest thing. Vati says to be patient, that she's not getting much sleep. That having the baby is harder than she thought it would be. But I know better. Mutti's always been temperamental, even before Bruno was born, and I'm used to the ever-changing storm clouds that open without warning, then dissipate just as quickly.

I slip the money and stamps into my purse, then drop it into the pram near my brother's feet. Bruno's fast asleep, his little finger curled in his rosebud of a mouth.

"We'll be back before lunchtime." I say.

Mutti goes to the stove where she refills her cup of coffee. "Good...tell Frau Wolff I'll see her at church tomorrow."

"I will."

As I push the pram out the back door, then precariously bump it down the steps, I try not to wake my brother. Looking back at the house, I see my mother standing in the window, staring into space, her arms crossed, her eyebrows furrowed. For a moment, she doesn't resemble the woman who has raised me.

In Mutti's face I see someone altogether unknown and it frightens me.

Bruno gurgles with delight as I lift him from the pram and set him on my lap. It took a while to reach the park and by the time I found an empty bench near the pond, my brother had woken up, his eyes wide and bright.

"Did you finish your bottle?" I ask, searching the blankets for it. "I'll bet not." Sure enough, I find it tucked between the thin, cloth-covered mattress and the pillow.

Bruno grabs it with both hands and shoves it into his mouth, sucking hungrily.

"You're a little piggy," I tell him sweetly.

As always, S.S. officers are everywhere, some men talking among themselves, some enjoying a quiet cigarette on their own. Families pass by. A group of children throws rocks in the pond. I watch the ripples on the surface of the murky water widen, then disappear. Close by a little boy pokes a stick into the muddy bank while his parents sit on a blanket sharing a late breakfast of rolls and fruit.

The sky isn't as blue as it was last month. October winds have blown billowing clouds across the horizon and I know it won't be long before the first snowfall. I wonder, *Will we spend one more winter at war? When will the Zweigs be able to leave the theater and go back home? Will we ever see Herr Zweig again? Will Baden Baden be destroyed by bombs or spared as it was during The Great War?*

Too many questions for a young girl to ask, especially when living as we do...day to day, never knowing what might happen next.

I hear a voice behind me. "Fraulein Vogel...Karin."

Turning, I see it's Stefan Roth. His uniform is starched and sharp edged, the red-banded swastika in sharp contrast to the grayish-green material. It's hard to believe he's only twenty-one as he looks much older than that with his closely cropped hair and hardened eyes.

I nod coolly, but my heart thumps loudly. "Good morning."

"What are you doing here?"

"What do you mean?"

"Why aren't you home with your mother?"

"I'm taking the baby for a walk."

"Where is your father?"

"At the theater."

Stefan sits next to me on the bench and I can smell his strong, bitter aftershave. "Why aren't you at the Jungmadel meeting?"

"There isn't one until next Tuesday," I tell him plainly.

"There is always a mandatory meeting on Saturdays," Stefan insists. "I'm certain of that."

I shrug. "It was cancelled."

Stefan laughs bitterly as he knows I'm lying. Attendance at the meetings has been poor for the past few months and I've convinced Vati and Mutti that once a week is plenty enough for me. No one's bothered me about it.

Until now.

"Maybe you're one of the weak ones who needs to be chiseled away as the Fuhrer demands," Stefan says, narrowing his eyes.

I shake my head. "Mutti needs me to take care of the baby...Jurgen is sick and Vati must work today. There's a new film and..."

"Yes, I know," Stefan spits. "But that doesn't mean you're allowed to shirk your duty."

"My duty is to my family first," I say a little more boldly than I should.

"Your duty is to the *Fuhrer* first!" Stefan grabs my arm and squeezes tightly. "To speak otherwise is to show contempt for the Reich."

Bruno lets out a yelp of fear, then starts to bawl.

"Make him stop!" Stefan orders as he lets go of me.

I try to push the bottle back into Bruno's mouth, but he shoves it away and clings to my jacket. Tears roll down his face as he howls, burying his face in my shoulder. He kicks his feet and one of them pushes into my pocket where Georg's book is hidden.

Stefan sees the red ribbon and before I can stop him, he jerks the package away from me. "Who's Georg?" he asks, reading the gift tag. "Your boyfriend?"

I shake my head, but say nothing.

"A classmate?"

I shake my head again, rubbing Bruno's back as he quiets down.

"Who then?"

"My cousin."

"Where does he live?"

"Freudenstadt."

"You're lying."

The sinister look on his face makes my skin crawl. "No, I'm not," I say, my voice quivering. "He lives with my Tante Sabine and Onkel Erik."

"You *lie*...they live in Stuttgart," Stefan says plainly. "You forget I know everything about your family. It's my job to know everything about every family in this district."

"They moved last summer."

"Really?" Stephan says, an evil smile crossing his lips. "To Freudenstadt?"

"Yes."

"Did they register when they moved?"

I shake my head. "I don't know...I suppose so."

"So why do you carry Georg's gift if he lives so far away?" he demands. "I doubt you'll be walking all the way to Freudenstadt today, especially with that brat."

I gently bounce Bruno and he whimpers softly, sticking his fingers into his mouth. "I'm taking it to Vati at the theater so he can mail it for me."

"Is that so? When?"

"Now."

"I'll escort you," Stefan growls so I know that it's not an offer, but a direct command.

Nervously I tuck Bruno back into the pram and hand him his bottle. He gums the nipple furiously, staring at Stefan with wide eyes.

We say nothing on the long walk to the theater. The pram bumps and jostles over ruts in the sidewalk, but Bruno thankfully keeps quiet, too. Stefan is a few steps ahead of us, his boots clicking on the concrete, his gait razor sharp.

"Schneller!" he says, looking over his shoulder. "Sich beeilen!"

*Faster...hurry up!*

When we reach the theater, Stefan tries the doors, but they're locked, so he bangs on the glass, shouting, "Vogel! Raus hier!"

*Vogel...get out here!*

I see Vati walking quickly from the back of the lobby. When he sees me with Stefan, he looks confused. Pulling keys from his pants pocket, he quickly unlocks the doors.

"Karin...are you alright?" Vati asks, pulling me toward him. "Is Bruno alright?"

"Yes...we're fine," I tell him. "Stefan saw us at the park and...well, I had this gift for cousin Georg in my pocket...and I wanted to bring it to you so you could take it to the post." I pull the little package from the pram and hand it to him.

"Oh, yes," Vati smiles. "Isn't it nice of you to remember his birthday?"

I nod, but say nothing.

"I'll get this in the post just as soon as I can."

"She's lying and so are you," he says with contempt. "Where's your phone?"

"In the office," Vati answers. "Why?"

"Do *not* question my authority," Stefan says, pushing his way past my father into the theater. "Follow me...both of you!"

79

By the time I'm able to maneuver the pram through the doors, Stefan is in Vati's office barking orders to whomever is on the other end of the line.

"Yes! The entire squad," he shouts. "And bring the dogs!"

An hour later I'm sitting with Bruno on my lap locked in Vati's office while he paces the floor. We can hear the S.S. shouting to each other and thumping on every wall, every floorboard. The German Shepherds howl as they sniff their way through the theater.

"Vati...I'm so sorry," I cry. "I only kept Georg's gift in my pocket for safekeeping. I wasn't going to bring it to you."

Vati says nothing.

"I promised Mutti I wouldn't and I meant to keep my promise," I say, wiping tears from my cheeks. "But Stefan..."

Vati stops and puts a hand on my shoulder. "Stop, Karin. It's not your fault. The Gestapo has been watching me closely for years. They've been laying in wait for news of Herr Zweig. This is not unexpected."

"What do you mean?"

"The Nazis are notoriously scrupulous...they keep impeccable records," he whispers. "Leonard is not in a camp. He's been in hiding since Kristallnacht...the Gestapo knows this because he escaped from the train when it stopped on its way to Weimer."

"But Vati...how do you know this?"

"He has been writing to me under an alias...a false name."

"All this time?"

"Yes."

"Does Mutti know?"

Vati shakes his head. "Only I know...and once I read his letters, I burn them immediately."

"Have you told Frau Zweig?"

He nods.

"And the boys?"

"They know their father is somewhere safe...that he's alive."

"Where is he?"

Suddenly a dog barks fiercely in the basement beneath the lobby. I'm frozen in fear when I hear S.S. men shouting to each other, their voices muffled beneath the floor.

"Wait, Karin...wait," Vati says calmly. "They may not find them. Heinrich and I made that wall air tight."

"But the dogs..."

"I know...just wait."

Bruno wriggles in my arms, desperate for a diaper change, but I haven't brought an extra one. Fussy and overheated, he begins to whine and pull my hair.

"Shush, Bruno," I say, kissing his forehead. "Shush."

Moments later we hear a rhythmic thumping sound followed by a loud crash. Mrs. Zweig's terrified screams fill my ears, then I hear her beg, "Nicht meine Kinder!"

*Not my children!*

Heinrich, Georg, and Fritz cry for their mother in a horrific chorus of terror. The sound of bullets rips through air...then an eerie silence.

Vati's face turns white when he gathers me in arms, pressing Bruno more closely to my chest.

In seconds the door bursts open and a furious guard thunders in yelling, "Vogel! You're under arrest! Don't move...don't say a word, you traitor!" He handcuffs my father and takes him from the room.

Bruno bursts into tears, shrieking at the top of his lungs. There's nothing I can do to soothe him as a host of men march into the office, tearing it apart before our eyes.

"Shut him up!" one of the S.S. shouts at me.

"I can't," I cry. "You're scaring him."

He smacks me sharply across the face. "Don't talk back to me!"

81

My hand flies to my cheek where the skin burns beneath my fingertips. Bruno arches his back and howls all the more.

"Shut him up or I will!" the S.S. threatens.

I back into a corner where Vati keeps his coat rack. His hat is still perched on one of the hooks and when I bump into it, the fedora falls to the floor where it's swiftly stomped on by heavy-heeled boots.

Bruno screams and bangs his head against my shoulder.

"Let me have him!" the S.S. demands.

"*NO!*" I shout, shaking my head.

The guard pulls on one of Bruno's ankles and his leg twists in a nauseating angle. "Give him to me!"

I cannot let him go...I cannot give him up.

Still, the S.S. pulls all the more as my brother screams in pain, the dreadful sound a sharp knife in my soul.

In an instant Bruno is silent, his lifeless body sprawled on the floor. His little face is covered in blood, his tiny leg torn away and thrown against the brick wall where seconds earlier the guard had viciously hurled Bruno, smashing his skull, killing him instantly.

I sob uncontrollably as I fall to the floor. Gathering my brother into my arms, I wail, "Why?! *Why* did you do this, you monster!?"

He stands over me, his gun at the ready. "Halt den Mund...oder du bist nachsten!"

*Shut your mouth...or you're next!*

I gasp, feeling something indescribably heavy lodge in my throat - a stone of sorrow that will remain for years to come, silencing me in the face of unspeakable torment.

*\*\*\**

Maria looks at me with compassion for she knows the horror that I had witnessed on that dark afternoon in October of 1941, the inconceivable pain I have endured. She knows that the Zweigs were gunned down in cold blood in the theater, a lesson to everyone in Baden Baden who would dare to hide Jews. She knows that Vati and I were made to stand and watch as Bruno's body, along with Frau Zweig's and her sons, was thrown onto a truck bed on its way to an unknown destination. And she knows that my family was taken that day and immediately deported to Auschwitz.

Maria knows all of these things through my mother's stories, for I have been a silent sentry to every moment since my brother's death. The story of what my life has become in the camps isn't echoed in what I say, but in what I create with my hands. Each piece of lace contains my memories, my anguish, my grief. I constantly weave in thoughts of those whom I have loved and those who have loved me. Those I despise and those I revere. Those who have beat me for their own pleasure and those who have treated me with uncommon kindness.

I don't know if I will ever speak again, for perhaps now my liberation can only be found in silence.

# Sapphire

Massa pull up in front a our shack 'stead a the barn and hobble Pete to the maple tree that shades our shack. "Ruby, let me help you and Sapphire down."

"Ain't you gone take him to get watered?" Mama ask.

"Not yet...I have to go to Mr. Birch's." He grab me 'neath my arms and gently set me on the ground. "There you go," he smile. "You can show your new doll 'round the place."

"Yes, sir," I smile back. "She say she like it already."

Massa chuckle at this. "What's her name?"

"She ain't got one yet," I tell him, hugging her close. "She gots to grow on me first."

Massa reach up a hand for Mama and she take it, hitching up her skirt. "Sapphire, put that dolly in the shack and go fetch some water for the folks in the fields," she say. "It getting warmer by the minute."

"Yes'm," I nod. "You want some for cooking?"

Mama turn to Massa. "You be eating with us today?"

"Just leave a plate for me in the cooler," Massa tell her, pulling the satchel from 'neath the seat. "I have to speak with Mrs. Settler before I leave...I imagine she'll be ready for dinner when we're through."

Mama pick up the calico. "I jest put my things in the shack and be right with her."

Massa glance in the back a the wagon. "Sapphire...when you go to the fields will you ask Keen to come see me in the big house? I've been forgetful lately...and just realized I didn't pick up the dry goods at the store."

*I's wondering how long it take for you to notice,* I think. But 'stead of saying it out loud, I ask, "Is Keen going with Pete?"

Massa shake his head. "No...I need Pete to go to Mr. Birch's. I'll send him with Nat and a skiff."

"Want me to go, too?" I ask, cutting my eyes to Mama.

She be frowning as if to say, *Now don't you get any such idea. You's staying right here with me.*

Massa pat my braids. "Thank you, no, Sapphire. Missus needs you in the house this afternoon. Her parents will hopefully be able to arrive in time for Easter."

I look at him confuse, 'cause didn't he jest say Missus and the chil'ren be going to see *them* soon? Then I 'member Massa be getting all kind a things mixed up in his head these days, like he don't even know what day *it be* sometime.

I like Missus' folks. They be jolly and laughing all a the time 'bout this and that. Plus they never call me nothing but "Sapphire", and they ask me to read from my little books 'bout what Mister McGuffey done think is proper for kids to learn.

Last time they come Mama let me stay up late and show 'em how I know all a my letters. I even wrote 'em a little note and read it to 'em all by myself while they's setting on the back porch enjoying the evenin' breeze. It say:

*Dear Massa and Missus Hamilton,*

*Thank you for my new Peter Parley book. Soon I will able to read it. Then I will write you one more time to tell you how I like it.*

*Thank you kindly,*
*Sapphire*

Missus' daddy say to not call him Massa. I ask what he want me to call him and he say sweetly, "Call me *Mr.* Hamilton. You're not my slave, just a nice little girl who plays with my grandchildren."

My eyebrows pop when he say this 'cause I know he ain't only saying it to be kind to me. Mister Hamilton done give Massa a sly look that say I ain't gone be his slave for much longer neither.

Massa jest cut his eyes away and sip his whiskey.

I want to say, *Well, I's Missus' slave sure enough when she ask me to fetch her some tea or tote water up to the bath or pick peas from the garden.*

But I don't say nothing 'cause Missus thank me for all the things I do for her and Little Sam and Marybelle. She thank me for making the beds and sweeping the floor and dusting the bookshelves. I may be her slave, but she treat me like a person, not a thing, and that be better than most folks has it.

Now Massa clear his throat. "The Hamiltons will be taking the train to Columbia in a few days and I'm going to send Keen with a note to pick them up with the wagon."

"Why you not going?" I ask like it be my business, which I know it ain't.

Massa don't seem to mind my questions. "I have other things to take care of. Keen's been on the road to Columbia more times than I can count."

*Never by hisself,* I think, setting my hands on my hips like Mama do when she getting ready to fly off the handle. *What you thinking, Massa? Sending Keen to do your business like he ain't likely to get hisself in a heap a trouble.*

Massa don't pay no 'tention to me now 'cause he turn to Mama. "How much money have you saved, Ruby?"

"Why you want to know?" She don't say it mean-like, jest like she curious why he asking her today.

Massa know she been saving for her freedom for near five years, since the first time she took some a her lace to town and sold it to Missus Snow. But he ain't never asked her nothing 'bout it. Now that I think on it, Mama say it be *Missus* who tell her that her stuff be good enough to sell all over Lincoln County. She tell Mama if she sell lots a her curtains and shawls and things, she could buy her freedom and mine, too. Massa get wind a this pretty quick, but he don't say she cain't. And he never say how much she got to save for us to be free. Maybe the price be too high and he don't want Mama to fret 'bout it. Or maybe the price be low and she done already got enough for the both a us and he ain't wanting us to leave.

"I'm just wondering," Massa say, rubbing his neck. "The war's going to end soon...looks like the Rebs are getting beaten up pretty badly."

My ears perk up right quick. "When it gone end?"

"I'm not sure," he say. "But pretty soon slavery will be a thing of the past."

"What we gone do then?" I ask, looking to Mama and back to him.

"I'm not sure of that either," Massa say plainly. "I'll still need help running the farm, but I don't know how I'm going to be able to pay anyone at first. The past three harvests have been mighty slim."

He don't have to tell me twice. Keen say if this year be like last, the farm be 'bout to bust. He say Massa's barely breaking even as it is. I don't know what that mean, but it don't sound good to me, no suh. I know it been a long time since Missus gone into Star City to buy new fancy things. She say she make do with what she already got. Plus her mama send her nice books and writing papers so she can keep on teaching Little Sam and Marybelle and me.

Last year Massa done sold one a his horses to pay taxes, 'cept I didn't know what taxes is, so I ask Keen one day when I was poking 'round the henhouse. He come over to say, "Howdy" and ask can I could fetch him a drink from the well 'cause he too hot and tired to get it hisself.

I say I get it in a minute, once I done seeing what Gertie got going on 'neath her rump. "You know what taxes is?" I ask him. "I hears Missus talking 'bout 'em to Massa this morning."

Keen scratch his prickly beard. "It be when you has to pay to live on the land you already own."

"That be crazy," I say, shaking my head. "Why you got to pay for something more'n once? And who getting all that money anyway?"

"Massa say he pay his taxes to the city and the state and that what he owe be going sky high to pay for the war."

"Yeah, but who get to spend all that money?"

Keen shrug and wipe his brow. "I guess it go to buy more guns and bullets and such for the Rebs."

"So Massa paying to keep the war going?"

"Yep...I suppose so...not directly, but who know what them mens in power do with what Massa and everone else done give 'em."

"Taxes is *bad*," I say, pulling a little brown egg from Gertie's nest.

"Taxes ain't what's bad," Keen say, shaking his head. "Massa say they pays for the post and the fire brigade and for that bossy little teacher at the schoolhouse. They pays for all kind a things that help run Lincoln County. But what *is* bad is when you ain't got no choice in how them taxes is spent."

I scratch a skeeter bite on my arm. "Who get to choose that?"

"Massa say the pol'ticians."

"Who they be?"

"Mens who think they knows ever little thing 'bout how to run the state, but they don't know squat 'bout how to work a plantation or what it take to scrape together enough money to pay what the Massa owe. All they knows is how to spend, spend, spend."

Which is why I's glad Mama know how to save, save, save.

Now she take my hand and tell Massa, "We be right back...tell Missus I have her dinner ready in two shakes."

I notice she don't say nothing 'bout how much money she got saved and Massa don't ask her 'gain.

"I will," he say. Then he walk toward the big house, that satchel tight under his wing. He ain't moving like no cock on the walk though...more like a tired old dog with his tail 'tween his legs.

Mama open the door a the shack and prop it with a chunk a brick. "Whew! It be stuffy in here," she sigh. "Springtime is coming, thank the Lord!"

"Yes'm," I say, looking 'round for a good place to set my dolly. "Mama...can I put her on the shelf over the bed?"

"Sure you can," Mama smile as she unwrap the calico. "She be safe all day long and at night she can come right down and sleep with us like she part a the family."

The material Massa done bought for us set on the bed, its pretty green and white colors sharp and clear 'gainst the faded blues and yellows a the quilt that Mama say be older than her. It so nice to know that some day soon, I gone have a brand new jumper to go with my fancy shirt, and my dolly will, too.

"Sapphire...change out a those clothes 'fore you head to the fields," Mama tell me. "I don't want you messing up that pretty shirt."

"Yes'm," I say, pulling the old jumper over my head. It get stuck 'neath my arms and don't go nowhere. "Mama! Help!"

She laugh as she wriggle me loose. "Lord, girl, you *is* growing like a weed! This thing be ready for the rag bag soon."

I laugh, too, and take off my shirt, then fold it up like Mama done taught me. She slip out a her going-to-town dress and change into the one she wear ever day -- the brown calico with yellow lace at the collar so nasty, it be unraveling nearly all 'round to the back. She don't want to get rid a it, though...and it ain't never going in no rag bag neither. Mama say it belong to her mama and be the only thing she got to 'member her by. They ain't no shiny pearls like Missus has. They ain't no paintings or fancy rings or nothing else to show Mama where she come from. Jest a old ratty dress that nobody want 'cept her.

Sometime when I be knitting in the kitchen, I watch Mama when she peeling carrots and such. I watch the seams in the sleeves pull a little more ever day. I see how the elbows been worn through 'til they nearly threads. I see how the collar get more stretched out and floppy.

But Mama don't care. She wash it ever week and wear it over and over 'gain. I wonder what she gone do when she make our new dresses, if she gone make something out that old dress like curtains or a little quilt or maybe something for my new dolly.

Now as she doing the buttons, she say, "You know, Sapphire, I think it time to make something new outta this dress a my mama's. I'll jest wear my town dress while I's making our new ones."

"What you want to make first?"

"How 'bout a wrap for your dolly so she won't be cold?"

"Thank you!" I grin, 'cause this be another one a them times when Mama and I thinks jest the same. "Now she gone have *two*!"

Mama pull off her old dress real careful. "And I think there be enough good material to make a nice headwrap for Opal and a cute little shirt for Pearl's new baby. Then all my girls has something from they grandmama."

"Can I help you cut out the pattern pieces?" I ask. Mama know how I love to work the scissors.

"Yes, baby girl," she say, rubbing my cheek. "We get started on it after dinner."

"Ya hear that, Ida?" I say to my dolly as I put her on the shelf that sit over my lump of a pillow. "You gone get some new clothes real soon."

"That be a fine name, Sapphire," Mama say as she fold up that old dress nice and neat. "Where you hear that from?"

"Ain't that what I always say when you ask me what I be doing when I's playing in the yard all by myself?" I giggle. "I always say, 'Ida know.' Now that she here, maybe Ida finally gone give me an idea or two."

"You is funny, baby girl," Mama laugh. When she turn to get her town dress off the bed, I see her back all scarred up with twisty welts that look like grapevines. I seen them ever time she get dressed, but she never say nothing 'bout 'em. I never ask neither, but today I be brave.

"Mama...why you got them scars?" I ask. "I ain't never seen you get whipped."

"It happen 'fore you was born...when Big Massa was still alive."

"He done it?"

"He done it."

"How come?"

Mama pull her town dress over her head and button up the bodice. "He got his reasons."

"What they be? You run off or something?"

"No, I ain't run," she say, smoothing the skirt and fixing the cuffs. "I was jest being myself."

"What you mean?"

Mama sit on the edge a the bed and pat the spot right by her so's I know to sit down, too. When I do, she chuck her finger 'neath my chin. "You's jest like I was when I was a bitty thing," she smile. "But you lucky 'cause Massa don't mind when you ask questions and speak out a turn."

"Big Massa mind when you did?"

Mama nod. "He mind that I be breating."

"How come?" I frown. "I figure he want you to stay alive and keep on slaving 'til the day you pass."

"Big Massa be different than Massa Sam," Mama say, twirling one a my braids 'tween her fingers. "He be mean and uppity like having white skin be his birthright to beat me."

"What he beat you for?" I ask. "You musta done something."

"Sapphire, you gots to learn that some mens...some *peoples*...get it up in they heads that they got a right to beat you jest 'cause you different...not 'cause you do something they don't like." Mama look out the door where the sun be shining down on everthing. "It don't matter if you be black or poor or from a place ain't no one want to claim. They beat you 'cause they think they got the right."

"That don't make no sense."

"Don't have to when they's the Massa," Mama whisper. "You lucky you ain't never seen it happen on Massa Sam's place...but it happen all a the time when I was a girl. These scars on my back be nothing when I think on other things I done seen." Then she pinch my cheek real gentle-like. "C'mon, baby, I tell you the story 'nother time when we ain't got work to do."


"Samuel, that's just not right!" I hear Missus yelling like she ain't never done 'fore.

She and Massa be in the dining room where Missus soon gone be eating her little bowl a soup. Mama standing at the kitchen stove, stoking the fire. When she see me coming through the side door, she put a finger to her lips.

"You *cannot* make that kind of deal with Mr. Birch...he's taking advantage of you!" I hear Missus shout.

"He's *not*!" Massa yell back. "This is the only way I can pay off my debt."

"But you can ask my parents for a loan."

"The hell I will," Massa growl. By the dirt in his voice I 'spect he start on his drinking early today.

"You're too proud I suppose," Missus say in her lilty voice that mean she gone start crying soon.

Massa stand his ground. "I'm proud enough to take care of my own business and not ask for a handout."

"It wouldn't be a handout," Missus argue. "Father would be happy to help you."

"You mean he'd be happy if I were in debt to *him*!"

"What's that mean, Samuel?"

"He's hated me from the moment we met," Massa say, his words starting to slur a little. "He hates that I dragged you all the way down here to live on this plantation. He hates that we're raising Samuel and Marybelle among slaves." Massa take a long drink a something, then he shout, "I'll be damned if I'm going to ask him for *anything*!"

"So you'd rather bow to a man who wants nothing more than to see you fail...who wants to take everything you've got just because you can't humble yourself and ask for help?!" Missus start crying real loud. "Do you know what this means, Samuel? We need that extra land for next season, especially when the war is over. We can't pay Keen or Albert or anyone else to work for us, but we could give them some of that land for plowing and planting."

"We can sharecrop the land we're already planting," Massa say like it be the last thing he want to do.

"There aren't enough crops now to pay the taxes and everything else we need to keep this place running." Missus sniffle a little, then she say, "Maybe you should just sell *all* of the land and be done with it."

I look to Mama 'cause this sound like crazy talk. Mama jest turn her head from side to side and roll her eyes.

"Jean...*stop*," Massa say. I can tell he fixing to get real mad. "I'm just giving Birch the northern twenty acres."

"Oh, *that's all*?" Missus snort. "You may as well be giving him the keys to our kingdom, because Lord knows he'll ask for that next."

"He knows better than to ask for anything else," Massa snap back.

Missus bide her time and I can tell she getting her courage up. Then she say real smarmy-like, "Is that *right*? Just like he asked for Juniper two years ago?"

Massa clear his throat. "He didn't ask for Juniper...he wanted someone else."

"Who?" Missus say.

Massa clear his throat 'gain. "Ruby."

I look to Mama who standing still as can be, her eyes wide, her face frozen.

"*Ruby*?" Missus say, surprised as we is.  "Why would he want Ruby?"

Massa sigh real deep.  "Because she's high yellow.  You know what Birch does with his mulatto slaves.  I couldn't let that happen to her.  I couldn't take her away from her children."

I peek through the crack in the door and see 'em setting at the table, one across from the other.  Missus' face curled up like she gone vomit.

"So you just gave away her husband instead?" she spit.

"I didn't have a choice," Massa tell her.

"Yes you did...you could've made a different deal."

Massa shake his head.  "No, I couldn't."

"You always have a choice," Missus say.  "*I* have a choice...I choose to live in this God-forsaken place because I love you.  I choose to teach Sapphire how to read and write because it's the right thing to do.  *You* could have freed all of your slaves when I moved here, but you chose not to because you didn't want to sell your father's land.  I've chosen to stand by you even though it's been hell on earth sometimes."

"What do you want me to do about it now?!" Massa shout.  "I have a debt...I have to pay it.  The war's over, Joan.  Lee's already surrendered to Grant in Appomattox.  I need to square things with Birch *now*.  What else can I do but give him the twenty acres?"

"Sell my rings," Missus say, pulling them pretty diamonds off a her fingers.  "You could get at least half of what you owe him."  Then she walk to the chiffarobe where the silver coffee tray be setting, ready to serve her mama and daddy when they come to visit.  "And sell this, too.  I don't want it.  I don't want anything that belonged to your father!"

Missus start to rant and that ain't nothing I ever seen or heard 'fore 'cause it always be Massa who do the yelling.  I ain't sure how long this fight gone go on, but I know in the end, Mister Rotten gone be the winner.

Mama pull on my arm and whisper, "It ain't polite to be eavesdropping, and we done heard enough. Let's get some flowers for Missus' dinner table." She sound like she 'bout to choke.

Mama shoo me out the side door and plant me in the wildflower patch. Then she start sobbing and go to the fence by Missus' little garden. She lean on it hard, her whole body shaking.

I watch and wait for her to say something 'bout how Mister Rotten be wanting to take her and not Daddy.

But she don't.

I pick a bunch a lavender stalks and think Mama gone tell me that be enough, and to choose some other flowers that ain't smell so strong they gone perfume up the whole house.

But she don't.

I think she gone say something 'bout us being free any day now.

But she don't.

Mama jest cry 'til they ain't nothing left inside a her heart that like to be so heavy sometime she can barely carry it.

When Mama finish sobbing, she come over to where I is and snap off a few Queen Anne's Lace even though they be short little things jest coming up out the dirt.

Handing 'em to me, she say, "You big enough to get Missus' dinner on the table, Sapphire.   And make sure you put these flowers where Massa gone see 'em, too."

Then she walk toward our shack, her shoulders soft and low, cradling her face in her hands.

By the time I bring Missus the vase a flowers, Massa be long gone.  When Mama send me into the kitchen, I seen him get in the wagon and smack poor old Pete's rump with the reins.  Missus be setting in the dining room crying.  I don't say nothing, jest do as I's told and get her dinner ready.

When I bring it to her, Missus say, "Thank you, Sapphire."  She looking out the window where Massa be shrinking in the distance as he drive off. "Did you hear all of that?"

"All a what?" I ask. Mama done told me a bunch a times to act like I don't hear nothing that go on 'tween Massa and Missus, or 'tween the chil'ren neither. She say ain't none a my business what go on with the white folks.

"Mr. Settler and me arguing."

"No'm," I say, shaking my head.

She look at me and lift her chin. "I'm not hungry anymore, Sapphire. Do you want my dinner?"

I's hungry 'cause the only thing Mama done give me be a carrot and some leftover cornbread, but I shake my head. "No'm, but thank you."

"Maybe Ruby would want it," Missus say, getting up from the table. "I'm going to lay down for a while."

"Yes'm," I say. I see her rings still be laying on the table like Little Sam's marbles that he leave all over the floor a his room so I got to be careful not to step on 'em when I make his bed. "Missus...you wanting these here rings?"

Missus look over her shoulder and shake her head. "Just leave them for Mr. Settler."

"Yes'm," I say, picking up the bowl. I carry it to the kitchen where I pour it into a pail and plop in another ladle of soup chock full a vegetables. Then I tote it out the door and head to the shack where Mama be laying on the bed. She ain't crying no more, jest staring at the wall like she do sometime when she sad.

"Mama, you hungry?" I ask real quiet-like. "Missus say she ain't want her dinner."

"You have it, Sapphire," she say. "I ain't hungry neither."

So I grab my wooden spoon from the shelf and sit on the bed shoveling in the hot vegetable soup full a peas, carrots, and beets Mama keep in the cellar all winter long.

"They still fussing?" she ask.

"No'm, they ain't."

"Where Massa be?"

"Guess he went on to Mister Rotten's place."

"Mister *Birch's* place," Mama correct me, setting up on the straw mattress. "I done told you...you ain't *never* s'posed to call him that. What if someone 'sides Massa Sam hear you say it? You get a whipping for sure...and it ain't matter how little you be. They do it jest the same."

I drop my chin and set the pail on the floor. "I's sorry, Mama."

"Don't be sorry...jest don't do it no more. I don't never want to see you get whipped, you hear me?"

"Yes'm."

Tears fill her eyes 'gain. "You gone leave this place without scars, baby girl...I's gone see to that."

I nod, but don't say nothing.

Mama turn so she setting right next to me. "Yes, ma'am, I's gone see to that...no matter what I got to do."

"How you get them scars on your back, Mama?" I ask, quiet-like, hoping she finally tell me the story.

Mama give me a sad smile. "I guess you old enough to know the truth 'bout a lot of things."

"I *is*, Mama," I tell her. "I is and that a fact."

"Alright," Mama smile. "I tell you." She set me on her lap and begin the story.

"Little Massa Sam and I was talking in the yard one day when Big Massa come out and yell at Sam to get to the fields right quick. We was only a little older than you is now...ten I think. During the harvest, Sam had to work in the fields jest like all the slaves, chopping and hauling and everthing. Even though he jest a boy, Sam was made to work like a dern dog."

"Why that?"

"'Cause his daddy like everone out the way of the big house when his Missus be sleeping. 'Specially on that day, but I know she ain't sleeping then." Mama sigh. "Big Massa Samuel jest pretending so's he can get me alone."

"Why he want that?"

Mama don't say why, she jest keep on telling the story. "When Massa yell at Sam to get to the fields, I seen his Missus be standing in the doorway watching all three a us with them beady eyes a hers. She got her face all puckered up and I knows trouble be brewing."

"What Sam...I mean...what *Massa* Sam do then?"

"He do like his daddy say," Mama tell me. "He hightail it to the fields 'cause he know a beating be coming if he don't. Then Massa jerk me by the arm and drag me over to Missus who be smiling like a cat that jest ate a big, fat mouse."

"What that mean?"

"She satisfied I's gone get what she thinks I got coming to me," Mama say. "She always be making a fuss 'bout how I clean the house or cook the food. One time she even make me sweep the porch *four* times 'til she satisfied I's good and shamed. This time Massa say Missus tell him I done stole a ring from her jewelry box, but I ain't. Missus say she send my sister, Jasmine, to find it in the shack and she came right back with it."

Mama stop for a moment and run her hand 'cross her eyes like she don't want to see no more a them memories. I lean 'gainst her chest and rub my head on her soft skin, hoping she keep telling the story...and she do.

"*'Jasmine ain't found nothing 'cause I ain't take nothing!'* I tell Massa with a heap a sass in my voice. Missus be lying her fool head off and he know it, but that don't matter none. He jest drag me to the fence and tie my arms with a leather strap. Then he rip open the back a my dress like it ain't nothing." Mama stop for a moment and I hear her heart beating like a drum. Then she say, "I hear Missus shout, 'Make sure she feels *every* strike! I want to hear that whip *sing*!'"

Tears fill Mama's eyes. "That whip sing sure enough when Massa thrash me 'til I scream and cry and nearly pass out. Ever one a them strikes is still echoing ever time I feels them scars...but that ain't the worst of it, Sapphire."

"What is?" I ask, not really wanting to hear no more.

"Little Massa Sam come running when he hear me screaming, and Big Massa tell him if he don't get back to the fields, he gone get a whipping, too." Now them tears start to spill down Mama's cheeks. "Sam don't listen to his daddy...he run to me and try to untie my hands, his mama yelling at him to stop, his daddy whipping his hide something fierce. Both a us got lashes 'cross our faces and Sam get a real bad one on his right ear. That how come he don't hear on that side. It like to knock him senseless."

When Mama tell me that part, my eyes be full a tears, too. She hug me close. "Missus jest say to keep on beating Sam 'til he learn how to respect his daddy. She say to give me a few more lashes for good measure. 'I hate the sight of her,' Missus say. She call me *tar baby* and *pickaninny* and *ugly nigger*. She say it a good thing my mama die 'cause she'd be shamed to know what kind a smart-mouthed gal I turn out to be. She say she glad my mama dead, too, and ain't it too bad that murder ain't legal 'cause I be the first nigger she like to see lynch."

Mama wipe her eyes, then she wipe mine. "But that old bat die in her sleep three days later. Big Massa get it up in his head one a us slaves done poison her food, but the doc say it be a heart attack or some such. After that, I ain't never got another beating and neither did Sam. But still...damage already be done."

Then Mama wait a long time 'fore she say, "And I see it ever time Massa Sam come walking by. I hear it ever time he talk. I know him like I know my own chil'ren. Massa ain't a bad man, but he don't really know how to be a strong man neither. That how come he drink."

She stop for a moment, thinking on what she done told me. "But he did save me more'n once, didn't he, Sapphire? Least he tried to when I was getting whipped...and he save me from Mister Birch, too. He save me from living the res' a my life without you and Pearl and Opal."

I nod, but don't say nothing 'cause I's wondering what our future gone look like when freedom finally come like Massa Sam say it will. When I look into Mama's eyes as she staring into the bright sunbeam that shine through the door, I know a piece a that new story be in the old one she thinking on right now.

# Karin

Grese stomps in and orders us to stop working. "Get back to your barracks!" she shouts. "Schnell! Schnell!"

I dart my eyes toward the doorway where I see a rush of S.S. moving past, all talking at once.

*"Get the orchestra ready!"*

*"We need another detail by the crematoria!"*

*"Kommandant Kramer will be inspecting in twenty minutes!"*

*Inspecting what*? I wonder.

The camp has been a flurry of activity since the evacuations and it seems the S.S. cannot bury the evidence of their crimes fast enough. Since early January, typhus has killed thousands. Unlike Auschwitz, there's no gas chamber here and only one crematorium that cannot keep up with the ever-mounting piles of corpses we must live among…and die among.

What will Kommandant have to inspect? Germans pride themselves on efficiency and order, but what's happened over the past few months has turned this place into utter chaos. Worse than Auschwitz. Worse than Buchenwald. For almost a week there's been no running water. No food or supplies. Perhaps the Kommandant will be inspecting the absolute ruin of what Bergen Belsen has become.

Through Vitya I've heard rumors that the British are not far away, that Auschwitz was liberated in late January and Buchenwald just a few days ago. The prisoners who work closely with the S.S. burying the dead have been spreading tales of imminent freedom and, like Renatta, I'm terrified that the Nazis will burn this place to the ground before they will ever surrender. They've exiled thousands more on death marches. They've kept the crematorium burning day and

101

night so the entire camp is coated in ashes that float to the ground like a sickening snowfall.

So maybe the war is finally over.

Maybe that's why Herman insisted I say he's been a good man. Soon we will be free and he, along with all the rest of the guards, will either escape or be arrested. But there will be no real justice for any of them, for even if they are sentenced to hang, they can only die once.

I cannot say Herman is a good man. A good man doesn't kill for his own pleasure. A good man doesn't beat someone for not being able to stand up at Appellplatz when he's cold and hungry. A good man doesn't threaten to shoot me if I take chocolate or milk from his cabinet.

A good man provides food and shelter. He looks after his wife and her loved ones. He keeps her safe from those who would harm her. In some ways, in many ways, Herman has done all of these things for me. Being in his debt has given me extra showers, a warmer place to sleep, work indoors where it is safer...and my life.

Although I cannot say Herman has been a good man, I cannot say he's been completely evil either. I no longer have to fear that I will be killed, but I fear what Herman might do if I tell the truth. And so I decide to do what I have done ever since he discovered me sifting through suitcases in Auschwitz: I count my blessings and remain silent.

Still, the rumor that Kommandant Kramer has agreed to turn the camp over to the British could just be a lie to keep our hopes up, to keep us working. We're all famished. We're filthy. We're fearful. But what we're most starved for is hope...and the Nazis know it. They prey on it in much the same way a viper stalks its victim, then strike quickly, poisoning us with their vicious fury.

As Simka and I hurry across the camp toward our barrack, she moans, holding her belly. The pain is getting worse, but I've said nothing to Grese. She would send Simka directly to the hospital where I know they will inject her with phenol to kill both her and the baby that floats in her belly, ready to be born too soon.

I listen for the sound of gunfire, for an explosion of bombs, but hear nothing. I squeeze Simka's hand and pull her further along.

"I'm trying, Karin," she groans.

*Why don't they come?* I wonder. *Why don't the British come* now?

If the baby could wait a little while longer, it would be born into freedom, not certain death, for I've seen what happens to babies born in concentration camps. I know for certain what happens if any woman dares to try and come between the S.S. and her child. Chaos or not, neither will survive.

Mutti told me when Jurgen was born that every child is an extension of their mother's body, that the soul of the newborn will always be linked to the soul of the mother. I wonder if Jurgen's soul cries out to her in the night, longing to be held, to be loved. And I wonder if Mutti can find his spirit while she lies in the dark stillness of sleep.

As I hold Simka's hand, I can feel her urgency in wanting to give birth, but I know that unless I can keep them both in hiding, she will never be able to hold or love her baby…at least not in this life.

"Oh!" she cries out, doubling over.

Blood and water trickle down the insides of her legs. More spatters on the dry earth as she squeezes my hand. "Is anyone looking?" she gasps.

Grese stands several yards away, barking orders at some poor girl who stumbles beneath the weight of a heavy basket. Brandishing her whip, Grese strikes her several times until the girl drops the basket and cowers. I watch Grese strike the poor wretch repeatedly until she collapses to the ground. Still, I do nothing, feel nothing, for this is commonplace – and not as bad as it could be.

S.S. guards rush here and there with prisoners who are able to work, shouting always to *"move faster!"* The camp orchestra plays Wagner while corpses lay strewn on the ground, an eerie audience of silent spectators, their mouths agape, their eyes vacant and glassy. The music is a bizarre and haunting backdrop to the horror all around us.

No one has time to notice Simka and me.

I wrap an arm around her shoulders as we near our barrack. Its fetid stench makes my nose curl and I feel as though I'm going to vomit, but I can't. Not now. Guiding Simka through the door, we see a large group of women dozing on their bunks. Several are talking among themselves, scratching their dirt-caked bodies, picking lice from their hair and clothing, then pinching them between callused fingers. Some are speaking German, some Russian. I look around the room at the dirty, hollow faces of the women I've lived among for months and wonder how any of us have survived this long.

One of them looks up when we enter. "Simka!" Esfir cries, sitting up. "You're bleeding! What did they do to you?"

"Hush," Simka scolds. "My baby..."

"It's coming?"

"Yes."

"Now?"

"Nyet," Simka grimaces. "But soon."

Esfir looks at me, her face smudged with sweat and dirt. "What are we to do?"

I shake my head as if I don't know.

Esfir works in the vegetable garden and is often sent to the cookhouse where Vitya keeps her informed of what she overhears from the S.S. Yesterday Esfir, along with all of the other workers, was ordered to stay in the barrack. I have no idea why. Just as I have no idea why Simka and I were ordered to sit and make lace for hours while the rest of the camp staggers under the weight of dragging countless emaciated, decaying corpses to open pits, and burning

104

evidence of the Nazi's crimes. Not that it will do any good. There must be thousands of half-rotting men and women's bodies strewn all over the camp.

Katarine sits in the corner, picking lice from her tattered dress, then biting them between her yellowed front teeth. She's mumbling to herself in Russian, so Simka translates some of her rantings to me, but none of it makes any sense. Stricken with grief, Katarine watched both her mother and father taken to the gas chambers at Auschwitz, then witnessed the murder of her sister a few months later. She's constantly carrying on a conversation with one or more of them, begging for their forgiveness because she continues to live.

Simka thinks Katarine's going insane, but I know she's coping in the only way she knows how. It would be easier to run against the barbed wire fence and electrocute herself. It's much harder to live with the memories of ones she loves. I've seen plenty of women commit suicide rather than endure one more day of grief. And I've seen even more lose their minds. When I start to lose faith, Mutti tells me that I must think about what freedom will look like when it finally comes.

"What will you eat, Karin?" she asks me. "What clothes will you wear? Will you travel to see Cousine Helga in the United States? Will you go back to our home in Baden Baden?" She tells me to picture it in my mind and when I do, I feel more at peace.

As I help Simka to her bunk, more blood oozes down the inside of her legs. I use the hem of her dress to mop it up as best as I can, but I can't stop the constant fluid that leaks from her body, soiling her tattered blanket and the straw mattress.

"Leave it, Karin," she says, easing onto her side. "There will only be more."

"Can we at least get some water for her to drink?" Esfir asks. "I can run to the kitchen to see if Vitya can boil some."

Simka shakes her head. "Not yet...not yet." She cradles her belly and winces, another pain rippling through her body.

"But aren't you thirsty, dorogaya?" Esfir asks.

"Nyet," she says, shaking her head.

Esfir looks at me, her face sallow, her eyes hollow in their sockets. "I don't care what she says...go get water...and some scissors. *Now*."

"Nyet...*nyet*," Simka moans. "Don't leave, Karin."

"*Go!*" Esfir hisses.

I squeeze Simka's hand and gently pull the matted hair from her forehead. She looks at me anxiously, but I listen to Esfir and kiss her good-bye. Picking up a discarded metal pail, I rush toward the door.

"Hurry!" I hear Esfir call to me.

As I leave the barrack, I watch for the S.S. who swarm here and there, barking demands at prisoners. I walk quickly and with purpose as if I've just been ordered by Grese to return to Herman's room. I make eye contact with no one, looking at the ground, trying to make myself as small and invisible as possible.

Darting across the main road toward the cookhouse where Vitya works, I see the door is open and the scent of roasting vegetables fills the air. Turnips. Again. But they aren't for the prisoner's. If we're lucky, we might find a scrap of rotten turnip tossed haphazardly on the ground. Slinking in the door, I see Vitya stirring a huge pot on the gas stove. I sidle up next to her and hold out the pail.

"Water?" she whispers.

I nod.

"What for? You know I can't give water to every person who begs. You're not here for Dieter are you?"

I shake my head.

"Grese?"

I shake my head again and place a hand near my belly, holding it away from me as if to cradle a baby.

Vitya's eyes widen. "Simka?"

Wrinkling my brow, I nod, almost imperceptibly.

Vitya takes the pail and pulls me into a storage room where barrels of water line the walls. She plunges a dipper into one that's open and scoops up ladle after ladle of water. My dry mouth feels even more parched as I watch her.

Handing me the pail, Vitya dips the ladle one last time and holds it to my lips. I gratefully slurp up the metallic tasting water in one gulp.

"It may be a while," Vitya says. "Her last baby took a long time in coming."

I nod.

"You take that back to her and make sure she has only a little bit at a time." Vitya covers the pail with a grimy rag. "Dip this in the water and have her suck on it. Not too much, mind you. Just enough to wet her mouth." Then she shoves a crust of bread into my hand. "Give her a bit of this if she'll take it. She's going to need all the strength she can get."

I nod again, quickly shoving the bread into my pocket.

"I will come when I can," Vitya says, going back to the stove. Then she pauses and takes my hand. "You come get me sooner if she's in trouble, okay?"

I squeeze her palm, nodding.

"Whatever you do, *don't* go looking for Klein," Vitya warns. "Don't you let him touch her."

I shake my head, silently promising to keep Simka and her baby out of the hands of the sadistic camp doctor who's taken more lives than he's saved. I should know. When I was imprisoned at Auschwitz, Klein sterilized me at Herman's command.

He was different than charismatic Mengele, who selected many for work, not for the gas. Silent upon entering the operating room where I lay strapped to the table, Klein didn't speak to the nurses as he systematically injected me with chemicals that spread like liquid fire and eventually rendered me barren. As I lay there, writhing in pain, Klein left quickly and without ceremony, much in the same way I hurry from the kitchen on my way to tend to Simka, remembering the day blood ran down my legs while Mutti held my hand and whispered, "Don't let go."

***

October, 1941

Mutti stands next to me in the cramped boxcar, cradling Jurgen and staring in to space. A steam whistle blasts through the murmuring voices, drowning out everything with its shrill, jarring eruption. Yet the noise does nothing to jolt my mother out of her stupor.

Vati wraps an arm around me and kisses my forehead. I stand nearly as tall as his shoulder and realize how quickly I've grown up since the war started. But I cannot remember when I changed from a young girl into the young woman my father clings to in desperation. Streaks of tears are dried on my face as I clutch the satchel filled with my books, my clothes, and my knitting. Vati stands next to a suitcase stuffed with all of the things he thinks we will need upon arrival at wherever this horrible train will take us.

There are rumors we are being expatriated from Germany, but I know that's a lie. The Nazis would never release a prisoner, especially Vati, who has been charged with high treason. Murdering Bruno wasn't enough of a punishment, so all of us are made to suffer as we wait for the inevitable unknown.

As more people are packed onto the train, Vati and I step closer to the wall where others solemnly stand coughing, crying, and moaning. Vati calls to Mutti to come with us, but she doesn't move.

A woman near her says, "Ma'am? Your husband needs you."

Mutti looks at her with glazed eyes. "Who?"

"Your husband."

Mutti sighs deeply, but says nothing.

The woman gently nudges my mother closer to us, then moves beside me with a young girl who looks utterly forlorn. "I'm Liege...Liege Daiga," the woman says to Vati. "I think my husband did some work for you at your theater. You're Henry Vogel?"

"Ja...is your husband Hans Daiga?"

"Ja."

"A good man...and a good carpenter."

Frau Daiga smiles sadly.

"Where is he?"

"Dead...the S.S. came in the night a few days ago and took him," she says somberly. "He was working for the underground and somehow they found out. They tortured him to try and get information, and when he wouldn't speak, they shot him." Frau Daiga's eyes are sad and swollen, but her jaw is determined. "Then they came to the house and ransacked it until everything was destroyed. My daughter and I were taken and held until the transport was ready." She pauses for a moment before she says, "We're going to a place called Auschwitz."

"Where?" Vati asks, gently nudging Mutti to sit on his suitcase where she can hold Jurgen more comfortably.

"Auschwitz," Frau Daiga says once more. "It's supposed to be a place where Jews are sent to work and receive vocational training."

"Only Jews?" Vati asks.

"I'm not sure...that's what I heard while our papers were being prepared. One of the female guards said my daughter and I would receive good care. That the doctors at Auschwitz would know how to help me when my time comes." Frau Daiga opens her coat to reveal a rounded belly.

Her young daughter stares at me with wide, brown eyes. Her hair is woven into thick braids along each side of a neat part and she's dressed in a woolen skirt and jacket, just as if she were ready to go to Temple for the Shabbat.

"You're Jewish, ja?" Frau Daiga asks.

"Nein," Vati replies.

"Then why are you here?" she asks.

Suddenly an S.S. guard shoves even more people into the boxcar, sandwiching us together until it's hard to breathe. "Sich bewegen!" he yells. "Jetzt!"

*Move! Now!*

Frau Daiga is pushed closer and her daughter lets out a yelp of pain as someone jams an elbow into her face.

"Da bin ich, Anya, meine Liebling," her mother says, holding her closer. "Da bin ich."

*I am here, my darling. I am here.*

Then the heavy door slides shut and we are plunged into darkness, the dank stench of sweat and fear permeating my senses. I hear a loud *clunk* when the door is locked. Only two small windows are stationed on either side of the boxcar at eye level, but my family and I are nowhere near them.

The poor souls who are able thrust their arms out of the windows, shouting, "Bitte...lasst uns heraus!"

*Please, let us out.*

As the steam whistle blares once more and the train lurches forward, I know all hope is lost. We will never see our home again. We will never be able to give Bruno a decent burial. I will never read books in my bedroom until well after sunset or walk through the park on a cool, autumn day.

As the train gathers speed, hurling us toward an uncertain fate, I cling to my father and stifle my tears. Closing my eye, I remember the horrible moment when Vati and I were escorted by Stephan back to the house where we were ordered to pack a bag.

"One *only*," Stephan warned. "But bring your valuables...anything you can sell or trade."

As we stepped through the side door, we found Mutti standing in the kitchen, a wooden spoon coated with applesauce in her hand. "Where is Bruno?" she cried when she saw my blood-stained clothes.

"He's gone," Vati said, tears filling his eyes. "Come...

"What do you mean *he's gone*?" Mutti asked, frantically looking from me to my father. "Karin...what happened?!"

"Come, Josephine...come let's go upstairs."

Stephan stood in the doorway, his rifle at the ready, glaring at us. "You have ten minutes!"

The three of us quickly climbed the stairs.

"The S.S. stormed the theater and found the Zweigs," Vati whispered. "And then...they...they took our Bruno from Karin..."

Mutti let out a frightening howl of anguish.

Vati pulled her up to the landing. "Shush, Josephine!"

"I told you to stay away from the theater, Karin!" Mutti hissed at me. "I *told* you!"

"Nein, Josephine," Vati said calmly. "She didn't come to the theater. Stephan found her at the park."

"Then how...*why* did she end up there?" Mutti asked, glaring at me.

"A package...something Karin had for Georg," Vati explained. "It was in her pocket and Stephan took it. She told him I was going to mail it, but he didn't believe her."

Filled with fury, Mutti's eyes never left mine. "Why did you defy me, you insolent child?" she spat, then smacked me across the face. "They took *my* baby...they murdered him...and it's all your fault!"

I burst into tears, but no sound escaped my mouth. Placing my hand against my cheek, I felt the warm imprint of my mother's palm.

"It's not Karin's fault," Vati said firmly, grabbing Mutti's wrist so she couldn't strike me again.

"It *is*," Mutti insisted. She looked to Vati. "You started this whole mess years ago, and now your daughter has finished it for us. For *all* of us. Are you satisfied now?"

I was gasping for breath, but Mutti didn't seem to notice.

"Josephine, *no!*" Vati said, shaking his head. "This is not Karin's doing...it's my fault. I knew it was a risk from the beginning. We both did."

Mutti's face curled up into a hideous scowl. "We both knew it, but in the end, it was *your* choice...not mine!"

Vati pulled Mutti toward their bedroom where Jurgen lay feverishly sleeping. While they packed a bag, I stood in my room, tears falling down my face. I could hear Mutti yelling at Vati, terror in her voice. She wailed and screamed that she wanted to see her son. That she wanted to spit in Hitler's face. That she wanted to drag Stephan into the street and beat him with a shovel.

All of a sudden, Stephan's heavy footfalls thundered up the steps toward my parent's room. "You better shut your damn mouth or you'll meet your son in hell!"

From my doorway I saw Vati stand in front of Mutti, begging Stephan to forgive his wife, to have pity on her as she was filled with grief over the loss of their child.

"Hurry up, you crazy woman!" Stephen ordered, banging the butt of his rifle on the wooden floor. "Before I change my mind!"

For days Vati, Mutti, Jurgen, and I are forced to stand in the jostling boxcar for hours on end. My legs ache and my back screams with pain. We take turns sitting on Vati's heavy suitcase, but even when I lean against my father I cannot find relief, nor can I sleep for more than a few minutes at a time.

To make matters worse, my period started and I can't stop the steady flow from soaking through my underclothes and stockings, mixing with the horror of being stained with Bruno's blood. I stand in the sticky mess, crying silent tears. I can't tell Vati. I *won't* tell Mutti. Ever since Bruno's birth, she mourns for her lost uterus every time I menstruate. She tells me to keep it to myself, that it's not considerate to remind her that she's barren. And so I feel the blood gush out of me in waves, fearful Mutti might see, anxious that the odor will give me away.

Frau Daiga notices on an afternoon so bright that the sunlight shines through the slats in the boxcar with ferocious intensity. Her daughter, Anya, leans against her, clutching her dress, moaning for water.

"Liebling?" she whispers, touching my shoulder. "Do you need a handkerchief?"

I shake my head and bury my hands in my pockets, desperate to hold my coat together in front of my soiled dress.

"I have one in my purse," Frau Daiga offers. "It's no bother."

I shake my head again and look to Mutti as she sits on Vati's suitcase with Jurgen in her lap. She's wrapped her Queen Anne's Lace shawl around his fragile body, and rocks from side to side as the train makes its way onward.

Jurgen lifts his head and looks at me with sleepy eyes. His lips are parched and his skin is pale. Realizing where he is, he starts to bawl. "Are we there? Are we there?!"

"Nein, Liebling," Frau Daiga says, touching his cheek. "Here...let me hold you." She holds out her hands.

Mutti wordlessly passes him to her, then sits as still as a corpse as the train moves on.

Jurgen cries almost constantly when he's awake and it's a blessing when he finally falls asleep, exhausted and beyond consolation. His fever makes him edgy and uncomfortable. Whenever Mutti tells him we will get there soon, he asks, "Where? Where are we going?"

None of us can tell him for certain.

There's no water. There's no food. There's no toilet, save for the small bucket in the corner that soon overflows with filth. At each stop, it's emptied, along with those who have been smothered to death or died of a heart attack or of grief and fear. It startles me to see so many of them hauled from the boxcar by the S.S. and thrown into a wagon.

"Fifteen less for the gas," one of them laughed.

***

Finally the boxcar stops and the sound of a steam whistle fills the air. I wonder if this will be a sojourn to empty the slop bucket and carry out the dead or if this is the end of our long, horrendous journey. Jurgen dozes in Mutti's arms while Vati tries to console her. The past few days have diffused all of her anger and grief, hollowed her out until there's nothing left but an empty, vacant shell.

A woman tells my parents, "I've heard about these places...these camps. You need to look as healthy as possible." Her crimson hair flows onto her shoulders and she pushes it off her face as she demonstrates. "Pinch your cheeks. Bite your lips to bring color into them. Stand tall. And for God's sake, don't tell them your real age. If you're forty, tell them you're thirty."

"Why?" Mutti asks.

"Because I've heard the old ones go away and never return," she explains. "But the younger ones have a good chance."

"A chance at what?"

"Life."

Mutti pulls Jurgen closer as he sleeps on, feverish and exhausted.

Anxious murmurs ripple through the boxcar as we hear Nazi officers shouting over the din of their barking of dogs. Horror ripples up my spine. I'm terrified of German Shepherds, for I know the S.S. wouldn't hesitate to sic their dogs on any of us if we step one toe out of line.

"Heraus! Heraus! Schneller!" the men shout while the dogs snarl in a chorus of vicious savagery.

*Get out! Get out! Faster!*

Men, women, and children are pulled from the train. They cautiously step over the bodies of those who perished the night before, some sobbing, unwilling to leave their mothers or brothers or grandparents behind.

The Nazis yank them through the doorway and onto the plank shouting, "Herunterkommen! Jetzt!"

*Get down...now!*

As Vati hands me my satchel he whispers, "Be brave, Karin. Be brave."

I nod and follow Mutti toward the shaft of sunlight filling the boxcar. It hurts my eyes, but it's warm and comforting, too. As I make my way down the wooden plank, an officer yells, "Manner auf dieser Seite...Frauen und Kinder auf der anderen!"

*Men on this side...women and children on the other.*

Gravel crunches loudly beneath our feet, the sound of it echoing in my throat. I feel the small bits of rock through the soles of my shoes and know that whatever happens next, I will soon forget what it means to be human.

Frau Daiga moves quickly, Anya clinging to her skirt. Vati carries her suitcase, along with his and sets it on the side where we have been instructed to stand.

"Auf der andere Seite, du Arsch!" an officer yells at my father.

*The other side, you ass!*

His dog lurches at Vati as if any moment it will snap the leash and devour him.

Hugging me close, he whispers in my ear, "Gute nacht, meine Liebling...du lebst...du lebst."

*Good night, my darling...you will live...you will live.*

To Mutti he simply says, "Ich liebe dich, mein Engel."

*I love you, my angel.*

Vati quickly kisses Jurgen, then is torn from our side by the S.S. guard who smacks him with a wooden stick.

"Henry!" Mutti shrieks. "Henry!"

"I'm fine, Liebling," Vati replies, getting into the men's line not three feet from where we're standing.

I look to my father, knowing this is the last time I will ever see him. I try to memorize his face, his profile, the scent of his clothing, the sound of his voice.

A smartly dressed officer walks toward us wearing his hat at a jaunty angle. It's as if his entire countenance tells us, "I am the Power." He waits with calm satisfaction until all of the prisoners have been separated, then walks to the front of the women's line. Spending less than a minute with each person, he then sharply says either "to the left" or "to the right."

When it's Frau Daiga's turn, the officer sees that she's pregnant. "To the right," he nods with his head. "You and your daughter will have a nice bath and then go to the hospital wing until your baby comes."

"My friend's son is ill," Frau Daiga blurts out. "He needs medicine."

"Who?" the man asks.

Frau Daiga looks to Mutti and Jurgen.

The man steps over to us. "Is that right? Is your son ill?"

Mutti nods. "Yes...he has a fever."

"Give him to her," the man orders. "He will be well cared for."

Mutti hesitates, but then the man chucks Jurgen under his chin and says, "I'll see to it myself."

"Ja," she says. "Please help him be well."

I wrap the shawl more firmly around Jurgen's shoulders to keep him warm. Kissing his cheek, I whisper, "I'll see you soon."

Mutti doesn't have time to say good-bye as Frau Daiga takes Jurgen and is shoved by a female guard who yells at her to keep moving. The grief etched in my mother's face is heartbreaking. But there's no time for mourning...not now.

The officer quickly looks Mutti up and down. "How old?"

I notice the woman with the red hair pokes Mutti in the back, reminding her of their conversation on the train.

"Thirty," she lies. She's thirty-seven.

Then she nods toward me. "I'm her sister," she lies again.

"To the left."

"When will I see my son?"

"Soon," the officer smiles. "He will be well cared for. I will see to it personally. Have no fear."

The officer inspects me, pausing for a brief moment when he sees my blood-caked stockings. "To the left."

As I walk to the line forming on the other side of the train station, for the first time I see the barbed wire fences, the guard tower hovering over us like a hungry vulture. Armed men stare at us with menace, their rifles poised. I look over my shoulder one last time to try and find my father in a sea of men, lined shoulder to shoulder, waiting for their turn to be told where to go...left or right.

Mutti grabs my hand and pulls me toward her. "Nicht lolassen," she tells me. "Ich brauche dich."

*Don't let go...I need you.*

\*\*\*

Vitya's voice rouses me out of my memories, "Now go! If you get caught, just tell them you're taking this to Dieter."

Careful not to slosh the water, I hurry out of the cookhouse. I'm thankful none of the other women seem to notice me as they mindlessly chop turnips and wilted greens. They stare into space as I do when I'm knitting, their eyes vacant, their expressions stoic.

Before I make my way back to the barracks, I stand in the doorway and watch for Herta Bothe, one of the guards who beats sick prisoners for her own pleasure. I've seen her shoot at them while they carry rations from the cookhouse to the barracks. Once Bothe shot a woman in the throat and as the poor creature fell to the ground, others scurried to gather up the scraps of bread and cheese while the woman bled to death at their feet.

There's a company of prisoners dressed in striped uniforms walking by with shovels. All of them are haggard and weak. None of them notice me, thank God, and it seems they barely notice they're alive.

117

The S.S. in the rear shouts, "Erhalten zum Krematorium...schneller!"

*Get to the crematorium...faster!*

They shuffle off as fast as they can down the main road. Once they've passed, I scurry across it.

"Halt!" Grese snarls from behind me, smacking her whip into the palm of her hand. "What are you doing, Schweine?"

I turn to see her contorted scowl.

"Oh, it's *you*, 811933," she sneers, pushing her face close to mine. "Taking water to Kapitan, are you?" Her dog stands by her side, licking his chops.

I hesitantly nod, keeping my eyes on the muddy ground, keeping my hand clenched around the scrap of bread in my pocket.

"You're lucky he's kept you for his pet," she says, spittle flying everywhere. "Otherwise, I would have gassed you long ago."

I set my jaw, but don't lift my eyes. I don't dare.

Grese will use any excuse to beat me. She's been ordered not to kill me, but torture was never specifically outlawed. "Get moving!" she snarls. "Before I sic my dog on you!"

I scuttle toward the barrack, my heart pounding in my chest, my eyes filled with heavy smoke, my throat parched by the odor of rotting flesh. Once more I cautiously step around the corpses, not spilling a drop of the precious water.

"Beeilen!" I tell myself. "Simka brauchst du."

*Hurry! Simka needs you.*

# Sapphire

I's toting my knitting basket to the fields where Mama say I can set and work in the afternoon sun. They's a heap a stuff to do in the big house, but it feel nice to jest leave it for a while. Plus Mama say if I keep on with my cleaning, I might wake Missus from her nap, so we can save it for later once Marybelle and Little Sam come home from school.

Now I get to enjoy the wonderful green grass and the warm, damp soil that Keen and Hale been tilling for weeks. It smell like a miracle out here. After the winter we done had, I thought that snow ain't never gone melt. But it sure has and now they's a bunch a brand new things popping everwhere. The lilac bushes fill the air with they heavenly scent. Them daffodil bulbs Mama and me done planted last fall be blooming. And I's jest passing by a pussywillow with its little fuzzy buds coming on real good.

I love springtime 'cause it feel the start of a brand new year, not like in January when it be cold, dark, and ugly. Everthing be gray and sad in winter, but in spring, everthing and everone get to be reborn brand new. This year I feel like I want to be a little bunny rabbit like the ones I seen hopping 'round the edge of Missus' garden. Mama bunny got three kittens and they all be jumping like little frogs in the clover. So I put my knitting basket on a rock and hippity-hop 'round the yard for a spell, jest 'cause they ain't no one to tell me not to.

At times like this I almost know what it mean to be free.

When I done, I hightail it to the fields 'cause Mama say I got to ask Pearl do she need a lie down. Mama say when a woman be near her time, the baby be pressing hard on her back and it sometime feel like fire.

"Tell her I come out there and do her work if'n she need me," Mama say.

But I know Pearl ain't gone be asking. She be built like one a Massa's horses, strong and steady, and she ain't gone ask Mama for nothing 'cause she know they ain't enough time in the day for all our mama got to do. Still, I's toting a little extra cornbread for Pearl in my basket 'cause I know she always be hungry. Maybe I should pick her a few a them spring peas to suck on, too.

All of a sudden I hear a rustling in the brush 'long the side a the dirt path and think it might be a 'coon or a skunk or some such. Mama say if I ever come 'cross a skunk to jest stand still and let 'em pass on by. She say that if they start pounding they paws on the ground to slowly get back 'cause they getting ready to spray and I gone smell like the dickens for days.

I freeze and wait while the rustling keep on going. Then jest like that, they's a grown man standing 'fore me, his clothes all tatty and his dirty old toes poking through the holes in his boots. His red hair be a mess a tangles and so's his beard, with brambles and such sticking to him all over. He carrying a rifle and a knapsack that look empty to me, jest as empty as his face that 'mind me of the skull Massa done found in the fields one time.

"Who you?" I ask, crossing my arms. I ain't s'posed to be talking to no white mens, but I ain't gone pretend I ain't seen him neither.

"Is this Lincoln County?" he ask, his voice scratchy like one a them brambles be stuck in his throat.

"Why you want to know?"

"I don't mean you no harm...honestly," he say. "I'm just trying to find my way home."

I narrow my eyes. "You a Reb?"

He nod and wipe his face with a filthy rag.

"The war be over?"

"Should be by now," he say. "I left a few weeks ago."

"How come you leave when the fighting ain't over?"

Tears fill up his eyes and he start crying like a little boy. "I couldn't stand it no more." Then the Reb set on the ground 'cause it seem like holding hisself up be more than he can take. "All the killing and dying and starving. I missed my mama. I missed my home. I couldn't do it no more."

"What your name?" I ask.

"Jimmy Ashby," he say, wiping his eyes.

*Jest like Jimmy from the McGuffy Reader*, I think. Then I wonder if he like to watch the sun come up in the morning and count his blessings. I don't ask him though, 'cause he might guess I can read...if'n he learned from the McGuffy Reader, too.

"Who are *you*?" Jimmy ask. For the first time in my life a white man ask my name, not who I belong to.

"I's Sapphire."

Jimmy scratch his dirty beard. "Well, Sapphire, am I in Lincoln County?"

"Yes, sir," I say. "Where you coming from?"

"Alabama."

"You tired?"

"Yes, ma'am, I sure am."

*Ma'am*? He calling *me* "ma'am?" That be a first, too.

"You hungry?" I ask. "My Mama got some soup in the kitchen."

"I'd thank you kindly for that, miss."

"Come on," I say, nodding toward the big house. "I take you."

Jimmy limping something fierce and can hardly keep up with me. I got to slow down my hippity-hopping jest so he don't think I's running from him. I ain't gone get shot in the back by a Reb, no suh. He may talk polite, but you never know what some peoples gone do when you ain't looking.

"Mama!" I holler when we get near Missus' garden. "Mama! They's a man here needs some food."

Mama come to the door, wiping her hands on her apron. When she see who I got with me, her face fall and her eyes go wide.

"This be Jimmy," I tell her. "He a Reb, but he say the fightin's all but done now."

"Good afternoon, ma'am," Jimmy say, taking off his hat.

Mama look at me, then back to Jimmy. "Where you get them manners?"

"My mammy always said it's polite to speak to ladies with respect," he say, grinning. His teeth be yellow and crooked, but that don't matter none 'cause he got a nice smile anyhow. Jimmy look down at me. "Even if they are *little* ladies."

"You look like you ain't had a meal in a while," Mama say. "Go on and wash up over yonder at the pump and I'll fix you some soup and biscuits."

When Jimmy do what Mama say, she lean over and whisper to me, "Go wake Missus. I ain't having no strange white man here without her say so."

I set my knitting basket on the kitchen table where Mama has the pretty calico laid out ready to cut into pieces for our dresses. I see she already got a little shawl started for Ida, the tiny hem halfway done with Mama's pretty blanket stitch.

Passing through the dining room into the foyer, I then tiptoe up the twisty staircase to where Missus be resting in her bedroom. The shades be drawn, so it mighty dark in there. Tapping gently on the door, I open it jest a crack. "Missus?" I whisper.

She don't move.

"Missus...there be a strange white man outside," I say louder. "He say he a Reb."

"What? What did you say?" she mumble, rolling over to one side. Her dress be spread out all over the bed and she look like the big, fluffy birthday cake Marybell done had at her last party.

"I say a strange white man be outside."

"Who is it?"

"Jimmy Ashby."

"Ashby?" she say, sitting up. "What's he want?"

"He say he looking for Lincoln County. He run off from the army to get back home to his mama 'cause he tired a all the killing."

Missus rub her eyes. "That's understandable."

I take a step closer. "Mama say to come up and wake you 'cause she ain't having no white man 'round here 'less you say so since Massa be gone."

I's wondering if Mama already done pull the big knife from the box and hide it 'tween her apron and her dress like she do whenever a stranger come on the place. She ain't never had to use it, but she say when Massa ain't home and the mens is in the field, us women gots to protect ourselves.

"I'll be right down, Sapphire," Missus yawn. "Ask him to wait outside and give him some food if he's hungry."

"Mama already getting it ready."

"Good. Give me a few moments and I'll come speak to him."

"Yes'm," I nod.

Once I close the bedroom door, I look down the stairs to see if Mama be watching for me. She ain't, so I climb up on the bannister backward and slide on my drawers all the way down to the bottom. It be one a the best things 'bout polishing day! That waxed wood be lickety-split for such things, but I know Mama'd make me set in the corner for a spell if she ever caught me. It be worth it, though 'cause I feel jest like a little bird swooping from the upstairs to the entryway as fast as I can.

When I get to the kitchen I see Mama standing outside talking to Jimmy, one hand tucked 'neath her apron. "How long you been on the road?" she ask him.

"Oh, 'bout a month, I'd say," he tell her, slurping up some soup. "This is wonderful, Miss Ruby...and I thank you for it. I've not had a hot meal since I can remember."

"You're welcome," Mama say, leaning in the doorway. When I sidle up next to her, she ask, "Missus coming?"

"Yes'm," I tell her. "She say she be down shortly."

"Whose plantation is this?" Jimmy ask. "Am I getting close to the Norton's?"

"Yes, sir." Mama point toward the north with the hand that ain't clutching the handle a the knife she hiding. "They be up the road a piece that a way."

"You know them?"

"Massa Sam knows Mister Norton," Mama nod. "I ain't never met him, but they do a little trading sometime."

"He's my uncle," Jimmy 'splain. "He can take me the rest of the way to Jasper...that's where I'm from."

"That's quite a ways east," I hear Missus say. She come up 'hind us, her skirts rustling.

"Yes, ma'am," Jimmy say, tipping his hat and bowing jest a bit. "Thank you kindly for the food."

"You're welcome...do you need clean clothes?"

Jimmy shake his head. "No, ma'am. These'll do just fine until I get to Uncle Edward's home. I'm sure Aunt Penny will make me scrub 'til my skin turns red...which would be a blessing with all the bugs I've got crawling all over."

I wrinkle my nose and make a face.

"Sorry, Sapphire," Jimmy say, his eyebrows arching. "That's not polite conversation to have in front of a little lady."

Mama pat my back. "You go on and see to Pearl like I told you. I ring the bell when it be time for you to come help with supper."

I want to hear what else Jimmy got to say. I want to ask questions like, "How many a them Yanks you kilt?" and "What it like to shoot a rifle?" and "Has you met Mister Lincoln?" I want to know if Mama gone have to use her knife, but by the looks a Jimmy, I know she ain't.

And I also know when Mama say to get, I got to get. Grabbing my knitting from the table I walk past Jimmy on the way out.

"Nice to meet you, little lady," he say, tipping his hat once more.

"You, too," I giggle. 'Your mammy done teached you real good manners, Mister Jimmy!"

Mama suck in her breath. "Sapphire, you get going right *now*."

So I hippity-hop off toward the fields, leaving Mama and Missus to do the asking.


Pearl and Isaac be bent over planting a mess a tobacco seeds in the middle of a long row that seem to stretch all the way to the edge a the earth. Pearl say she be fine, that Mama ain't got to spell her any time soon 'cause Lord knows she be working hard in the big house.

Opal and Hale and Old Albert be working in they own rows, humming and singing. Old Albert wearing Daddy's straw hat and it make me smile to see his head bobbing up and down while he planting. It make me miss my Daddy something fierce, too, but that don't matter none. I's used to that little bitty hole in my heart by now.

I see Keen on the edge a the field, riding old Nat, the mule, and toting bags a seeds to the others, asking how many more they think they gone be able to plant today. Massa say tobacco be the best chance he have at a cash crop this year. Some he sell in town, some to Mister Rotten, and some he even send up north to Missus' family. Last year the crop be smaller than the year 'fore, but that don't mean Massa ain't gone try 'gain. He say he ain't never gone give up 'til he make the plantation a success.

I wonder how he gone know it be one. When he got a heap a money in the bank? When Mister Rotten stop stealing everthing he got? When he don't gotta worry every dern day 'bout paying taxes and such? And then I wonder if them be the very things Mama gone worry 'bout when we ain't slaves no more and gots to figure out how we can survive on our own.

It be a lot on my mind, so I find a little patch in the grass near the edge a Pearl's tobacco row and pull out my knitting. I's making new booties for Marybelle's shiny-face doll baby. They has lace cuffs to match the little lace blanket I done made her last winter. As I work them stitches back and forth, my fingers find the rhythm and soon I feel better. I know I ain't got to worry long as Mama be 'round.

Pretty soon Opal start singing "Do, Lord, Remember Me." I love that one and pick up on it right quick. Opal look up when she hear my voice and we sings at the top a our lungs:

> *I've got a home in gloryland that outshines the sun*
> *I've got a home in gloryland that outshines the sun*
> *I've got a home in gloryland that outshines the sun*
> *Way beyond the blue*

"When you get here, lil' bit?" Opal ask, shading her eyes from the sun that warming my skin 'til it shine with sweat.

"Not long," I say, knitting two stitches together, then passing a slip stitch over 'em. "Ida been here sooner 'cept I had to show a runaway Reb back to the house." I say it like I bring home strange white mens for Mama to feed ever day.

"And I's s'posed to be the big fibber 'round here," Opal tease. "You's jest telling a story, Sapphire."

"No, I ain't," I say, sassy as you please. "His name be Jimmy Ashby and he has red hair and a beard so dirty, you can pick things out a it. Plus he gots a rifle and shoes so holey you can see his naked toes peeping out."

Opal plant her hand on her hip. "Oh, really? And jest what is Jimmy Ashby doing on Settler's place?" She like to call Massa Sam "Settler" 'hind his back, like she some big thing.

126

I shrug and finish the row I's working. "He don't know where he at, so I told him he in Lincoln County."

"Where he from?"

"Some place call Jasper," I tell her. "Missus say that be a far piece from here."

"Ida know 'bout that," Opal say, going back to her planting. "But if a Reb be stopping here all by hisself, the war got to be over. He say so?"

"Massa say we gone be free *any day now*." I say it like I's the Queen of Everthing.

"Oh, did he, Miss High and Mighty?" Opal smirk, rolling her eyes. "And how do he know that?"

"'Cause he stop at the telegraph and the bank when we was in town." I scratch an itch on my head. "Guess the war already done ended at some place called Appy-mattix."

"'Where that?"

"Ida know."

Opal rub her low back hard. "Lord, I's tired as all get out today."

"How come?"

"It be my time."

"Time for what?" I ask, my needles and yarn flying fast.

"My women's time."

"What time women got that different than mens?"

"Sapphire...ain't Mama done told you yet?" Opal frown, shaking her head.

"Tell me what?"

"When you get bigger you gone have a woman's time, too," she say. "Ever month you gone bleed 'tween your legs, but it ain't 'cause you hurt or nothing. It be 'cause you getting ready to has a baby."

"Like Pearl?" I ask, real excited. "She has her woman's time, too?"

"No, Sapphire," Opal say, shaking her head. "When you get your women's time, that mean you *ain't* gone have a baby."

127

"You confusing me," I scowl.

"It like this...when you old enough to has a baby, ever month your body get ready for the seed to be planted, jest like I's planting these seeds in this here soil Hale done tilled up. But if they ain't no seed that stay planted, then your body lets go a the blood...that be like the soil...and the whole thing start over 'gain."

"So womens be like a field?" I ask. "We get seeds planted 'side a us and grow babies like this here field gone grow tobacco?"

"Something like that," Opal nod. "But *I* ain't...not 'til we free."

"Well, looks like you can do more'n plant tobacco seeds if'n Massa and Jimmy be right."

Opal stop for a moment and look at me real hard. "You sure they say that the war be over?"

"Uh huh."

She take a deep breath and look at the row a pine trees growing near the edge a the plantation that be warming in the afternoon sunshine. It smell like Christmas time out here in the spring, even though Jesus' birthday be nearly a year away. Opal don't say nothing, she jest look and look and look at them trees 'til tears be flowing down her cheeks. Then she turn and walk off toward Hale who nearly done with his row. Opal hug him close, whispering in his ear. Hale kiss her cheek and whisper something back. Make me feel like I's eavesdropping to see such a thing, so I cut my eyes toward the big house.

In the distance they's Massa pulling up in the wagon near the barn. He get down and unhitch poor, old Pete who been walking 'round all the dern day. I bet he need some hay and water, so I gather my knitting and skip back to the barn in no time.

"Afternoon, Massa Sam," I say.

He put Pete into a stall where he now taking off his bridle and bit. "Hello, Sapphire."

"You see Mister Jimmy when you drive in?"

"Who's that?"

"He run off from the Reb army."

Massa rub Pete's nose. "Is that so?"

"Mama and Missus be talking to him outside the kitchen," I say, scratching a scab on my knee. "He was hungry, so Mama give him some soup 'fore he head over to Mister Norton's farm. He say that be his uncle."

Massa nod. "I knew Norton had a nephew in the army, but they hadn't heard any news from him in over a year. I'm glad he's alive."

"Mister Jimmy still here?"

"I didn't see anyone outside and the chimney's smoking, so I know your mama's cooking supper," Massa say. "Maybe he went on his way already."

"He weren't scary or nothing," I say, puffing up my chest real proud-like. "I can tell."

Massa smile. "I'll bet your Mama had that knife hidden in her skirts all the same."

"You don't miss a trick," I laugh. "How you know 'bout that?"

"'Cause she hides it in there whenever Mr. Birch comes on the place."

"She do?"

"Yes," he say softly. "She doesn't know I know it, but I saw her pull it out from behind her apron once after he got on his wagon and figure she keeps it handy...just in case."

"In case a what?"

"In case he wants to take away one of her girls." Massa look at me directly now. "But you don't have to worry...I won't ever let that happen."

I feel my throat stick. Massa and I don't never talk 'bout my daddy being dead. He don't say nothing and I know it ain't my place to ask questions 'bout it. But after hearing what Massa done say to Missus today, after Mama tell me that story 'bout when they was young kids, I know Massa Sam

129

gone protect my mama, no matter what. And if for some reason he cain't, Mama sure will take care a herself.

Massa go back to unbrindling Pete, so I put my knitting basket on a shelf so the cats cain't get into it.

We got a mess a new kittens this spring and they be good mousers, too, but they also like to mess with my yarn, so I got to be careful. Massa say I can name 'em myself and that be so much fun! One be Sunny, 'cause she a yellow-striped tabby. One be Blueberry, 'cause he shiny black and 'mind me of how them berries look when they get good and ripe. One be Honey 'cause she so sweet. And the last one named Rascal, 'cause that jest what she be, an ornery little kitten who need to learn some manners. Mama say cats has nine lives, and I's sure Rascal done gone through eight a 'em already.

"Can I feed Pete?" I ask Massa.

"Sure you can," he smile. "Will you get him some water, too?"

"Yes, sir."

Massa Sam still looking mighty sad. Tired, too. But I cain't tell if he been drinking with Mister Rotten or not. He ain't slurring his words no more, so maybe he sober up on the ride back.

I dipper up some cool, fresh water for Pete and pour it into his trough. He slurp it up real fast, then bump his head into my shoulder like he asking for more and I's happy to get it for him.

"Not too much," Massa warn. "I don't want him getting a bellyache."

"He working hard today, though, ain't he?" I ask, dipping jest one more cup.

"Yes, that he has," Massa say, slipping his hand into a curry brush. He start grooming Pete, which I know be one a his favorite things. I can tell 'cause he do it the same way I take to my knitting. Slow and steady, Massa brush and brush and brush 'til Pete be as shiny as them pennies I done give Missus Snow for my dolly. All the while Pete be munching on a bunch a hay with a handful a oats I always like to throw in for a treat.

I forgot 'bout the cornbread I has in my pocket. "Can I give this to Pete?" I ask Massa, pulling it out and showing him. It be crumbly and soft, but it still good.

"Isn't that yours?"

"No, sir. Mama say give it to Pearl, 'cept I forgot."

"Won't she want it later?"

"Naw."

"I'll send Keen into town shortly to pick up the dry goods and some tack for pancakes," Massa say. "You want him to get some dried fruit? Raisins maybe?"

"Oh, yes, please!" I grin.

Massa know I love oatmeal with raisins 'cause sometime he set in the kitchen and eat his eggs with me if it be too early for Missus to rise. We eat breakfast and chat 'bout books and animals and such. Mama be standing at the stove while we carrying on. She look over her shoulder at us ever once in a while, smiling at Massa Sam like she ain't his slave, but something else altogether.

"So can Pete has this?" I ask, standing near the horse's snout that be sniffing and snorting at the goody. "I ain't want it no more neither."

"Sure he can," Massa smile, then go 'round to brush the other side.

Pete gobble up the cornbread in one bite, then go back to his hay.

"He a pretty one alright," I say, admiring Pete's glossy brown fur and his shiny black eyes.

"What's that?" Massa ask.

I walk 'round 'til I be on his good side so's he can hear me. "I say Pete be pretty."

"That he is," Massa agree.

"Why you name him Pete?" I ask. "Why you name all them animals real names?"

"What?"

"Why you name him a man's name and not 'Banjo' or 'Thunder' or something like that?"

"I don't know," Massa shrug, smoothing down Pete's mane. "I guess because they're a living being just like me. It makes them seem more human I suppose."

I think on this a moment. If Massa Sam be figuring his horse be human, what he think I is?

Jest now Blueberry come darting into the barn and skid toward my feet with Rascal close on his heels. I scoop him up and cuddle him 'gainst my cheek. He start purring real loud and that make my heart melt. Then Rascal see a piece a hay fluttering in the soft breeze and chase after it into the yard.

"I ain't named my kittens like that," I say, real soft.

"Well, they're *your* kittens, Sapphire." Massa say like it be true. "You can name them anything you want."

"You sure they mine and not your'n?"

Massa stop grooming Pete and look down at me. His green eyes soften a might and for a second it like I be gazing in the mirror at my own eyes. I take a good look at 'em ever time I be polishing Missus' mirror on her vanity. It be so strange to see my light brown skin with them bright green eyes staring back at me 'cause I's used to jest seeing 'em on Massa's white face.

"Of course they're yours, honey," he say, smiling.

Since my Daddy gone, Massa sometime call me "honey" and that be one more reason I want to name my kitten after that sweet thing. It be like a bit a Daddy coming through Massa and I like to hear it...like to say it myself. And it make me want to forgive Massa a little bit more for taking Daddy from me.

Maybe this what Mama mean 'bout listening with them different ears.

"You thinks I's a whole human being, too?" I ask Massa.

"Yes...I do." His voice get real low when he say, "I've always felt that way."

I ain't know what to say now...and that almost never happen.

Massa stop grooming and kneel down in front a me. "Sapphire, you're just as human as I am. Just as human as Mrs. Settler and Little Sam and Marybelle." He pet Blueberry's ears real gentle. "Being a slave doesn't make you less human, but in many ways, being a slave owner does."

"What you mean?"

"It's not right to own another person," he say somber-like. "It's never been right, even though I've done it ever since my father passed. I felt it was something I had to do as owner of this plantation, as a southerner." Massa sigh real loud. "But I can see now how weak I've been in not giving your Mama her freedom when I could have. Everything could have been different for all of us. I could have set you all free before the war. I could have sold the plantation and moved north... but I didn't."

Massa stand up and go back to his grooming.

Cradling Blueberry like a baby, I rub his chubby little belly and wait for Massa to say something else.

But he don't.

He jest keep on brushing Pete even when he long past clean, rubbing and polishing and smoothing his coat 'til it look like the shiny bannister I done slid down not an hour ago. When he finally done, Massa rest his head 'gainst Pete's shoulder like he trying to soak in some a his strength. The lonely look on Massa's face make me wonder how it feel to be a man, and that be something I ain't never thought 'bout in my whole life.

But I 'magine Massa be thinking on things he ain't never done thought 'bout neither, 'cause in a few days, everthing gone be different for all a us whether he want it that way or not.

# Karin

Simka is quiet as I sit by her side, the filthy, damp rag in my hand, ready to offer it to her when she wakes. Esfir says she's been asleep for a few minutes, and to just let her rest before the contractions start again. The barrack rumbles with the sound of women snoring, women murmuring and bickering among themselves.

Even though I bathe almost every day, I still feel dirty whenever I return to this hideous place where excrement fills nearly every bunk since most of the prisoners are too weak from dysentery and typhus to sit up, let alone make it to the latrines. The female guards used to inspect our barrack regularly, but have ceased their daily torture since there are too many crammed into a place too small to hold us all.

It's both a mercy and a terror.

I lean against the wall and close my eyes. In the dull roar of voices, I hear Katarine talking to Magda, her invisible sister. "Kazhdyy den' kto-to drugoy...kazhdyy den' kto-to drogoy, Magda," she chants. "Kazhdyy den' kto-to umret."

Esfir says she's saying, *Everyday someone else will die.*

Katarine waits patiently for Magda to respond.

"Da, no vyvstretite menya vest?" she then pleads.

*Will you meet me there?*

Again, another pause.

Katarine's voice elevates in pitch and volume. "On budet umirat' v etom strashnom meste. Eto uzhasno, uzhasno, uzhano mesto!"

*It will die in this horrible place! This horrible, horrible, horrible place!*

"Shut your trap, you crazy lout!" a woman yells from the other end of the barrack. "Some of us are trying to sleep!"

"Shut yours, you ugly beast!" another voice answers. "You're not helping any!"

Katarine hears neither of them. "Da, da, yest'...ryadom s ney, ona yest."

*Yes, yes, she is. Right next to her, she is.*

Another pause.

"Ona, ona, yesli vy sprosite yeye," Katarine says quickly.

*She will, she will if you ask her.*

Another short silence.

"*I* shall ask her then," Katarine replies, speaking in German. She walks the short distance to where I'm crouched on the floor. "You're to sing to her, Karin. Sing! Sing! Sing!" she insists.

I sadly shake my head.

"You must! You must sing when it's her time." Katarine nods her head ardently, her eyes bright in their sunken sockets. "Magda says you must!"

I shake my head again.

"When you sing, you will help to bring the baby," Katarine explains. "When you bring the baby, you must sing!"

Esfir sighs. "She's crazy...just forget about her."

"Nicht verruckt!" Katarine spits. "Nein! Meine Schwester will Karin zu singen!"

*Not crazy! No! My sister wants Karin to sing!*

"Where's your sister then?" Esfir asks, looking wildly around the barrack. "Where is she? I don't see her. Do you see her, Karin?"

I look from Katarine to Esfir and back again. I cannot see Magda, but I know where she is. I know how she speaks to her sister so clearly that Katarine must listen and do what she says.

I know because Mutti is in the same place speaking to me. She tells me what do to, how to stay alive. And even though I can no longer see her, I hear her voice all the better, for now she can never leave me. Still, the intensity of Katarine's eyes and the way she implores me to sing, remind me of a time when singing to Mutti was the only thing that had kept her alive.

***

October, 1941

"Don't leave me, Karin," Mutti begs. "Please...you're all I have left."

I hold Mutti's hand as the long line of women is directed toward a building with a sign outside the metal doors: Anmeldung.

*Registration.*

"Leave your bags on the lorries and follow me into this building!" an S.S. officer orders. "LEAVE EVERYTHING!"

A woman behind us whispers, "But my mother's pictures...they're all I have left of her."

"Silence!" the officer shouts, smacking her across the face so hard her skull cracks into mine.

Tears fill my eyes as Mutti and I set our satchels on the lorry. I'm too exhausted to care when I'll get to read my books or write letters to Tante Sabine or finish the cabled sweater I had been knitting for Bruno.

Just the thought of him makes my heart want to burst.

One by one we enter the building. One by one we're asked our name, our birthplace, our heritage. I have no identification card and I won't speak, so the S.S. interrogating me slaps me a few times to loosen my tongue.

"My sister is mute!" Mutti cries from the next table. "She's *mute!*"

"Why wasn't she taken in the other line then?" the S.S. frowns. "The Reich has no use for her."

Mutti shakes her head. "No! The man in charge told her specifically to come here with me."

"Get over here then!" the S.S. yells, motioning with his hand. "Name?"

"Mine or hers?"

"Hers!"

136

"K...K...Karin Vogel," Mutti stutters.   "Karin Elaine Vogel."

The S.S. types this information, then asks.  "Age?"

"Fifteen...almost sixteen."

"Birthday?"

"November 26, 1925."

"Birthplace?"

"Baden Baden."

"Religion?"

"Christian."

With this, the S.S. looks up from the typewriter and frowns.  "Christian?"

"Yes...Lutheran."

"Why were you sent here?"

Mutti doesn't answer.

"I'll only ask you one more time," the S.S. threatens. "*Why* were you arrested?"

Mutti looks nervously to me, then back to the S.S. "Political reasons...my husband...."

The S.S. quickly types something onto my record.  He then quickly takes Mutti's mostly false information and directs us toward a female guard standing near the doorway.

"Rotes Dreiecke!" he shouts.

*Red triangles!*

I don't know what this means and Mutti dares not ask.

We're led to another building where I'm tattooed, but not completely, as Mutti frantically reminds the sadist with the needle that we are German Christians.  I don't understand why the S.S. doesn't finish the job, but I'm thankful.

We endure having our heads completely shaven...to prevent lice we're told.  As my blonde locks fall to the floor, silent tears slide down my cheeks.  Every woman, every girl looks less human somehow.  Less alive.  But being stripped of my hair isn't as bad as the humiliation of being ordered to undress in front of everyone...the other prisoners, female guards, and even the male S.S. officers.  No one has ever seen me naked, and the humiliation of blood running between my legs is almost more than I can bear, especially when a rough and careless S.S. shaves me there, all the while telling me what a dirty whore I am. He slaps my bare scalp a few times, reminding me that I'm nothing more than a number now.

"Forget your name," he snarls cruelly, wiping the bloody razor blade on a grimy rag. "I'm surprised they let you live, you filthy animal."

It's then I'm certain that Frau Daiga, her daughter, and my Jurgen are all dead. I almost collapse, but Mutti comes from behind, holding my arm and guiding me out of the room and into the showers where we're ordered to wash thoroughly before being given dresses and shoes that don't belong to us.

"Where are our things?" Mutti asks a woman next to us. "Will they be placed in our rooms?"

"Rooms? This isn't a hotel! There are no rooms here!" she laughs bitterly, her Polish accent making her hard to understand.

"How do you know this?"

"Do you know where you are?" the woman asks.

Mutti's eyes are filled with tears. "No...I don't."

"In hell."

But it's worse than hell when we're finally marched into our barrack by the kapo, our sadistic block leader. Stubenaltester Yenta is large and loud, with buckteeth and an angry scowl. She shouts at us to line up alongside the narrow wooden shelves, stacked four high. She demands we follow her every command or risk the consequences.

As we're herded inside the cramped, drafty building, one of the women is so utterly exhausted, she falls to the ground. The kapo angrily beats her until she passes out, blood pouring from her nose and ears. Still, the kapo continues to thrash her until, minutes later the poor woman is dead.

"Let this be a lesson to all of you!" she shouts, spit flying from her rubbery lips. "You will obey me in every turn, or this sub-human's fate will be yours as well!"

By the time she's halfway through her speech about the mandatory Appell - the roll call - my ears ring and itch from the loud din of her maddening voice. Blood still trickles down my legs and as the kapo passes by me during her long, tedious speech, Mutti grabs my hand once again. The brute passes us and my eyes meet Mutti's. She nods slightly and rubs her thumb along my fingers, reassuring me.

But on her way back, the Yenta stops in front of me and turns, scowling at my shorn hair and terrified expression. She then looks down and sees the spatter of red on the floor between my feet. "Clean it up!" she yells at me. "Clean up your mess, you filthy pig!"

I quickly kneel on the ground and use the hem of my thin, threadbare dress to try and mop up as much as I can. The kapo kicks my leg with her steel-toed boot.

"Faster! Faster!" she spits. "I don't have all day!"

Furiously I scrub harder until the spots are smeared into the thick layer of grime coating the hard cement floor. The blood stain on my dress nearly matches the red triangle sewn over my left breast.

When I stand up again, the kapo smacks me across the face for good measure, to make sure I don't forget that to be alive is a gift Yenta's given me just now, a gift she can revoke whenever she sees fit.

As the kapo finally leaves the room, a painfully thin woman wearing rags assigns us to our bunks. The woman who had spoken to Mutti on the train stands nearby, silent and somber. Her long, beautiful red hair is gone, and her hands absentmindedly touch her scalp as if to constantly remind herself that she's not dreaming. That this hell is real indeed.

Mutti sneezes, then wipes her nose on the back of her hand. "That smell," she says, frowning. "What is that unbearable smell?"

"Didn't you see those chimneys when we arrived? Don't you know what they're for?" The woman looks at Mutti and her eyes seem to darken when she says, "That smell is your son's corpse...burning."

Later that night when the lights are out, the barrack is pitch dark, but not silent. A soft moaning can be heard from every corner of the drafty building, women crying out for their husbands, their mothers, their children.

Mutti lies next to me, holding me close. We stink of disinfectant and the musty, scratchy clothes we've been given. My bald scalp bristles against my forearm that I'm using as a pillow, and I shudder beneath the thin blanket we've been given to share. We're on the top bunk, so the ceiling is mere inches from our faces. We cannot sit up and we cannot climb down until morning, or risk certain retribution.

I'm cold and tired and hungry, for the meager rations we were given this evening were next to nothing...a scrap of black bread and a mug of something the kapo called coffee, but it was tasteless and bitter, so I gave mine to Mutti. Now my stomach cramps, but I'm thankful I'm not bleeding as much, that my dress has soaked up much of what the kapo would surely punish me for in the morning.

"Karin," Mutti whispers. "Karin...are you still here?"

I touch her face with my fingertips, but still, she cries out. "Karin! Where are you? Are you here?"

I press my forehead to hers and feel the tears spilling down her cheeks, but in her shock and anguish, Mutti cannot feel my presence. In less than a week, Bruno has been murdered, the Zwiegs, systematically executed. We've been taken from our homes with next to nothing and endured the horror of an endless transport, not knowing what would happen next. Vati and Jurgen have been taken from us, and I know for certain we will never see either of them again.

Mutti is beyond consolation as she starts sobbing loudly, "Karin! Karin! Where are you?"

Soon another woman starts screaming in Polish. Another in Yiddish. Yet another in German. Their voices create a cacophony of torment that echoes from every corner.

I'm frightened that the kapo will return and beat us all to death, so I do the only thing I can. I comfort my mother. At first I simply hum "Brahms's Lullaby." Then I sing "Stille Nacht," which slows Mutti's tears. From a few bunks away another thin, reedy voice joins me, then another, then another, and soon the unsettled voices in the barrack are quiet as we all softly sing:

*Sleep in heavenly peace,*
*Sleep in heavenly peace.*

"Mehr, meine Karin," Mutti whispers, her eyes closed, her hands reaching for mine. "Bitte...mehr."
*More, my Karin. Please...more.*

And so I choose her favorite song, one that Mutti would ask Vati and I to perform at the Volkslieder. Softly I croon "Thoughts Are Free" in her ear:

*Thoughts are free, who can guess them?*
*They fly by like nocturnal shadows.*
*No man can know them, no hunter can shoot them*
*with powder or lead: Thoughts are free!*

By the time I finish, Mutti has drifted off to sleep, her hands still clutching mine.

***

Now Katerine grabs my hand and nods. "Sing, Karin! Sing for the baby."

Simka frowns in her sleep as her chest rises and falls with labored breathing. She doesn't stir when I gently mop the sweat from her brow and softly sing another verse of Mutti's favorite song:

*So I will renounce my sorrow forever,*
*and never again will torture myself with whimsies.*
*In one's heart, one can always laugh and joke*
*and think at the same time: Thoughts are free!*

As I continue singing, my thoughts freely wander to that first day in Auschwitz. The day Jurgen died. The last time I saw my father. I remember seeing the sign above the gates: "Arbeit macht frei...*Work makes you free.*"

All these years later I realize that work has kept me alive...but it has not set me free. Only seemingly insignificant moments like this, when I can sing a song which meant so much to my mother, when I can soothe my friend, while I let the verses speak for me since I cannot find the words myself...this is when I am free.

# Sapphire

Ain't nothing to do 'til Marybelle and Little Sam come home from school, so I leave Massa to his chores and skip back to the kitchen. Maybe Mamma need my help with supper, and if she don't, I can work on my knitting a bit 'fore my reading lesson.

Mama be setting at the table peeling 'taters. "Hey there, baby girl," she smile. "You been busy in the fields? Let me see what you got done."

I hand her my basket. "I ain't done much. Pearl say she be fine in the fields, so I was in the barn helping Massa take care a Pete."

"That nice," she say, looking at my work. "You need help with the heel on this one?"

"No'm," I tell her plainly. "I can do it."

"You getting mighty independent there, Miss Sapphire."

"What that mean?"

Mama hand me back my knitting. "It mean you can do things all by yourself."

"I can do lots by myself," I say, setting on a stool. "I can feed Pete and pick peas and sew curtains and even peel them 'taters if'n you want me to."

"No, thank you kindly...I do it." Mama pick up the 'tater she been peeling and get back to work.

I get busy, too. These baby booties ain't gone make theyselves, or so Mama always tell me.

"What else you want to learn, Sapphire?" she ask.

"I don't know...I wish I could drive the horses and the wagon to town." I give her a sly smile. "That way I can get out a here whenever I want to."

"Not whenever you want to, baby girl," Mama chide. "Massa has some say in that."

I look 'round the kitchen and through the window. "Where Mister Jimmy go?"

Mama keep on peeling. "He go on his way to Massa Norton's place."

"He seem like a good man," I offer.

"Good and filthy," Mama say. "He need a bath something powerful."

I nod. "You think he got them bugs?"

"I do indeed."

"What kind a bugs do peoples get?" I ask. "They get fleas and things like cats and dogs?"

Mama shake her head. "Fleas can bite peoples, but mostly what bugs they get called lice and they like crawling all over they hair and such."

I make a nasty face.

"You ain't got to worry 'bout that, Sapphire," Mama say, pointing her peeler at me. "You jest keep on taking your bath with that lye soap. I know it ain't the best smelling stuff, but you ain't gone get no bugs if'n you do."

"I *know*, Mama." I roll my eyes 'cause I *hate* that dern lye soap. It sting my eyes something fierce and stink like the devil to boot.

She pick up another 'tater. "I ain't having none a my babies dying a typhus like my mama done."

"That how she die?"

"Uh-huh," Mama nod. "It be a cold winter when I was 'round six. We spent most a the time in the shack when we weren't cooking and cleaning in the big house. Mama and Jasmine and me done huddle up together under the quilt to keep warm. We all got them lice that year, but Mama...she be the only one who got sick from 'em...and die from the typhus."

"Where she now?"

"My mama?"

"Uh-huh."

"Her body be buried in the yard 'hind the shacks, but her spirit be free to fly with Jesus."

144

I scratch my forehead. "We grow wings when we dead?"

"Not real ones."

"Then how we fly?"

"Maybe an angel come down and give us some wings." Mama shrug. "Alls I know is when my mama die, her body get lighter somehow...like something jest lifted on out a her."

"You think she and Daddy see each other in heaven?"

"I hope so."

We set and work for a while, neither of us saying a word. I hear the birds chirping outside the open window and feel a nice, cheerful breeze blowing them curtains so they flippity-flap on the sill. I smell the warm, wet earth a Missus' garden where them baby bunnies still hippity-hoping 'round the snow peas.

Watching Mama peel them 'taters, I see her brow all curled up like she thinking on something. Her face still streaked a bit with them tears and her eyes be tired.

"You thinking on your Mama?" I ask, real quiet.

"Uh huh," she nod. "I's thinking how Massa Sam's mama done laugh when she find out my mama be dead." Clearing her throat, Mama look at me. "Missus laugh 'cause she glad she ain't gone have to look at her one more day. She say that right to my face."

"That real mean," I frown.

"That ain't all," Mama say. "Missus tell me and Jasmine that my mama be a thorn in her side from day one and that Big Massa Samuel should a left her on the plantation with Mister Norton."

I sit up tall. "Grandmama come from over there? She know Mister Jimmy?"

"No, baby girl," Mama say, smiling real gentle. "She ain't know him 'cause he ain't been born yet."

"Oh."

"She been sold to Big Massa Samuel when she be 'bout your age."

145

"How come?"

"The way Mama tell it, they be too many chil'rens running 'round on Mister Norton's place." She peel the 'tater right quick. "She say he be too busy in the slave quarters and not busy enough in the fields."

"What *that* mean?"

Mama stop working for a moment. "I ain't gone tell you the whole story 'til you bigger, but I tell you this...Mama say Mister Norton be her daddy."

I wrinkle my brow. "How that be?"

"It be 'cause it take a mama and a daddy to make a little baby," Mama 'splain. "Jest like it take a daddy cat and a mama cat to make that litter a kittens you got in the barn."

I grin. "Yeah...Henry and Mabel got a bunch a cute kids, ain't they?"

"Yes'm, they sure do," Mama say, smiling. "And Mister Norton got a bunch a his kids slaving on near ever plantation this side a Lincoln County."

My mouth open wide. "How come?"

"He be the daddy and his slave womens be the mamas."

"Them kids be both colored *and* white?"

"Yes'm," Mama nod. "That what *mullatto* mean."

"Ain't that what Massa Sam call you?"

"Uh huh."

"Grandmama be colored even though Mister Norton be her daddy?"

"Yes, baby," Mama say, getting back to her peeling.

I chew the side a my cheek for a moment, then ask, "So Mister Jimmy and me is *kin*?"

Mama nod. "They's white somewheres in my blood...and your'n, too. That why you's lighter than your sisters. I 'spect they gots more a your daddy's blood in 'em."

I stop my knitting and look out the window where I see Massa pitching hay down into the barn. Look like he gone clear ever piece from the loft. "Do Massa know?"

"Yes, he do."

I look at Mama. "So I's got *white* blood in me...for sure?"

"Yes, baby girl...you and Opal and Pearl." She quiet for a moment, then say, "All a us coloreds gots some white blood mixed in, and I 'magine lots of them white folks in town gots a little bit a colored, too."

I's quiet for a moment, thinking on that one *real hard*. After a while I say to Mama, "Maybe all a us is a little bit of everthing."

"Yes, chile...you right, we is." She get up to put the 'taters in the boiling pot.

"Mama...what white blood look like?"

Stirring the 'taters in the pot, she say, "It be red jest like everone else's."


Missus got me setting near the sunny window reading Massa's King James Bible while she go in the kitchen for a cup a tea. I ain't know who King James be, but secretly I call it the King Jimmy, 'cause I like the way that sound a heap better, 'specially after meeting a white man named Jimmy who be my secret kin and call me "little lady".

Marybelle and Little Sam be changing out they school clothes upstairs and I can hear 'em yelling at each other. They come in the house squabbling and jest keep on going as they climb the big, twisty staircase to the second floor where they bedrooms be. Each got they own bed, they own little desk, and even a heap a clothes in a thing called a chiffarobe. All I got is a peg near the door a the shack where I hang my dress at the end a the day. That be where my raggedy nightie dangle, too. It waiting for me right now, sagging and sighing 'cause it ain't fancy or nothing.

Marybelle say she gone give me one a her old nighties jest as soon as her grandmama come to visit. She say she wrote to Missus Hamilton and tell her she need some new clothes from up north. Marybelle say everthing down here in Tennessee be old fashion and she want some new styles.

I don't know what *style* mean, but the way Marybelle tell it, I guess it be something worth having.

Now Little Sam come thumping down the stairs, his brown hair flying everwhere. "Sapphire, where's Mama?"

"Who Mama?" I ask, grinning.

That be our little joke. He call my mama "Mama Ruby" and his mama jest plain old "Mama".

"*Your* mama," he smile. "I need her to cut my hair. That darn Douglas Pritchard called me a sissy girl on the way home from school."

"You whip him good?"

"Naw...he's not worth it," Sam say, pulling his books from the shelf and tossing 'em on the fainting couch. "Papa would whip my hide if he ever found out."

"No, he wouldn't," I sass. "Massa don't whip nothing or nobody." I's flipping pages a King Jimmy 'cause I cain't find nothing to my liking. I already done read 'bout Matthew and Mark. Luke and John look to be the same old story 'bout Jesus' life. I already know He been born in a barn and made to hide from some mean old King who kill all the babies 'cause he done be 'fraid they take his power away. I know Jesus be teaching all kind a folks 'bout God and saying, "His Kingdom is within you."

But I don't know what that mean. How can God be inside a me and also inside a Little Sam and Mama and the baby Pearl gone have soon? Then I think maybe God be a little like Queen Anne's Lace. Maybe that little spark a life that keep 'em coming back year after year be what inside all a us...and it also what God truly be.

I watch Little Sam jump 'round, his blue eyes snapping 'cause he pretending to be smacking some invisible person. Little Sam a heap different from his sister, jest like I's different from Opal and Pearl. Then I think on Mister Rotten and Mister Jimmy. On Mister Norton and all a his kin. I think

148

on Missus and her mama and daddy who be coming soon. I think on *my* daddy and Mama's mama and all a them Yanks and Rebs who ain't alive no more.

*God love a great diversity*, I think to myself. I know what *diversity* mean 'cause Missus done tell me. I 'member how she say all of nature be diverse, that it be made up of a whole bunch a different things. Diff'rent plants and trees and animals and insects.

*And peoples, too,* I tell myself.

I flip through them pages real fast 'til King Jimmy open to a chapter called 1 Corinthians. I don't know how to say that big word, so I ask Little Sam.

"That says 'First Corinthians, chapter twelve, verse thirteen," he tell me.

"I know how to read them numbers," I shoot back. "I only asked you how to say the *big word*."

Little Sam make a silly face. "Well, *pardon me*, Miss Sapphire."

"You excused," I say real sassy.

"Good...I'm getting something to eat."

I wave him off as I set my eyes on them words from Corinthians:

*For by one Spirit are we all baptized into one body,*
*whether we be Jews or Gentiles,*
*whether we be bond or free;*
*and have been all made to drink one Spirit.*

*What be a Jew and a Gentile*? I wonder. I know what being in bondage mean...and hopefully gone learn what it mean to be free someday soon. *Is drinking one Spirit mean we all the same, no matter what we look like? Maybe that how God get inside all a us.*

Missus come in, her skirts a swirling. She ain't got on her hoop 'neath 'em and they kinda droop on the ground like Little Sam's long hair droop on his shoulders. They look alike, her and Little Sam. They gots the same blue eyes and browish hair. The same thin, pink lips. The same long, spindly arms and legs. Marybelle look more like Massa Sam, 'cept she ain't got green eyes. She gots blue, too. Her hair be blonde and straight as a stick, so she keep it pulled back with ribbons. Not like Sam who let his hair go ever which a way.

"What did you find today, Sapphire?" Missus ask.

"Something from Corinthians," I tell her. "You know what a Jew and a Gentile be?"

Missus move Little Sam's books and set on the fainting couch. "A Jew is someone who is Jewish and a Gentile is someone who is not...someone who is Christian like us."

"What Jewish?"

"To be Jewish is to believe in a certain religion," Missus 'splain. "It's an old religion...thousands of years old."

"Is the Gentile religion ol,' too?"

Missus shake her head. "When Jesus was born... actually when Jesus started teaching and people followed him, that's when the new religion was started."

"How long ago that be?"

"1800 years."

"That be a long time?"

"Yes...a very long time."

"Did Jesus tell everone they's Christians?"

Missus take a deep breath, then let it out. I can tell she ain't know how to answer that one. "Actually, Jesus was a Jew," she finally say.

"How can Jesus be a Jew, but start a whole new religion so's we'd follow him?" I ask. "And what 'bout this here Bible verse that say we's *all* born a the same Spirit no matter who we be. What that mean?"

Missus smile at me. "You're full of questions today, Sapphire."

Now Marybelle come down the stairs wearing one a them old fashioned dresses. It red with white roses all over and look to be a size too small, so I guess it be a good thing she gone get some new styles. Maybe she pass that pretty dress on to me, too. Don't know where I'd wear it, but all the same, it'd be nice to hang on my peg and look at on Sundays when I ain't got no work to do.

"Mama, may I have a cookie 'fore we start?" Marybelle ask.

Missus nod. "Yes, please tell Little Sam it's time for our lesson."

"I will." She flit on by and don't pay me no mind today.

Marybelle be like that sometime. One day she be my friend, the next she say she too old to play with the likes of me. I don't know if it 'cause I colored or 'cause I younger than her. It don't seem to matter to Little Sam, but I's more likely to climb trees and shoot marbles with him than I is to talk 'bout styles and such with Marybelle.

Missus take the King Jimmy and put a little bookmark on my page. She say I can go back to it when my chores is done after supper. "It's time for Mr. McGuffey's work now," she smile, handing me a brand new book. "I think you're ready for this one."

My eyes get wide, 'cause it be the *third*, not the second.

"You've been practicing," Missus say. "I've heard you reciting while you're working, and I'm very proud of your progress."

My heart rise up and feel like it do when Mama say I be getting independent. I take the book from Missus and run my fingers over the word *eclectic*. "What this word mean?"

Missus look where my finger be. "That word is *eclectic*." She say it real careful. "It means to be varied...to have a lot of different stories included in the same book."

I nod. "That be like *diverse*, right?"

Missus smile real broad. "Yes! Exactly! My, you are bright, Sapphire."

"So this could say 'McGuffey's Third *Diverse* Reader' and it be the same thing?"

"Yes, in a way."

I open the stiff, white pages and see a little boy setting in a tree, reading a book. I wonder what his name be and what he reading. Maybe it be the very same book I got in my hands. I look through the story titles in this eclectic thing and don't know how I's gone be able to read 'em all. But I got through the second reader alright, and I 'spect I can do the same with this one here.

"Which story do you want to start with, Sapphire?" Missus ask.

I look up from the book. "Ain't I got to do all a them exercises in the beginning?"

"No, I think you can pass by those for a while," Missus tell me. "If you have trouble, we'll review them."

I go back to the stories and see one called "I Will Think of It." I like the sound of it 'cause I always be thinking on something and I wonder what old Mister McGuffey gone say on the subject. "This one here," I say, pointing.

"Go ahead and find the page, Sapphire," Missus smile. "I'll go and fetch those children of mine. I'm sure they're eating up all of your Mama's cookies."

She go on to the kitchen while I flip through the pages 'til I find the one I wants, then I get to reading. The story be 'bout how all kind a people solve big questions by thinking on 'em. A man named Galileo done seen a chandelier swinging this a way and that and he think up a way to make something called a pendulum. And here come another James who figure out how to make a watch all by hisself. He be independent jest like me.

But I don't like the end of the story, no suh, 'cause it say:

> *Boys, when you have a difficult lesson to learn,*
> *don't feel discouraged, and ask someone*
> *to help you before helping yourselves.*
> *Think, and by thinking you will learn*
> *how to think to some purpose.*

I don't like that Mister McGuffey jest write *boys* and not *girls*, too. I's been sep'rate from folks jest 'cause I colored, and even though I's used to it by now, I still don't like it one bit. Now I's thinking it gone be the same 'cause I's a girl, too.

White *or* colored, womens cain't do what mens can. Even I know that by watching how it be on Massa's plantation. And when I's in town, I watch how it go on in Lincoln County, too. I 'spect this how it be ever other place, no matter where it be.

Mens run everthing.

But they cain't ever make me stop thinking and wondering.

# Karin

Simka's feet are inflamed and red. Blisters cover her heels where ill-fitting shoes rub them raw. Her ankles have disappeared in the soft flesh surrounding them, and her calves are swollen. She moans in pain, clenching handfuls of her dress in tight fists.

"Karin...help me...please," she begs.

I don't know what to do. I'm not sure Simka's even conscious, or if she's calling out to me in delirium, something many of the prisoners often do in the middle of the night.

But it's not nighttime...not yet. The sun is high, and scant light marred by smoke shines through the open door of the barrack. A light breeze blows in now and again, bringing with it ashes, dust, and the incessant odor of death.

Katarine has gone back to her bunk and mumbles to herself, words Esfir and I cannot hear.

"Leave her to her madness," Esfir scowls. "She'll be dead before the day is done. The typhus will take her quickly enough."

Looking at Katarine, I feel nothing but pity. For weeks I've listened to her babbling. She's trapped in an ongoing conversation that endlessly spins its wheels until sleep eventually finds her. But even then I can often hear Katarine mumbling in Russian, her sister's name tangled among the foreign words.

I don't have conversations with Mutti. She simply tells me what I need to do: "Use loose tension when making lace curtains and tighter tension when making socks." "Take Simka and hide in the pantry." "Don't eat too quickly or too much when the camp is liberated."

Her voice is always the same. Strong. Deliberate. Clear.

154

It's not at all the way it was four years ago when we were sifting through a sea of luggage in "Kanada" and discovered the hidden treasure that would return to us a sense of being human beings...not just prisoners. Back then neither of us knew how determined and unrelenting Mutti could be in saving both of our lives.

***

November, 1941

In the weeks that follow our arrival at Auschwitz, my mother and I, along with dozens of other women, are made to work outside in the increasingly bitter cold. Icy winds and frigid rain fall on us as we haul coal from building to building. Our bellies nearly empty, our hearts full of sorrow, we pull carts carrying fuel for the Nazis to keep their offices and barracks warm and comfortable, while at the end of a long, fourteen hour day, we go back to our own frigid barrack for a small tin of watery soup and a meager crust of bread.

The kapo, Yenta, yells at us to eat quickly and get to bed, for another day of hard work will soon be upon us. "And no talking!" she orders. "For every person who speaks, ten more will be beaten!"

The red-headed woman spits on the floor when Yenta's not looking. "Bah! I'll beat you with this!" Johanna whispers, covertly brandishing a chunk of wood from a bin near the stove that scarcely heats our side of the room.

Mutti grabs her wrist and hisses, "Put that down! You'll get us all killed!"

Johanna scowls, but shoves the wood into the stove instead of down Yenta's throat like we all wish she would. Then again, we might get someone even worse than her...or maybe Johanna would be called upon to be our kapo. That's the way it works here. The criminals, the sadists, the most inhumane rise in power, and woe to the creature who falls in the ranks. I've heard of kapos who were stripped of their

155

position, then handed over to the prisoners who would beat them to death in retaliation.

Even though I hate Yenta, hate the sound of her callous voice, the sight of her ugly face, and the smell of her fetid breath, I don't think I could ever bring myself to kill another human being.  Then I would be just like the S.S., like Hitler, and anyone else who zealously believes Germany is becoming more powerful by eliminating the Jews and all those who they deem to be sub-human.   It's at moments like this when I realize how well my father has taught me, and I wonder where he is.

Is he still alive?

The next morning, we're awakened by Yenta's ruthless demands. "Get out of those beds, you lazy beasts!" she hollers, smacking her whip into the palm of her bare hand.  "Get up! Get up!  Get up!"  Just for fun she thrashes a few prisoners until their faces are striped with blood.

Quickly Mutti and I make our bed, turning down the blanket in military fashion.  Then we stand at the end of our bunks, ready for inspection, while our daily ration of "coffee" is distributed.  I cannot stand the taste of it, but am so hungry, I slurp the foul liquid, marveling at how something so sickening can feel so wonderful sliding into my stomach.

Mutti tries to give me her ration again, but I push it away and shake my head.  She never says a word about my self-imposed silence.  Never asks me to speak.  Never asks why I don't.  She watches how the system works around here and reminds me to remain as invisible as possible, for the ones who are not noticed are not beaten.  The ones who are quiet are often overlooked.  And so far, except for the first night, Yenta and all of the other guards have left me alone.

As we march to the Appellplatz, Mutti never leaves my side.  She cannot hold my hand, but I often look over and see her silhouette, once soft and supple, now angular and indifferent.  I've watched her labor continuously, clamoring to do her work to avoid a beating, to avoid being separated from me or sent to the gas chambers. For by now, we all know what happens to prisoners who dare to disobey. Who dare to fall behind. Who dare to collapse from hunger or exhaustion.

Mutti and I stand in our places, staring straight ahead while thousands of others follow suit. My legs ache. My arms are numb. My eyes see nothing but gray, gray, gray everywhere, and my ears hear nothing but the loud voices of the S.S. ordering everyone to move faster. Stand taller. Keep their eyes front.

This morning it takes nearly an hour for the barracks to empty and the Appell to be assembled. But finally, when everyone has been accounted for, when the dead have been dragged from their barracks and heaped onto carts, when the ones who have collapsed in their lines have been carried away to meet their doom, a voice on the loudspeaker orders us to sing *Horst Wessel*.

With our right arms raised in the *Heil Hitler Salute*, our scores of fractured voices join as one as we sing Germany's national anthem. New prisoners who don't know the words are pulled from the ranks and thrashed. Those who don't sing loud enough are cursed and beaten. Those who sing too loudly are punished as well.

I stare at the bald head of Johanna who stands directly in front of me and sing as clearly as I can, even though the lyrics make my skin crawl. Minutes later, when we're ordered to raise our right arms once more for the fourth verse, I'm thankful these will be the only words that will pass my lips for the entire day.

A tall S.S. officer paroles the ranks while we sing, eyeing the women. I notice him out of the corner of my eye. His short, brown hair. His fiercely focused eyes. His strong gait. He stops in front of Johanna and grabs her face, turning it to his.

"Dieses ein!" he tells another officer who follows behind with a clipboard.

*This one.*

The officer pulls Johanna out of line and writes down her prisoner number.

Next the tall officer towers over me and grabs my arm. Immediately I stop singing. His blue eyes seem to deepen as he stares into mine. I quickly look at my feet.

"Schau mich an!" he commands.

*Look at me!*

I lift my eyes.

"Dieses, auch," he tells the man with the clipboard.

*This one, too.*

I frantically look toward Mutti and the man notices. "Sie ist eine relativ?"

*Is she a relative?*

Darting my gaze toward the ground, I nod.

Lifting my chin with his fingertips, the man smiles. "Ich werde sie nehmen, auch."

*I will take her, too.*

Mutti steps out of line to join us and I grab her hand. I don't know where we're going -- if we'll be sent to a different workplace or to the gas. All I know is that I cannot leave Mutti to suffer alone in this hell on earth, and if we're going to walk toward our inevitable deaths, then at least we'll walk together.

When the officer turns to select more women, the loudspeaker demands another round of the national anthem. "Ihr seid still!" he yells, wheeling around to point his baton at us.

*You are silent!*

"Kapitan Dieter!" another S.S. shouts, running toward him. "Only five this time!"

Dieter nods and quickly chooses two more women. I'm by far the youngest and feel strangely out of place. *Where are we going?* I wonder.

"Folge mir!" Dieter shouts.

*Follow me.*

As we shuffle by the poor souls made to sing for what I know will be more than an hour, I hear Dieter say to the S.S. with the clipboard, "Sicherzustellen, das junge Madchen bekommt mehr Futter."

*Make sure the young girl gets more food.*

We're taken to a new barrack with running water and *real soap*! After a hot shower, we're given clean dresses, kerchiefs, and even warm coats. We're told by an S.S. guard that we will be allowed to grow our hair. That we will no longer be beaten. That we will have access to running water and latrines that fuction properly.

"You are in what the prisoners call 'Kanada,'" the guard says, motioning with his head. "Go outside and see the officer by the gate for your assignments."

Mutti and I walk into a yard filled with bags and boxes, satchels and suitcases. Dozens of women sift and sort their way through the enormous mountain range of luggage that lines one entire side of the large open space. There are piles of wicker baskets. Bins of toothbrushes. Stacks of books and a wheelbarrow filled with wire-rimmed eyeglasses.

We follow Johanna as she walks toward a man with a clipboard in his hand. He looks identical to the one who assisted Kapitan Dieter at the Appell. "Numbers?" he asks Mutti, scribbling something on a chart.

"711564," she replies quickly. "And my sister's is 811993."

The man jots them on the chart, then points in the direction of the far side of the yard. "You're to go over there and begin sorting. Ask the other prisoners where to place money, jewelry, and other luxury items. The rest you can figure out on your own."

"Thank you," Mutti replies, taking my hand and walking toward one of the mountains stacked high with dirty duffel bags. "Do you know how lucky we are, Karin?" she asks. "Better barracks...more food...even warm clothes!"

It's the first time I've seen even a hint of a smile on her face. Perhaps there's a chance we'll both survive.

A woman in a brown frock walks over to us. "I'm Irena."

"Josephine," Mutti says. "This is my sister, Karin."

I give her a weak smile.

Irena nods. "It's pretty simple. Choose a bag and sort all of the items. Clothes here...." She points to a pile nearby. "Shaving supplies here....glasses here. Shoes here..." She looks at Mutti. "You get the picture."

"Yes...we were told to ask you where to place money and jewelry," Mutti says.

Irena lifts a brow and whispers, "If you have pockets in that coat of yours, see what little you can take for yourself, then put the rest in the locked box in the barrack." She looks toward the guard who is still making notations on his chart. "Find a safe place and keep what you can. It's good for bartering."

"Bartering with whom?" Mutti asks, perplexed. This type of bargaining is unheard of on the other side of the camp, at least in our barrack.

"The other prisoners, the guards, anyone who has something you want," Irena explains. "Or...you may have something *they* want and you can trade. But be warned - if you get caught, you'll be shot or sent to the gas. I've learned a thing or two in my time here in Kanada. The Nazis have no problem with committing mass murder, but pinching from what the Reich steals outright is treated like a federal crime."

Mutti sighs and chooses a duffel near her feet, then points to one beneath it. "Start with that one, Karin."

As we open the overstuffed bags and pull out clothes, watches, and shoes, I feel as if my heart is being crushed. After Mutti and I put our satchels on the lorry when we first arrived, I had forgotten about them completely. Now I realize where they must have gone: here, to Kanada, "the place of abundance and wealth". Our own things have long since been pilfered, piled away, and possibly bartered for money, for food, or for life.

It makes me wonder who discovered the little sweater I had been making for Bruno. Whose hands are completing the sleeves and collar...or has it been completely torn apart, just as I have been, utterly unraveled in the reality of a new and terrible existence?

I find a handful of tarnished silverware and toss it into a wooden box near Irena's feet. Then I pull out a pair of man's linen pants and shirt with a monogram neatly stitched into the collar..."rGl" is embroidered with stiff, black thread. I wonder to whom this shirt had once belonged...and is he still alive?

Next, I find a metal mezuzah, weathered, worn, and slightly dented. It reminds me of the one Herr Zweig nailed to the doorframe of their house in Baden Baden, a blessing for their home and for everyone who entered it. Frau Zweig had told me that whenever I came for a visit at the theater, she imagined a mezuzah on the false wall. Later, when I was able to smuggle in paper and some of Jurgen's crayons, Georg created a small, three-dimensional one for her, the letter "Shin" drawn in bright blue on a golden background.

Mutti is busy with her bag and Irena has crossed the yard to give some cigarettes to the officer with the clipboard. Darting my gaze around the yard and finding the guards preoccupied, I press the rusting piece of metal into my palm and slide it into an inside pocket of my coat. Now I will have a reminder of Georg and his mother with me...always.

Hour after hour we sift and sort through the piles of countless strangers' belongings. I find diaries and silver platters and even lightbulbs. Mutti comes across a duffel bag filled with ancient photographs, sepia-tinged and rotting. Old faces, young faces, and little babies stare at us from another time, another world.

"Put those in the trash bin," Irena tells Mutti. "The Nazis have no room for nostalgia."

When it's nearly nightfall, the guards tell us to finish the bag that we're sorting, then line up for our evening meal. My stomach is growling, even though the officer with the clipboard gave me an extra piece of bread when we arrived in Kanada. I tried to share it with Mutti, but she insisted I finish it myself. Now, after a long day of hard work, I'm exhausted and famished.

As we stand in line, huddled together to keep warm, Mutti places something in my hand, whispering, "I found food in one of the satchels. Here...take this and eat it when no one is looking."

It's a round, red apple, the first piece of fruit I've seen since our deportation. It's shrunken some and is riddled with bruises, but I don't care. My mouth waters as we wait for the rations to be distributed, and I wonder how I will ever bite into it without attracting attention.

Standing in silence I survey the heap of well-worn shoes and cannot fathom how many people they represent. Hundreds, maybe thousands, who had once worn them to work, to shop, and to play. I cannot imagine what the Nazis will do with all of these seemingly insignificant empty shells that bear the distinctive footprints of men, women, and children who are all now dead.

Then I wonder, *How many more will die before this madness will end?*

***

Gently holding Simka's feet, I rub her swollen ankles and think back on my first day in Kanada, the first time I had a glimpse of possible life in the midst of probable death. Esfir's eyes meet mine, and it's as if we're both thinking the same thing. *Will Simka survive the birth of her child?*

We can't ask for help and I don't know what to do other than sit with her and soothe her pain as the women surrounding us snore and moan and shuffle by on their way to the latrine to repeatedly empty their guts and their stomachs. It's then that I know this place is truly worse than Auschwitz.

Beyond the squalor we have to live in, there is little hope that any of us will be able to survive.

But as Simka rolls onto her back, pressing her hands to her belly, I see the gentle roll of a foot beneath her thin dress...perhaps a sign that indeed her child has the will to live.

So I sit and bravely wait for the future to come.

## Sapphire

I know Little Sam be bored with his lessons 'cause he standing looking out the window, watching his daddy in the barn. "Mama, why is Papa doing Keen's chores?"

"Because he sent Keen into town to fetch the dry goods," Missus say.

Little Sam look over his shoulder at me where I sit making my letters. "Sapphire...didn't you go to town with Papa this morning?"

I nod.

"Why didn't he bring the dry goods back then?"

"Ain't my place to say."

Little Sam narrow his eyes while he watch how Massa be working like a slave on his own plantation. "Why'd he pitch all the hay down from the loft?"

I shrug. "Maybe Pete's powerful hungry."

Little Sam roll his eyes. "Mama...I'm done with my lines. May I go out and help Papa?"

Missus look up from her book. "Yes...please tell your father that I'd like to see him when it's convenient."

"What *convenient*?" I ask.

Missus look at me. "It means when he can take the time to speak with me."

"Oh." I go back to my writing, but it hard to make them curvy lines Missus call "cursive". I's used to making them lines and ovals she say be called "print". But ain't they both printing since I's putting 'em on paper? I get bored with all the lines a "k's" and "l's" I gotta make and switch to printing my name, "SAPPHIRE SETTLER" in bold letters. I know to use only a big letter at the beginning a each name, but I like how it look when I put 'em all as capitals.

Then I jest write "SAPPHIRE...SAPPHIRE...SAPPHIRE" all over my slate 'til the chalk be nearly a nub 'tween my fingers. I ain't gone ask Missus for more 'cause she say I be wasting it writing my name. But how else I gone sign for things at the store when I be free and Mama and me head into town to buy our own calico?

Marybelle be sighing and heaving on the fainting couch where a book be on her lap, open to the middle. She ain't reading though...jest looking into space, daydreaming 'bout some boy at school. I hear all 'bout Phillip Henderson and Charles Stanforth, and even that old Douglas Pritchard sometime. She say one be nice, the second be handsome, and the third be a weasel. That make me laugh thinking on how a boy can be shifty and scheming, and who do whatever he can to get out a trouble.

They ain't no colored boys 'round here and I ain't seen many a 'em in town. From what Earle say, there be a few young ones slaving for Mister Rotten, and they be tough as nails and hard as iron, whatever that mean. I cain't 'member where Massa done got Hale and Isaac or even Keen. From what I know, they's always been here on the Settler Plantation.

Maybe I should ask Mama 'bout that. She say Big Massa Samuel done kept three gen'rations of my daddy's family here, way on back to Daddy's granddaddy. I be the fourth gen'ration, or so Missus teach me, and Pearl's baby gone be the fifth. But when I think on it some, I figure if the war be ending soon, that little baby ain't gone be no slave at all...and that be the best thing I can 'magine.

Missus say my name real sharp-like. "*Sapphire*! What are you doing?"

I's drawing all kind a birds and flowers and little baby bunny rabbits all 'round my slate 'stead a practicing my letters. My flowers look pretty good, but my baby bunnies all look like logs with long ears.

"'Scuse me, Missus," I say, feeling my ears and cheeks flame up. "I's done with my letters."

"So I *see*," she growl. "Why don't you go help Ruby in the kitchen."

Missus don't like nothing out a order. She don't like no waste. And she don't like me daydreaming when they's lessons to be done. I know Missus be mad at me for using up her chalk, but she don't say nothing. She jest look at me with them eyes that glow like two big, blue marbles when she be disappointed.

I put my things in the little chiffarobe by the fireplace and go to the kitchen where Mama be standing at the stove. On the table be that pretty fabric with pattern pieces pinned all over. I can tell Mama be starting with my dress 'cause the pieces be smaller, and I feel so proud that I gone have something that be made by my mama's own hands, not shipped from some fancy store up north.

It then I think that maybe style be something you feel and not something you wear.

"What you need, Sapphire?" Mama ask without turning 'round.

"Nothing," I say, setting at the big table and admiring the little shawl Mama done finished for my dolly. "This be real pretty, Mama. Thank you."

She look at me out the corner a her eye. "You's welcome. I thought that be a nice thing to start with so's I could check the tension a the stitches on that fabric."

"What *tension* mean?" I ask, fingering the delicate white stitches Mama done sewed careful 'round the edges.

"It mean how tightly you sew or knit...or how loose your stitches be," she say, coming over to set next to me. "See how I made them stitches 'round the corners tighter? That so the material don't unravel when you play with your dolly. Now if'n I use the same stitch in the middle a the shawl, it gone pucker up something fierce."

I know what *pucker* mean 'cause that how my fingers and toes be looking if'n I set in the bathtub too long or when Little Sam and I plays in the creek on a cold, spring day. My fingers plumb look like raisins when we splashing each other like little ducks.

166

"You need help with supper?" I ask.

"Not yet," Mama tell me, picking up the scissors and cutting on the bodice part a the dress pattern. "In a while you can cut up some carrots and steam 'em. Missus say when they gone want to eat? Look like Massa be outside working like a dog."

I nod, looking out the window toward the barn. Little Sam be cleaning out the horse's stall, tossing in fresh hay while poor, old Pete be hobbled to the hitching post. He jest stand there watching Massa with a strange look on his face like he saying, "This ain't what I's used to."

I knows jest how Pete feel. Massa ain't one to shirk his work, but he ain't never been one to send his slaves into town while he be slaving in the barn. Usually it be the other way 'round.

But Keen and Hale be trustworthy with the skiff and the old mule ain't gone get 'em too far if they decides to run off. Hale done love Opal too much to leave her here, so I know he ain't going nowhere. But Keen...well, I ain't know a whole lot 'bout what go on in his head 'sides what he say at night 'round the campfire. He talk 'bout what field work they done that day and what seeds they gone plant and all that kind a stuff. Work, work, work. That all he talk 'bout. And when he ain't talking, he jest be setting, staring into space, thinking 'bout things I ain't never gone know. Keen be a mystery...that for sure. Mama tell me it ain't my place to try and solve him. She say some people be so confusing, ain't no 'mount of insight gone be able to figure 'em out.

"Massa say he got to get the barn good and clean," I tell her, picking up my knitting basket. "He say it not good enough to jest give it a *once over*. What that mean, Mama?"

"That mean to do something quick...like when I look at your hair in the morning to make sure none a them braids come out." She pat my head. "I don't has to look real hard, I jest give it a quick look 'fore we get to work."

"I can do that myself now, cain't I, Mama?"

"Yes'm, you can," she smile, getting back to her cutting. "You ain't my baby girl no more...not really. Now you's getting to be a *little lady*." She teasing me 'cause that what Mister Jimmy done call me, but I hear a little truth in what she say. I ain't no baby no more, but I ain't grown up neither, and Mama say being stuck in the middle an affliction sometime.

Mama has me peeling carrots by the sink when Massa Sam come into the house, his big boots clomping up the wooden steps. His face be red and his hands be dusty and lined with dirt.

"Ruby, may I talk with you in private?" he ask.

Mama look at me, then back to Massa Sam. "Sapphire...you go on and take that shawl to your dolly, then bring me some water from the well."

"Yes'm," I nod, passing her the peeler. I move real slow, hoping Massa Sam gone start talking while I's still there.

But he don't.

Mama give me a look that say, *You scoot*!

So I scoot.

Little Sam be talking to Pete at the hitching post, feeding him a little, red apple. "Where are you going?" he ask me.

"To the shack to give this to my new dolly."

"You got a dolly?" he smirk. "When?"

"This morning," I say, puffing up my chest. "And I got her with my own money I done earn from all the knitting Mama sold to Missus Snow."

Little Sam lift his brow and nod. "That's nice. What's she look like?"

"Come and see."

So Little Sam follow me to the shack, but he don't come in 'cause his mama done told him it be alright if we plays together and all, but it ain't his place to be in no slave quarters.

I pull Ida from the shelf and bring her to the door, wrapping the new calico shawl 'round her shoulders. "See?"

Little Sam lean 'gainst the doorframe, folding his arms. "Yep."

"You like her?"

"I guess...what do you do with her?"

"Nothing yet," I shrug. "I jest had her since this morning. I 'spose I'll hold her and rock her and put her on a shelf and look at her sometime."

Little Sam sigh. "That's boring."

"Not to me," I say proudly. "'Cause she the first thing that be mine and mine alone 'cept these old rags I wear."

Little Sam shake his head. "Those aren't rags. You should see some of the poor kids at school. Their clothes are rattier than Pete's feedbags."

I look at my shoes where my toes be peeking jest a little out the tops. The soles be a mess and the strings been broke and re-tied so many times, I ain't got but a tiny bit left to make the bow. These ratty shoes be so old, whenever I walk, I can feel the footprints of all the girls who ever done wore 'em... Pearl and Opal and whatever slave chile be walking 'round in 'em 'fore me, all a us on the same path, but for different purpose.

"Want to shoot marbles?" Sam ask.

I shake my head. "Nah...I gots to get to the well and bring Mama some water."

"I'll help you," Sam offer. "Come on...maybe Mama Ruby'll let us play for a while before supper."

We race to the well and Sam only beat me by a hair this time. Even though my shoes be a sight, I can still run in 'em flippity-flap...quick as a jack rabbit. We fills up two big buckets in no time and since Little Sam be helping me, I don't got to make two trips to the kitchen.

Massa and Mama still be setting and talking. They be tears in Mama's eyes. She ain't crying real good, but I can tell by Massa's face, he be getting ready to bawl hisself. It been coming on all day for him I 'spect.

Little Sam don't seem to notice. "Mama Ruby," he say, setting his bucket near the stove where he know she gone need it. "Can Sapphire shoot marbles with me before supper?"

Mama wipe the corner a her eyes with her apron. "Go on," she say, looking away. "You play out in the garden where I can see you."

"I'll get my bag," Little Sam smile, running by me on the way to his room.

I stand in the doorway looking at Massa and Mama, the way they's setting 'cross from each other at the table. Massa's hands be curled up together tight and he clearing his throat. Mama pick up the scissors and keep on a clipping the fabric 'round the pattern pieces.

"Thank you 'gain for the new Easter dress," I tell Massa real soft.

"You're welcome," he manage to squeak out. Then he look at Mama. "I'll tell you more later...after the evening chores."

Mama bite her lip and nod. It not like her to be silent. She always got a thing or two to say 'bout everthing, but now Massa done made her mute.

He get up and cross the room where he stop by the dining room and turn 'round. "Ruby...I'm sorry...really I am."

"I know, Sam." For the first time since she beg for him to not let Mister Rotten take Opal or Pearl, Mama call Massa by his real name.

He jest nod and walk away.

Mama clip and clip and clip the calico while I stand in the door with my hands 'hind my back, waiting on Little Sam. It like to take him an hour to find his aggies and in the meantime, I ain't 'bout to ask Mama what Massa done said. It make my tongue feel like a rock to jest stand there and keep quiet.

Fin'lly Little Sam come through the kitchen and grab my hand. "C'mon, Sapphire!"

170

Feeling his sweaty palm in mine, I look at Mama who don't say nothing. Looking back to Little Sam I see the side a his face, and ain't it something that he look jest like his daddy. Make me wonder if'n years ago Mama and Massa be like Little Sam and me...and if'n years from now I's gone be setting at that kitchen table, cutting out pieces of a dress for my little girl, crying over something I cain't even understand.

# Karin

I'm barely awake when Vitya tiptoes into the barrack and sits down next to me on the floor. "How is she?"

I sigh and rest my head against the bunk's wooden frame, shaking my head as if to say, *I'm not sure.*

Esfir's asleep on the floor and most of the women in the barrack are quiet, dozing off and on or softly talking to one another in tangled conversations of Russian, German, and Yiddish.

Kneeling, Vitya takes one of Simka's hands and strokes her forehead that's beaded with sweat. "Her son took too long in coming," she whispers. "Poor baby...he died with the cord wrapped around his neck."

I look from Simka's strained features to Vitya's troubled expression.

Turning her eyes to mine, Vitya says, "This one might not be so lucky."

I frown in confusion.

"If the baby's born alive, who knows what they'll do with it," she explains, nodding toward the door where the din of shouting echoes into the barrack.

I nod, knowing what horrors the female guards are capable of...how they've made prisoners murder babies to save their own lives.

"I do, too," Mutti silently reminds me. "You mustn't let them have this child, Karin. Not this one."

"There's a lot of commotion out there...the kapos and block elders are gathering for what looks like an exodus," Vitya says, sitting next to me and pulling a chunk of bread from her pocket. "Perhaps it's true what I've heard about the British coming to liberate us." She hands me a small piece, then tears one off for herself.

I try to imagine what freedom will be like as I place the bread in my mouth, but I can't think of the future...only the past. Suddenly I'm reminded of my confirmation day when I was twelve. I remember the way the Eucharist felt on my tongue as I knelt at the altar and took communion for the first time. The way it melted into nothing as I swallowed it. The starchy aftertaste as I went back to the pew to sit with Vati and Mutti who smiled proudly at me. Later that day while we were having dinner, I told Frau Zweig about my initiation into the church, and how I was trying to imagine what it must have been like to be one of the twelve disciples at Jesus' last Passover. She explained to me that during a traditional Seder meal, a cloth bag with separate compartments holds three sheets of matzah...the unleavened bread. The piece in the middle is split, one half being broken and shared, and the other, wrapped in a napkin, hidden, and brought back after it is found.

Now as I swallow the small bit of nourishment, I feel as though I'm being completely broken in two...one part of me sitting in fearful anticipation of the birth of Simka's baby and our imminent liberation, and the other part shrouded in the past...trying to imagine what our lives would have been like if I hadn't wrapped Georg's birthday gift and hidden it in my pocket. And yet, I cannot change what I've done, but I can weave in memories of how my mother found ways to nourish and comfort me.

I can recognize that communion is anything that brings me closer to what Jesus must have felt on the night he was betrayed, and his acceptance and forgiveness of everything that followed.

*** 

April, 1944

Mutti and I have been working in Kanada for over two years when she happens upon a large tapestry satchel with a broken handle. I'm busy sorting through a man's suitcase, separating his shirts from his socks from his antique cufflinks when Mutti sidles over to me.

"Do you have room in your pockets?" she whispers.

It's mid-April and in the cool, damp morning air we often shiver in our coats. I'm glad it's still early spring because nearly every day we find some scrap of food to hide in our coats and smuggle back to the barrack: tins of meat, small boxes of biscuits, and napkins filled with broken crackers. I even found a small chocolate bar that Mutti and I made last for seven days as we cut it into small pieces and let the warm confection melt on our tongues like communion bread.

I nod, looking into the satchel Mutti is holding close to her body. There inside I see a small ball of yarn with a pair of rosewood knitting needles. Darting my eyes to Mutti's I see her gentle smile.

"You keep these," she whispers, sliding them into the oversized pockets of my wool coat. Then she pulls another ball of yarn attached to a circular needle with a hat that's nearly finished. "I'll hide this one."

I smile, closing the flap of my coat to conceal the evidence.

"If Kapitan Dieter comes, you give me your coat before you go with him," she demands.

I nod and get back to work, hiding my shame at the thought of it.

Kapitan Dieter has been ordering me to his room ever since we were transferred to Kanada. A week after our arrival, he was passing through the yard when someone mentioned it was his birthday. All of the women were ordered to stop working and sing in celebration.

Kapitan walked among us and made sure to pass in front of me at least twice. He leaned closer and whispered in my ear, "Lauter singen, mein Liebling."

*Sing louder, my darling.*

Eyeing the pistol tucked into his holster, I nodded and complied.

When we had finished, Kapitan ordered everyone to stop and I had to sing it once more alone. I was mortified, but did as I was told, my voice quivering as much as my stomach.

*Best wishes and many blessings*
*on all your paths,*
*good health and cheerfulness*
*be with you too!*

"Aufhoren zu arbeitne," Kapitan ordered. "Komm mit mir."

*Leave your work. Come with me.*

And that is how I unceremoniously became one of Kapitan's "best birthday presents", as he called me that day. He knows I'm German, that I'm Christian, and that makes me all the more desirable, as having carnal knowledge of a Jew is considered to be an abomination. There are rumors of a brothel at the main camp, but I'm not a prostitute for many, just for Kapitan, and for that, I am supposed to be grateful.

Now he calls for me several times a week and if I want to live, I have no say in the matter. I wash, am disinfected, and given clean clothes. Then I report to his room, lined with shelves of books and a glass cabinet filled with chocolates, gourmet biscuits, and cans of sweetened condensed milk that he uses in his dark, bitter coffee.

Kapitan tells me I can take whatever food I want from the footlocker, that the bread and cheese are mine to share, but I'm never to take anything from the glass cabinet or he'll shoot me on site and feel no remorse for doing so. How could he when I've heard he shoots prisoners for not doing their jobs well enough or fast enough, for daring to talk back, for stealing rations? How could my life mean anything to him?

But Kapitan says it does. He says he will take good care of my sister and me. I don't speak, other than singing songs he likes to hear before or after he's done what he wants to do with me. He doesn't know Mutti is my mother, not my

175

sister. He doesn't know her name, and he doesn't call me by my name either. He simply calls me by my number or "mein Madchen"...*my girl*.

A few months after Kapitan's birthday, I was bleeding when he called for me, something for which I've not been beaten in Kanada. Still, he ordered me to go directly to the hospital. Two days later I returned to the barrack in debilitating pain, having been sterilized without anesthesia so that Kapitan can have his way with me whenever he wants and there will be no evidence of his crime. But as long as I'm alive, my body will be all the evidence I need to remind me that in order to survive, I've given up a part of myself I can never reclaim.

It's a high price to pay for my continued existence, but I endure it over and over and over again so that Mutti also might live. She didn't ask any questions when I returned that first time on Kapitan's birthday. She simply marveled at the food I brought her, sharing it with Johanna in a corner of the yard as far away from the guards as possible.

"Where did you get this?" she asked.

I looked toward the main road.

Mutti saw the red blotch on my shoulder where Kapitan had marked me. Her face fell, but she took my hand in hers. "It's what they all want, Karin," she whispered. "They don't want an old woman like me. You're young and pretty...I'm sorry, but that's the way it is here. He's taking plenty from you, so take as much as you can from him in return."

"At least he's handsome," Johanna smirked, shoving a piece of black bread into her mouth. "Not like some of the other brutes around here."

I stared at the ground, tears flooding my eyes. My legs hurt, the place in-between as well. Bruises marked my arms where Kapitan had held me down, but no one could see them. Worse yet, my throat felt even tighter, the stone lodged more deeply in place by Mutti's cruel, yet honest words.

*By enduring this humiliation, I am now the provider,* I thought, shame and sorrow mixed together with a strange sense of satisfaction.

And yet, when I came back from the hospital and Mutti learned I had been sterilized, she didn't speak for a few days, but she also never left my side. She took on more of my work and gave me a portion of her food since I wasn't visiting Kapitan's room as he felt it prudent to give me time to heal.

Shortly after my visits to his room resumed, Mutti refused to take the food I brought her, pushing it back into my hands instead. "You eat it, Karin...I'm not hungry," she would say, her face drawn and tight.

Now I quickly shove the yarn and needles into my pocket and rest my hand on the soft wool. It feels like a dream to touch something that I used to take for granted, but have not held in my hands for years. Had I not given Stephan a reason to storm the theater, Bruno would be toddling around the house in his sweater and I would surely be knitting him some warm mittens to match. I used to spend my evenings sitting by the fireplace making lace for Mutti. Now I spend each night picking lice from my clothing and pinching them between my fingernails. Simply running my fingertips over the smooth rosewood needles is an uncommon reward for what I know will soon be coming.

But Kapitan does not call for me today. It's been nearly a week and as I sift and sort and separate the belongs of a complete stranger, I wonder if he's found someone else, a new girl to keep him occupied. Perhaps after all this time, he's grown tired of me, even though I stay clean and eat as well as I can. My hair has grown back and I keep it neat and tidy, tucked beneath a kerchief so the dust and grime of my daily duties don't soil it.

But there is hidden filth within me that no amount of water can wash away. Disinfectant cannot rid me of the gnawing degradation I bear every moment. The other women in Kanada know what Kaptian does with me. Many of them are jealous. Some have tried to beat me out of anger or rage. A few call me a whore. But Kapitan has ordered the guards to remove anyone who dares to harm me and send them to block eleven at the main camp. Everyone knows that block eleven means death...either by slow torture, starvation, or merciless execution.

When a pair of Hungarian sisters taunted me until I cried, one of the guards beat them senseless and sent them back to Auschwitz to suffer the consequences. Now I'm left alone, but no one will speak to me except Mutti and Johanna. I'm living in exile among a sea of women who would gladly take my place...and I would gladly let them if it weren't for the hope that when I'm being taken to Kapitan's room, I might catch a glimpse of my father. When we pass the gallows, I make myself look at the faces of the corpses dangling by heavy ropes. Every day there's another group of prisoners left to be an example for the rest of us.

So far, none of them is Vati, and I'm infinitely thankful.

Still, Kapitan told me my father is dead, that he was shot in one of the quarries and buried in a mass grave. I don't believe him. I think Kapitan tells me these things to hurt me, to keep me frightened and submissive. But the only time I am obedient is when he orders me to sing or to undress.

In every other moment I silently curse him, calling him by his first name and wishing he were dead. But if Herman dies, then I won't live either, so I swallow my prayers and suffer the consequences of being his chosen girl.

The day solemnly drags on and finally we're ordered back to the barrack for the night. It's Saturday, so there's a day of rest tomorrow. Rations are generous this evening with an extra spoonful of butter to smear on our bread. Some get a dollop of jam, but the kapos usually confiscate them, threatening to take away a prisoner's entire ration if it's not surrendered.

Mutti and I sit on our bunks, rubbing our eyes. The sound of the orchestra dies down for the night. They played constantly to drown out the screaming and clawing of the dying, as the gas chambers have been especially busy today because three transports arrived overnight. The crematorium has been running non-stop and the stench of burning flesh stings my nose and throat.

But it doesn't deter me from the task at hand.

We eat in simple silence, Mutti pulling a little tea cake wrapped in a handkerchief from her dress pocket. "It looks like a little birthday cake," she smiles.

I nod.

"Here, Karin...take it."

I'm incredibly hungry, but no amount of food can satisfy me. The fear of Herman calling for me has been trumped by the fear of him choosing another, so I sit and wonder if tomorrow will be different. Maybe I'll once again be roused from sleep by Irma Grese, the horror we call "The Beast." She heeds Herman's warnings, but often wakes me by striking my bare feet with her baton. After all, she knows I don't speak, so I won't tell, and Herman can't see the bruises. It didn't take me long to learn that no one can hide from her vicious threats, even the most obedient.

Mutti shoves the tea cake into my hand. "Eat this. You must...no matter what happens, you must survive."

I shake my head.

"I'll eat it," Johanna says, snatching it from my lap. She crams it into her mouth, chewing furiously. For two long years she's been more than willing to take whatever extra scrap of nourishment Mutti and I provide, yet never gives us anything in return. I'm certain that, like the rest of us, Johanna has found food hidden in the suitcases and duffel bags, but she's more stealth at hiding her secret stash.

I look to Mutti and point to the yarn in my pocket.

"Wait until after sunset, Karin," she says, sipping her watered-down coffee. "I don't think anyone would report you to the guards, but in this place you can't trust anyone."

"That's the truth," Johanna says gruffly, shoveling a spoonful of soup into her mouth.

I think of Vati and make myself eat the stale, crusty bread while I watch Mutti struggle to finish her ration, her eyes locked on the doorway. *What is it?* I want to ask. But I don't. Instead, I look and listen for what might be coming, but all I hear are the same sounds of women eating and talking, mumbling in a host of languages, most of them I cannot understand.

Mutti looks at me with sad eyes, then pats my hand. "He'll send for you tomorrow, Karin," she says flatly. "He will."

I can't tell if she's saying it with expectation or regret.

***

Vitya sighs, waking me from my memories. She tells me she has to get back to the cookhouse, that she'll come back when she can. "Give her this," she says, pressing a small photograph of a woman into my hand. "It's her mother."

The woman is wearing a long white coat with a silk scarf tied beneath her chin. She sits on a wicker chair in the center of lush landscape, casually smiling at the camera.

"It was her wedding day...right before she and her husband left for their honeymoon," Vitya whispers. "When we arrived here from Russia, Simka kept this in her mouth so the Nazis wouldn't take it. When we were transported here, she gave it to me for safe keeping."

I wrinkle my brow.

"She was always afraid that one of the guards would find it in the barrack or where you work," Vitya explains. "She knew that in the cookhouse I would be less likely to be questioned or searched."

Studying the photograph, I envy Simka, for there's nothing left of my family but my memories...and often they

180

fade into the haze and smoke of this horrible place where dying is often as insignificant as living.

"Simka will need this when it's time," Vitya says, nodding. "Tell her I will come for her."

I nod, watching her leave as she steps over the emaciated and diseased women who are barely breathing, barely able to move. And even though I am more alive than most of them, I still feel dead inside, as if my body hasn't yet discovered my own demise.

I gaze at Simka's mother, her round cheeks and cheerful smile, her lovely brown locks and gently sloped eyebrows. I can still see the light in her eyes echoed in her daughter's as Simka sits up and asks, "What time is it?"

I gently place the photograph in her hand, feeling her sweaty palm in mine. My heart aches for my mother, but like Simka, I know that profound longing will never be met. And yet I can do as Mutti had asked...and be the keeper of her memories as she had been for mine.

# Sapphire

I's setting on a stump, sopping up the rest a my oatmeal with a piece a stale bread. It taste like dirt...plain and nasty, 'cept for the drop a honey Opal done put on it. She share the last of her treat with all a us, but give Pearl a might more 'cause she got two mouths to feed. That baby be rolling 'round her belly plenty whenever she eat; I guess 'cause it be hungry, too, and I sure cain't blame it. Peas and carrots and corncakes ain't gone keep our bellies full with the longer days we gone be working this spring. Missus say she got a lot a seeds to put in her garden and Massa tell Keen they gone try and put in the corn a week early this year. Wheat, too, maybe. It be a heap a work with not much to keep us going.

Mama set near the fire, her shawl wrapped 'round her tight while she stare into the flames. She ain't said much since we fed the folks in the big house they supper...jest "Throw out the dirty dish water, Sapphire" and "Go on back to the shack for your own supper and I'll be there shortly."

I do what she tell me with no back talk. Fact, I don't do any talking 'cept to s'cuse myself to use the privy. I know Mama been thinking 'bout what Massa done said this afternoon. She ain't crying no more, but her eyes still look sad.

As the sun set on top a the fields and the stars start twinkling, Isaac talk to Pearl 'bout what they gone name they baby when it come. He say he like the name Juniper if it be a boy and *Tulip* if it be a girl.

I knows Pearl like the boy's name, 'cause that be our daddy's, but she laugh and say, "I ain't gone name no chile of mine *Tulip*! Where you get such a notion?"

"From them pretty flowers in Missus' garden," Isaac say, shoveling in some oatmeal. "You said you like the red ones."

Pearl nod. "Yeah, but not so much I's gone name my *baby* after 'em."

"You got a better idea?" he tease.

Pearl slip off her ripped-up shoes and wiggle her toes in front a the fire to warm 'em up. "Mama said if'n she hadn't lost her last baby, she was gone name her Amber. How you like that?"

Isaac set his hand on Pearl's big belly real gentle-like. "That be a nice name, Miss Ruby," he say, smiling at Mama.

"When you lost a baby?" I ask her. "Where it be?"

"Dead, baby girl," Mama say real low. "You was jest out your diapers when she come too soon."

"Too soon for what?"

"Babies gots to be inside they mamas for a long time 'fore they ready to get born." Mama look out toward the fields. "They little bodies ain't meant for this world 'til they can breathe on they own, and little Amber didn't even get to take her first breath 'fore God done call her home."

"Where she now?"

Mama don't say nothing. She poke a stick into the fire and it blaze with orange and red shooting up everwhere. The flames snap and pop something fierce, and I got to keep my feet back from the pit so's I don't get burned.

"Massa took the baby and put her in the little graveyard on the other side a the big house," Opal tell me. "You seen the one with the little bitty headstone that say *Baby Settler*? That be your little sister."

I look to Mama and don't know what to say. She looking mighty upset as it is, and I ain't gone go asking no more 'bout her dead baby.

"Sapphire, why don't I tell you all 'bout Brer Rabbit 'gain tonight," Old Albert say, patting his knee. He pretty good 'bout getting my mind off a things I don't want to think on.

I give my empty bowl to Mama and go set on Old Albert's knee where he stroke my braids like they be the tails a my little kittens. He ain't my daddy, but I still like to lean my head on his chest and listen to his heart go *thump, thump, thump*. His voice make a vibrating sound, and sometime I like that better than the stories. Tonight he smell like sweat and dirt and something else I cain't quite figure. Soil and manure maybe, but the good kind, like when Massa and Keen done fert'lize the fields on a warm, spring day.

He ain't shaved a lick since he got here, so Old Albert's beard tickle my cheek and chin. I don't mind. I like being tickled and this be one a the best parts of having him 'round. Plus I get to set and be like a white chile for a while, listening to tall tales and forgetting I's still a slave. But maybe sometime soon Old Albert and me's gone be free and we can set 'round and tell tales *all* the time.

"I's tired of Brer Rabbit," I tell him plainly. "You got a new one?"

Old Albert stroke his beard and think on it some. "How you like to hear the one 'bout how Mister Possum love peace?"

"A piece a what?" I ask, picking little brambles from his vest.

"Not a piece a something," he grin. "Mister Possom love *peace*...like concord."

I wrinkle my brow. "That a word I ain't never heard 'fore."

"It mean when they ain't no fighting. Like how we hears all them rumors 'bout the Rebs and Yanks gone stop they waring soon and have peace."

"You seen Mister Jimmy today?" I ask. "He a *runaway* Reb."

"No'm, I ain't," Old Albert say. "But I heard 'bout it from Opal."

"She heard 'bout it from *me*," I say proudly.

Old Albert peck my cheek. "You the original chatterbox."

"You stop teasing me," I say, snuggling in close. "Go on and tell me that story 'bout the Possom who love peace."

"Sapphire...you ask politely now," Mama chide. "Old Albert ain't your storytellin' servant."

"No matter, Miss Ruby," he say, pattin' my cheek. "She jest got a lot a spunk."

I smile real big. "That mean I's sassy?"

"It sure do," Old Albert grin. "Now you get comf'table and I'll tell ya the story.

And he do.

I hear all 'bout how Brer Coon and Brer Possum be friends and all, but then one day they be walking on the road and here come Mister Dog talking to hisself in the woods. Brer Coon say he stand by Brer Possum if'n the dern dog gone run up on 'em. But when the time come and Mister Dog done sail 'tween the two a 'em, Brer Possum jest fall down like he dead. Poor old Brer Coon got to take care a hisself and whip up on the dog 'til he get gone. After that Brer Possum sit up, make sure the coast be clear, then hightail it lickety-split back to his house jest like I hippity-hop to the fields.

When Brer Coon see Brer Possum 'gain, he be madder than a wet hen, or so Old Albert say. I know what that mean 'cause when Gertie be pitching a fit, I best get out the way or get me some hen-pecked fingers.

Old Albert make his voice real low when he pretending to be Brer Coon. "I ain't running with no cowards these days!"

Then Brer Possum get mad, too. Old Albert say in his silly voice, "Who be a coward?"

Brer Coon say that he ain't gone be friends with nobody who lay down and play dead when they's a free fight going on.

Brer Possum done laugh his fool head off when he hear that one. He say he weren't 'fraid, nuh uh. He tell Brer Coon that old dog weren't no match for him.

Then he say, "When Mister Dog pass by me, he tickle my ribs and I's the most ticklish chap you ever meet. I jest lay down laughing 'til I ain't had no use a my limbs. It be a mercy to the dog, 'cause I'd a et him right on up."

Old Albert smile big when he say in Brer Possum's voice, "I don't mind fighting, but I declare I cain't stand to be tickled. Get me in a fight where they ain't none a that, and I be your man."

"I don't mind no tickling," I say, scratching my head. "You believe him, Old Albert?"

"Who, chile?"

"Brer Possum when he say he jest pretending to lay down dead."

"Do you?"

I shrug. "I ain't never seen a possum close up 'fore...jest in the woods climbing trees."

Old Albert chuck my chin. "I s'pose most folks say anything to get theyselves out a trouble."

"What trouble that be for Brer Possum?"

Old Albert set me on the ground. "Well, it done look like he a coward, right? But when he 'splain why he jest lay there, it sound true don't it?"

"I guess it do," I shrug.

"That leave old Brer Coon standing there a scratching his head jest like you be."

I laugh then, cause ain't it the truth if I is.

"Sapphire, you stand too close to Mister Jimmy this afternoon?" Mama ask. "Maybe some a his bugs done jumped up onto you."

"No'm, I don't think so." I scratch some more and right quick wish I ain't 'cause I jest know what she gone say next.

Mama look me in the eye. "All the same, go on to the wash house and I be there shortly with the lye soap."

I make a wicked face and that make everone 'round the fire laugh.

"Too bad for you," Opal tease. "Mama gone scrub you bald-headed with that soap a hers."

I stick out my tongue real mean-like and she jest laugh all the more.

"Go on, baby girl," Mama say. "Untie them braids, too, so the job be easier."

I stomp off to the wash room like that dern Mister Dog who be blasting through the woods on his way to pick a fight. But I know my mama ain't gone play possum when they's a battle to be won.

Mama and me's setting up in bed, the lamp light glowing and wiggling on the walls. Shadows be dancing this a way and that, and they looks jest like black ghosts shivering in the cool evening breeze. Mama cover me up good with the quilt 'cause she don't want me catching no cold with my wet hair and all. She rub it dry best as she can with an old rag, but all the same, it still be smelling like pond water and lye all mixed together. It be sticking up all over my head, too, but I ain't itching no more, and that a mercy.

I's playing with Ida, putting on her shawl, then taking it off jest for fun. She look a might plain without it and I tell Mama so.

"She a pretty dolly," Mama say, smiling at me. "I's proud you used that money you earned on something that you can keep always."

"And I's gone keep this shawl always, too," I tell her. "'Cause it be what Missus call a *keepsake*. You know what that mean, Mama?"

"Course I do, baby girl," she nod. "Your daddy's token 'round your neck be a keepsake, too. Something to 'member him by."

"I wish I had me some tintypes like Massa got a Missus and Little Sam and Marybelle," I say. "Then I'd has something to 'member what he look like."

"You don't 'member no more?" Mama whisper.

"No'm...and it make me feel bad 'cause I love my daddy."

Mama smile real sweet. "Sure you do, baby girl. And your daddy love you, too." She running her fingers over the quilt where the stuffing be coming out in little white fluffs. "He be the strongest man they ever was. Kind and wise and a good daddy to you and the girls."

"You miss him, Mama?"

"Ever day."

I watch her face for a while, studying the way she look awful sad. I feels brave enough to risk one more question. "How come Massa made you cry? He mad at you?"

Mama shake her head. "No, baby girl. He ain't mad."

"Then what he say?"

"Massa Sam think he might lose the plantation."

"What that mean?" I ask.

Mama watch the lamp light get lower 'cause the kerosene be almost gone. "It mean he in a heap a trouble with paying taxes. With last year's crops not doing good and the war sending prices sky high, it like to break his back jest to put food on the table. He done give Mister Birch them forty acres to pay off some a what he owe, but if'n he cain't get out from under this season, he'll have to sell it all."

She look back at me and say real strong, "You *cain't* tell nobody, Sapphire...I mean it. Massa don't want nobody to know."

I wonder why he tell Mama, but I promise to keep my mouth shut. "What gone happen to us if'n he sell it?" I ask. "We's part a the plantation, too, ain't we?"

"Not when the war be over. Then we gone be free."

My chin start quivering. "But we ain't got nowhere to go."

"Massa Sam say he gone try and fix that," Mama sigh. "But I don't know how he can."

"What *he* gone do if he has to sell?"

188

"He say the Hamilitons be happy to has him and Missus and the chil'ren come up north and live with 'em in Ohio."

"They want us, too?"

Mama shake her head. "Ain't no place for us up yonder."

My heart start pounding and my stomach start aching while I think 'bout ways Massa can keep the plantation. "Why don't he sell Missus' rings like she say he can?"

"He too proud."

"Too proud for what?"

"Them rings once belong to Missus Hamilton's mama, so he figure they ain't his to sell...even though by law they is."

"You mean Massa Sam own everthing Missus got like he own everthing we gots?"

"Yes, baby."

I look at Ida, then back to Mama. "You think Missus Snow take this dolly back so's I can get my pennies and give 'em to Massa?"

"No, honey, that dolly be yours." She wrap an arm 'round me and hold me close. "Massa Sam want you to have it."

I think on that for a minute. "If'n he cain't pay taxes, why he tell you to buy us calico for our Easter dresses?"

Mama's warm breath dust my cheek. "That be Massa Sam's way. He say he went to the bank this morning to fix things so's he can try and pay off all a his debt."

"What *debt* mean?"

"What you owe folks...like money and such."

I think on how Massa know he owe Mama a husband and me my daddy. But ain't no 'mount a money gone ever bring him back.

I look up at Mama. "We got any debt?"

"No, baby girl," she say. "The only debt I got is to the Lord Jesus for giving up his life...for sacrificing Hisself on the cross so's we can 'preciate all He done and have a life that be more abundant."

"What *abundant* mean?"

"It mean we got plenty to eat and plenty to wear and plenty to be thankful for."

"I's thankful for my dolly," I smile. "And I's thankful for that new dress you gone make. So I got life abundant right now, ain't I, Mama?"

"Yes, honey, you sure do."

I think 'bout Jesus rising up from the grave and why we has Easter ever year...right at the beginning of springtime. That be when all things get made new. New bunnies and tulips. New snow peas in the garden. New green sprouts in the fields. Even the blue sky look brand new 'cause it no longer dark and gray.

"Mama? How come Jesus sacrifice His life?" I ask. "That mean He give it up 'cause He want to?"

"Yes, baby girl," Mama say. "Some things is worth dying for, and saving your sweet soul be one a 'em. I 'magine it weren't no easy thing for Jesus, jest like it ain't easy for all a them boys who been fighting for years to make our country one whole thing and not jest the north and the south. The Yanks done sacrificed they lives for folks like you and me...jest like Jesus done all them years ago."

"But Jesus come back from the grave," I tell her. "Ain't nobody else do that...right?"

"That right."

"Then He get on up to heaven and live with God, huh?"

"Yes, baby."

"When we die is we going up to heaven, too?"

"Yes, Sapphire, right back where we come from." Mama hold me closer. "We gone go where your daddy be. Where my mama and baby Amber and Jasmine is, too. All a us gone have the best abundant life then 'cause we finally be together always."

190

I hear a hooty owl in the woods calling for someone far away. Sound like he saying, "Whooo, whooo, whooo you?"

*I's Sapphire Settler,* I say in my mind. *Whooo you?*

He don't say nothing back...jest keep on asking who I is.

Mama lie down. "Turn off the lamp, Sapphire. It time for sleeping."

After I shut off the light, I sit in the dark, rubbing them tokens 'til the tips a my fingers mem'rize the letters that be carved in the stone. I get to wondering what it gone feel like to jest be who I is and not who I belongs to. Then I take them tokens off and set 'em on the shelf above the bed, right next to my new dolly.

When I snuggle in close to Mama, it feel like I can breathe on my own...for the first time in my life.

# Karin

It's nearly twilight.

Simka helplessly moans as the contractions keep coming one after the next. I sit nearby, anxiously remembering when Mutti was in labor with Bruno. She had planned to deliver him at home, just like she had Jurgen and me, but when the pain became unbearable, the midwife transported her to the hospital.

Thank God.

If she hadn't, both Mutti and my brother would have died. But now they're both dead anyway, and as I hold Simka's hand in mine, I wonder what might have happened if I had been left motherless four years ago instead of losing her last summer.

Simka squeezes hard. "Moy bog, eto bol'no!" she cries out.

Esfir darts up from her place on the floor and quickly moves to Simka's side. "Derzhat'sya...derzhat'sya." She looks at me. "She says it hurts."

I frown, wiping Simka's brow. With every contraction, more blood seeps from between her legs onto the straw. She screams in Russian until nearly everyone in the barrack is roused from their sleep. Some women shoot angry looks our way. Others shout for her to be quiet. Most weakly acknowledge where the noise is coming from, then go back to doze on their pile of rags.

"Karin," Simka pants. "Find the little hat. *Find it!*"

Esfir looks at me with questioning eyes.

"Find it!" Simka whimpers.

I pull a wicker basket from under the bunk and search through the soiled clothes for an infant's cap that Simka had made with yarn she stole from the workroom. For many nights she sat on the cold, hard floor of the barrack, her baby rolling in her belly, humming softly to herself while she created the intricate pattern. Stitch after stitch, she would sing Russian lullabyes, songs I couldn't understand, but knew were filled with love.

When the hat was finished, she proudly showed it to me. "My baby will be warm in this, yes?"

I nodded, fingering the delicate lace and cables.

Now, weeks later, it's tinged with grime and has a few holes where vermin have chewed it open. Still, it's a keepsake for Simka, a blessing in the midst of this torment. Her face has grown pale and her skin clammy. Still, she manages to smile.

"It won't be long now," she says, holding her belly.

Esfir elbows me. "Go get Vitya...she'll know what to do. She says she brought her last baby...let's hope this one won't be too long in coming."

We can hear the sounds of the S.S. shouting and stomping their way through camp as twilight nears. There has been no dinner ration. No supper either. No water. No medicine.

Nothing for nearly a week.

Perhaps I could smuggle in some food from the cookhouse. Dare I risk it? Looking from Simka, to Esfir, and then to Katarine, who sleeps fitfully in her bunk, I think, *How can I not?*

Pulling on my tattered overcoat, I go to the doorway of the barrack and search for Grese. She's nowhere in sight, although swarms of S.S. are ordering prisoners to continue dragging corpses across the yard. The number of officers has dwindled since early this morning, but still, there are enough of them for me to be leery of calling attention to myself. I go back to the bunk and grab the empty water pail.

Before I leave, I look to Katarine's bunk once more. There she lies motionless, her mouth agape, her open eyes vacant and glazed. Whispering a Kaddish prayer for her soul, I dart out the door and into the gathering darkness.

"Has the baby come?" Vitya asks when I arrive at the back door of the cookhouse. Her arms and the front of her dress are coated in flour and she smells like yeast. She's been making bread all afternoon and the dough is stuck to her fingers in yellowish-gray clumps.

I shake my head and motion for her to come with me.

"It is time?"

I nod, holding out the pail.

Vitya looks to her worktable where mounds of dough are waiting to be kneaded. Several women mill around the room gathering vegetables while others stand at the stove stirring huge pots of soup.

"I must go to Simka...her baby is coming," she says to one nearby.

"Da," the woman nods. "Ya rasskazhu vam."

"If they ask, tell them I have dysentery and didn't want to infect the food."

"Da," the woman says, waving her off. "Idti! Idti!"

Vitya rummages in the utensil bin for a moment until she pulls out a ball of twine, a pair of scissors, and a rubber spatula. "For the cord," she says. Holding up the spatula she explains, "She can bite on this if the pain gets to be too much."

Leading me into the storage room for more water, Vitya quickly fills the pail, then covers it with a rag. "Through the back," she whispers. "We'll have to go around the cookhouse to avoid the S.S. It's almost time for their supper, although not many will come tonight."

I look at her in confusion.

"Haven't you heard?" she asks, taking my hand. "Most of them have already left...the British will be here in the morning. By this time tomorrow, they'll have liberated the camp. Kramer is preparing to surrender right now."

I can scarcely believe it. Even though I've heard gunfire in the distance and know the allies are approaching, even though I've witnessed the flurry of activity to hastily bury the evidence of the Nazi's crimes, I can't quite trust that anything will change if the British arrive. What will we do? Where will we all go? Most of the prisoners here are like me...homeless, orphaned.

Utterly alone.

"Simka's baby will be born into freedom," Vitya says, giving me a sad smile. "It will be born in hell, yes, but with the hope of heaven close by."

As we quickly make our way back to the barrack, the orchestra plays on...Beethoven's Fifth, I think. The crematorium churns an endless stream of smoke and ash as the notes swirl higher into the early evening sky. My heart pounds with both anticipation and fear, for we are not free yet, and much will happen between tonight and tomorrow morning.

***

April, 1944

Johanna lies on her bunk idly plucking the buttons on her sweater while Mutti and I sit on a wooden bench, huddled together. We're knitting gloves so our hands can stay warmer, yet still be able to sift and sort efficiently. Our clothing here in Kanada is better than in Auschwitz...I've even been given underwear, socks, and a scarf. Still, I'm always cold, even on the sunniest of days.

Johanna watches us in fascination while our fingers fly back and forth, weaving the yarn around the needles. "I wish I could do that," she sighs, absentmindedly pulling a button loose and sticking it into her mouth. She sucks on it as if it were a lemon drop.

"I could teach you," Mutti offers, looking up from her work.

"I'm not coordinated enough," Johanna laughs, spitting the button into her palm. "My mother said I was all thumbs." She sticks them up for emphasis and I can see a huge wart on the tip of one of them.

195

Everyone here has a rash or a cough or some minor illness or injury. Lice are kept to a minium as we have running water and soap. Our rations are meager, but all of us supplement them with the continual food supply provided by the incoming prisoners. At first it made me ill to think that I was eating something that belonged to someone who was probably taken to the gas chamber upon arrival. It was overwhelming to see the mountain of suitcases every day and not think that each one represented another life lost.

But I'm still alive.

Mutti's still alive.

I hope and pray Vati is still alive.

So I must do what I can to keep on living. If that means I must steal from a stranger, than so be it. Johanna especially has no problem with it. She's stolen more than food, as her pockets of contraband grow heavier with every arriving train. Yet she won't tell us where it goes or to whom she's trading it...and for what.

Johanna has become thick as thieves with a couple of the female guards and that scares me. Maybe she's simply biding her time until the war is over. Or perhaps she's bargaining for another work detail, although from what I understand, it doesn't get much better than Kanada. Every so often Johanna will tell us stories about how Grese is just a country bumpkin, so stupid she wouldn't know how to tie her shoes without a manual.

"She's just is a puppet for the Reich," Johanna said one night over cups of lukewarm coffee. "Mark my words, Grese will hang one when this is all over."

As well she should, for as horribly as she treats me, I've seen Grese do much worse to some of the other prisoners. She shot one of them right in front of us at Appell, and the poor woman's brains splattered onto Mutti's clothes. Another she beat so fiercely, the woman collapsed to the ground unconscious. Still Grese wouldn't stop until the woman was dead.

"Noch Jude verschwunden," she muttered.

*One more Jew gone.*

And yet, it doesn't matter if we're Jew or Gentile. Athiest or Communist or anything else. The Reich knows no bounds when it comes to punishing those who they deem to be the enemy. The longer Johanna worms her way into the fold of sadistic women who would sooner sic their rabid dogs on us than look us in the eye, the more I wonder what she'd be willing to do to survive.

For days now, Mutti has watched me make mistake after mistake as it's been a long time since I've knit anything. Even longer since I've made gloves. The yarn is stickier than I imagined which makes slipping off the stitches a chore. More than once I've dropped a few along the way.

"No matter, Karin," Mutti smiles, taking my work. "You can just go back and start over again."

*But I don't want to start over,* I think. *I want to finish these before anyone finds out we took the yarn and needles.*

Having corrected my mistakes, Mutti hands the work back to me. "Here, Liebling. Now you try."

My hands ache from the damp chill, from long hours of work, from lifting heavy bags and boxes and baskets of trinkets the Nazis will sell or store for God knows how long. They don't waste a thing, and while I used to think that was simply being frugal, now I know it's more about greed than anything else. For what they blame the Jews, the Nazis are more than guilty of themselves.

Johanna sighs deeply, then gets up from the bunk.

"Where are you going?" Mutti asks.

"To see about a promotion," Johanna smirks.

Mutti looks at me and we both shrug.

The barrack hums as the women sit and talk about the day gone by. What they will eat when they can go home and cook a substantial meal. The comfort of warm bedding and proper shoes. A tinkle of laughter rises up from the far side of the room and I glance in that direction.

Before I know what's happening, Grese has pistol whipped the side of my face and I'm on the floor covering my head with my hands, blood oozing between my fingers. Next she visciously attacks Mutti, thrashing her mercilessly with a baton. Mutti cowers on the floor, covering her face with her arms. Skittering across the dirt, I cling to her as well, shrouding her body with my own. Blow after blow lands on my shoulders and arms. My ears and neck. The back of my head.

I can barely hear Grese when she shouts, "Dies wird dich lehren, nicht zu stehlen!"

*This will teach you not to steal!*

When the beating is finally over, Grese orders two prisoners to carry us to the washroom. "Warten dort, bis ich komme fur dich."

*Wait there until I come for you.*

As we're carted off, bloody and boneless, I hear Grese tell Johanna she's an asset to the Reich. Looking over my shoulder I see Johanna's open palm into which Grese drops a small sausage. There's no remorse in Johanna's face, no hint of guilt or shame as she eagerly shoves it into her mouth.


Two nights later, Mutti and I are loaded into a boxcar along with seventy other prisoners. We haven't eaten. Haven't slept. No one tells us where we're going or how long the journey will be. Like before, we're given a bucket filled with water and a bucket to fill ourselves when the time comes to use it as a makeshift toilet.

Mutti and I stand close together, shivering in our coats. We're lucky as we have our hair to keep our heads warm. Most of the others are bald or have only stubble covering their skulls. They look like walking skeletons and smell like a sewer, the poor souls. Some are too weak to stand and sit on the floor with silent tears rolling down their cheeks.

A shrill steam whistle blows and the locomotor begins to chug. Slowly, deliberately, the train rolls away from the platform, taking Mutti and me to a nameless destination, taking us away from the hope of ever seeing Vati again. Perhaps Kapitan was right and my father is truly dead. And so, like Jurgen and Bruno, I can carry the memory of him, desperately trying to remember what he looked like. The sound of his voice. The touch of his hand on my cheek. Sorrowfully, I find that in the confusion of the past few days, I cannot recall anything about him except for his last words to me: "Du lebst. Du lebst."

*You will live. You will live.*

And I have.

I continue to live in the horror of the unknown, watching over my mother as the train picks up speed and hurdles us onward into the darkness.

Two days later I'm awakened with a start as the train jolts to a stop. The brakes screech loudly, sending a wave of panic up my spine. Mutti clings to me and says, "I'm here, Karin...no matter what happens, I won't let them take you from me."

Our joints are stiff and swollen. Many of the prisoners have died on the journey and have been pitilessly pushed aside to make more room for the living. The rest of us lean against the walls or each other as we hear the door being unbolted. As it slides open, I recognize the sickeningly familiar stench of smoke and ash and burning flesh.

When the prisoners are ordered out of the boxcar, a familiar face greets us as Mutti and I gingerly walk down the wooden plank.

"Guten Abend," Kapitan Dieter smiles. "I've been waiting for you."

# Sapphire

I's dreaming of snow falling to the earth like little bits a ash when a scratchy little tongue wake me with a start. It be Blueberry licking my ear, then my nose, then my chin. I pet his little head and whisper in his ear, "What you doing up? It ain't time for eating."

He jest keep on licking and pretty soon here come Honey and Sunny. Ain't no sign a Rascal, though. That not be a big surprise. She always be getting into some kind a trouble. But then I hear Henry yowling outside the shack and I know something ain't right.

Mama still sleeping deep, her arm wrapped 'round herself like a belt. She sleep like the dead sometime and it scare me when I cain't wake her. Still, she always know when it be time to get up in the morning, even 'fore the old rooster start his crowing. I don't want to wake her now, so I shoo the kittens off the bed and real careful slip out from 'neath the quilt to see what going on. Jest in case, I take the kerosene lamp and a match, sticking it in the pocket a my nightie. It be cold, so I grab my shawl and wrap it 'round me real tight. Them kittens be right on my heels when I step out the door and into the yard.

Old Henry be yowling some more, but Mabel ain't nowhere to be seen. The full moon shining down on everthing, making long shadows in the yard. I hear something going on near the big house, so I set the lamp on the dirt, strike the match on a rock, then lift the glass and light it up.

It be then that I hear Pete stamping his hoof and grumbling to hisself. I walk closer to where he be and find him hobbled to the post by the kitchen door.

*Why ain't he in the barn?* I wonder.

Then I see all a the animals be hobbled here, there, and everwhere. Sue be mooing low near the snow peas. Nat be pawing at the dirt right by the sage. Timothy be chewing up a heap a grass where he tied to the fence, and Joan and Joanna be huddled together baa-baaing like they singing the gospel.

*What this mess?* I wonder. *And who done it?*

Them kittens run like the wind to they daddy to keep 'em safe from stomping hoofs and such while I carry the lamp to the barn where they's a light glowing inside. I try the door, but it be shut tight. It look like all a them animals done let theyselves out the barn and locked the door 'hind 'em. Still, I know they ain't no animal what can strike a match and light a lamp.

I goes over to the window and try to peep inside, but I's too short to see anything, so I set the lamp on the ground and look for a log I can stand on. Ain't nothing nearby, so I hightail it to the chopping block and find me a piece a wood I can carry back to the barn. It not be big, but it be big enough for me to get up a little higher so's I can see through the bottom of the window.

Looking 'round, I don't see nothing but a big old pile a hay and a lamp setting on Massa's workbench. His tools be gone. His saddle be missing. They ain't even a shovel or hoe to be seen.

"What going on?" I say outloud to nobody.

Looking to the big house, I don't see no lights. Don't hear nothing 'cept that hooty owl calling in the night ever once in a while. He don't care who I be no more...now he asking folks yonder in the woods.

Rascal dart out from 'neath the mulberry bushes and scare the dickens out a me. "Where you been?" I hiss as she fly by on the way to find more trouble.

Looking back through the window, I see Massa near Pete's stall. He looping a rope 'round and 'round 'til it look like a lasso.

"What you doing that for?" I whisper. "Ain't no work to be done in the middle a the night."

Then he hang the rope over his shoulder, pick up the lamp, and start to climb the ladder to the loft. Step by step, up he go real careful 'til he be standing in the empty space over Pete's stall. They's a big beam right near his head and I's surpised when he take that big old rope, throw it over, then knot it tight.

My eyes get wide when I see Massa get up on a milking stool and put the rope 'round his neck. It then I know he gone lynch hisself and I smack my hands on the window and yell at the top a my lungs, "NO, MASSA! NO!"

He hear me shouting and look toward the window where I's banging on the glass. Look like his tears done finally start falling as he throw the lamp down into the straw, then kick the stool out from 'neath him and lean out over the stall, his body dropping like a stone.

The lamp bust open and catch the hay on fire right quick and I know I ain't got no time to waste. I run to the shack screaming, "MAMA....MAMA....*MA-MA*!"

She up like a shot 'fore I can even get there and grab me up tight. "What is it, baby girl?"

"Massa!" I cry. "Massa done set the barn on fire and hung hisself!"

"*What*?!"

"Massa hung hisself!"

Mama don't ask no more questions, she jest run to the barn and bang on the door. Smoke be seeping through the cracks and it choke me something fierce. Mama run to the window and see Massa kicking and fighting the rope, but he still alive.

"Sapphire, you stay out here!" she yell at me. "Don't you come in that barn...you hear me?"

"Yes'm," I cry, tears dribbling down my face.

She pick up the piece a wood and start beating on the window 'til it break, then she crawl through into the smoke and disappear into nothing.

I run to get Hale and Isaac, but they already be coming, they nightshirts a flapping. Pearl and Opal be right on they heels.

Isaac yell, "What happen?"

"Massa set the barn on fire and hung hisself!" I cry. "Mama go in there to save him!"

"Lord a mercy!" Hale shout as a flame shoot up through the roof, making a hole that seem big as the moon. "Get back, Sapphire!"

Pearl and Opal grab me up and drag me toward the big house where Missus be running out in her nightclothes. Her hair a mess. Her face be a fright. When she see the barn, she fall on her knees and scream, "NO...SAMUEL!" It like she know 'zactly what Massa Sam done and she ain't even need us to tell her.

We standing there watching Hale and Isaac beat down the door and when it open, smoke come pouring out like big, black rain clouds filled with ash and soot. It stink like something I ain't never done smelled 'fore...like something out a one a my bad dreams.

I hear Mama coughing and screaming, "SAM! *SAM!* DON'T DO THIS! NO, LORD JESUS, *NO!*"

I don't think 'bout nothing 'cept trying to save my Mama. Wrestling free from Pearl's grip, I hurry to the barn yelling for her. Hale and Isaac be running in and out, coughing and hacking. Flames be licking up into the rafters, sending smoke up into the night sky.

When I get to the door, Hale push me back. "You ain't going in there!" he yell. "You *ain't!*"

"But *Mama!*" I scream. "I got to get Mama out a there!"

"Hale gone find her," Isaac say, picking me up and taking me back to my sisters. "He gone find her."

Isaac then run to the well with Keen and Old Albert, gathering buckets a water to put out the fire. They run back and forth 'gain and 'gain, but it don't do no good.

Missus be on her knees crying and praying to Jesus. Little Sam and Marybelle come stumbling out the house and run to her. They be shocked and silent to see such a thing 'cause it be like a horrible dream ain't none a us gone wake up from any time soon.

I's next to Little Sam with tears running down my face, mixing with the smoke and ash and all the things I ain't never gone forget: the way all a Massa's animals be surrounding us 'cause he made sure they be out a harm's way; the scary sounds they be making 'cause they scared, too; the heat from the fire that like to burn up my spirit right now, and the helpless feeling that I cain't do nothing to stop it.

I watch them ashes flying through the sky and falling down like snow on the new, green earth. In my mind I see the look Massa give me 'fore he drop, the tears and sadness in his eyes that no 'mount of drinking can bring. He mean to do what he done...and he mean to do it so's nobody can save him.

It then I know he dead.

My heart like to burst when I look to Little Sam and see that he know it, too. His face be squeezed up tight and his eyes be full a water. When he look at me, I know for sure both a our daddies be gone forever.

Little Sam grab my hand and hold it tight. "*Why*?" he ask, his voice spilling over with tears.

Wiping my face with the back a my hand, I keep my promise to Mama and don't say nothing.

For a long time we stands there waiting, long minutes that go on forever 'til finally Hale come staggering out the barn with Mama in his arms. She limp like one a Marybelle's ragdolls and her arm be hanging loose. Hale bring her to us and real gentle lay her on the ground.

I put my cheek to Mama's heart and feel it thumping. Her face be covered with soot and her nose and mouth be black as coal. Her breath be short and quick, but she still here.

"Mama?" I cry.

She try and reach up to pat my head, wheezing something awful. "Sapphire...you need to braid that hair," she say in a voice that sound like it coming from far away.

"Yes'm," I cry, wrapping my arms 'round her while Opal and Pearl set down with me.

Pearl leaning 'gainst Opal, cradling her belly, holding in her tears. She don't need to say nothing, 'cause her eyes tell the whole story.

"You do like I tell you, Sapphire," Mama say, blinking like she trying to see me better. "You be a good girl, you hear me?"

"Yes'm."

She touch my neck. "Where your tokens?"

"I took 'em off," I cry. "They by my dolly in the shack."

"Don't you dare put 'em back on," Mama say, her voice breaking. "You's free now." She look at Pearl and Opal. "All my girls be free."

'Yes'm," I cry. "You's free, too, ain't you?"

"Yes, baby girl," she say, stroking my cheek. "I's always been free."

"Mama...you ain't gone go nowhere," Opal say real strong-like. "You's gone stay *right here*."

Reaching over to touch my sister's hand, Mama say real calm, "No, I ain't...I's gone see your daddy real soon."

I hug her close and cry, "No, Mama...*no!*"

"Don't fret, baby," Mama whisper. "I's gone see you 'gain...in God's heaven."

"Please...please, Mama!" I sob. "Don't go!"

"It be alright, Sapphire," she say, looking in my eyes. "I ain't gone be far away."

Then, like her mama done 'fore her, Mama let go a her body, and it feel jest a bit lighter when she set her spirit free and fly on up to heaven.

# Karin

Ash falls through the chinks in the roof as Simka bears down with all her might. Vitya kneels on the floor between her legs, ready to catch the baby while Esfir and I sit by Simka's side.

"Push!" Vitya encourages. "Push *hard!*"

Simka scowls and tries to push, but she's not strong enough to do it for very long.

Vitya looks up at me and her eyes tell me what she dare not say. If Simka can't push, then both she and the baby will surely die. We won't ask for help from the doctors, who will just as soon let nature take its course than to do anything to help a prisoner and her child. What's one more body to them? Or two, if the baby is born, but doesn't survive?

"Think of Alexi," Vitya says, rubbing Simka's knee. "Think how this baby will look just like him...don't you want to see?"

Tears fill Simka's eyes when she hears her husband's name. Every single night, she says the Kaddish prayers for him and through listening and learning, I know them by heart, my favorite being the last two lines:

*May there be abundant peace from Heaven*
*and life upon us and upon Israel.*
*He Who makes peace in His heights, may He make peace,*
*upon us and upon all Israel.*
*Amen*

But there has been no peace to be found here in life and I wonder if Alexi found his in death. He died soon after their transport arrived at Buchenwald last August. The long journey with no food or water was doubly hard for him as he had recently contracted pneumonia from living in the squalor of the ghetto.  Upon arrival, he was taken away and never seen again.  Three weeks later, Simka told me she was pregnant and begged me to keep it secret.

I nodded an unspoken promise and to this day, have remained by her side through months of uncertainty.

Now Simka grabs my hand and cries out, "Karin, ostanovi eto!"

Esfir mops her brow and tells me she begging me to make it stop.

*The pain or the baby?* I wonder.

For on the day I met Simka, many lives were taken...and not just the ones we could see.  In the eight months since that horrible time, not an hour goes by that I don't think of Olga and her child, or of Mary and her daughter, Elizabet, as they were herded along with other young mothers to the firing squad where their wailing could be heard all over our side of the camp.  No amount of orchestral music could cloak the sounds of the bullets ripping them apart, their screams of terror, the inhuman sounds of suffering those women made while they were dying with their children in their arms.

It was on that day that I was grateful to be barren, to know that, no matter what Herman did to me, there would never be any evidence of my shame, nor any way I would ever bring a child into this world that's so filled with hatred and cruelty.

But Simka cannot stop her child from coming.  One way or another, it will be born.

Into this life.

Or the next.

***

November, 1944

Mutti and I sit in a gray, damp room knitting and watching the clock.  It's eleven in the morning and we've been working since Appell ended two hours ago.  It was longer than usual since three new transports arrived in Buchenwald

207

last night.  One from Auschwitz, two from places I can't remember.

I look at the new girl, Simka, who's not much older than me.  She's small and frail with black hair and bright, blue eyes.  She furiously works the yarn and needles until they are nothing more than a blur.  Simka arrived last week, while Kapitan was changing our barrack assignment.  Mutti and I stood watching the new women huddle in masses, waiting to be separated by the officers in charge.

Before the selections were completed, Kapitan ordered our kapo to clear the barrack and make all of us stand at attention outside.  It was then that I realized one of the women...Olga, I think...was pregnant and could no longer hide it.

Kapitan pulled her from the ranks and threw her on the ground near the line of S.S. guards.  "Heraus!  Brauchen wir night von dir."

*Get out!  We have no need of you.*

Then women were torn from Simka's line as well and shoved to the side with Olga.  All of them were holding small children or babies.  One of them screamed something in Russian and was immediately shot by one of the S.S.  Her child fell to the ground in her arms and was murdered as well.  I couldn't watch, but I heard the efficiently fired bullets, the eerie silence that followed.

Since that time, my mind doesn't work properly and I can't recall my age or the place I was born or how to cast on stitches.  Mutti doesn't know this, of course...except for my helplessness when knitting.  She simply casts on the stitches for me, then hands me the needles, saying, "Try again."

I do.  I try again and again and again, but nothing seems to make sense anymore.

Since we arrived in Buchenwald five months ago, Mutti and I have been shuttled to three different barracks until Kapitan  Dieter was satisfied that the kapo was treating us fairly.  When he discovered Grese had beaten us for stealing and planned to send us to the gas chamber, he demanded that she be disciplined and had both of us boarded on the next transport to Weimar where he had been transferred to work under Kommandant Pister. Now we sit in a damp warehouse, making lace for the Reich twelve hours a day, six days a week.

I'm still summoned to Kapitan's room nearly every morning. When he's finished with me, I always take bread and cheese and other food from his footlocker. After all this time, he never forgets to make sure there is extra to share with Mutti. Even though I can't recall how old I am or how to spell my brothers' names, I still remember to do what my mother told me and take as much as I can smuggle beneath my dress without rousing the suspicions of the guards, many of whom are worse than Grese.

Here we don't work outside, which is a blessing now that winter will soon be on the way. Cold winds blow through the camp and the prisoners who are made to labor in the quarry often arrive at Appell in the evening chilled to the bone, hardly able to stand. I've been able stay warmer wearing second-hand dresses Kapitan chooses for me from the piles of clothing the female guards abandon for the latest styles. They have a high time at their parties, drinking and smoking and dancing.

I know this because Vitya, a friend of Simka's from her village, works in the cookhouse and often serves the S.S. in the officer's club. They arrived just last week, Simka being sent to work with Mutti and me, Vitya to peel potatoes, chop onions, and, as she tells it, to also resist the temptation to put rat poison in the Nazi's food.

Except for Simka, Vitya, and Maria, a woman Mutti has befriended in our work group, none of the others will look at me. I'm a step up from the whores in the brothel, but still I sell myself in trade for food and clothing...and my life. I cannot tell these women it wasn't my choice, that given the opportunity, I would murder Kapitan in his sleep. But then I would be executed and Mutti would surely hang as punishment for my unpardonable sin.

So I work and eat and sleep and go to Kapitan. I live in a fog of existence, never really knowing what day it is, what time it is. As she can see I'm slowly slipping into delirium, Mutti tells me bedtime stories from my childhood to keep me connected to the living. She recalls tales of our life in Baden Baden before Jurgen and Bruno were born, before the war started, before everything that has happened since Herr Zweig was taken away. She never speaks of my brothers or of Vati, and I'm strangely grateful. For if she did, I would surely go mad.

Now as we sit anxiously watching the clock, Mutti says to Maria, "When will she come?"

Maria shakes her head. "I don't know...it may be a long while yet."

*Who is coming?* I wonder.

Mutti checks my work, correcting a mistake I've made in the lace. "Watch me, Karin," she says, taking the needles in her hands. "You just forgot again...no matter. I will show you how."

When she returns the lace, Mutti darts her eyes to the clock again. Her hands shake uncontrollably and I wonder why she's afraid. I look to Simka, then to Maria, both of them eyeing me carefully, watching my hands as they absentmindedly manipulate their knitting needles.

It's then I remember that one of the Aufseherin makes her rounds before the noon ration. I think it might be that woman...the former Kommandant's wife they call the Bitch of Buchenwald...what is her name? Koch, I think. But then I remember that she no longer lives here after her husband was arrested and taken to prison. They say she rode her horse around the grounds wearing suggestive clothing and flirting with the prisoners, then slapping them if they dared to look her in the eyes. One prisoner said she beat a man to death right in front of him.

There have been rumors of lampshades made of human skin that still sit on end tables in the Kommandant's house, frightening souvenirs from tattooed men that Koch hand-selected to be murdered, then flayed for her own amusement. In my confusion, I often think that the Aufseherin who inspects our work is actually Koch come back from her exile to taunt and torture us until we're dead.

The last time she was here, the guard grabbed the lace out of my hands, shouting, "Fehler, Fehler! Zu viele Fehler!"

*Mistakes, mistakes! Too many mistakes!*

The guard spat, tossing my work back on the table. "Das nachste Mal, wennst du nicht so viel Gluck! Wird es Konsequenzen geben!"

*The next time you won't be so lucky! There will be consequences!*

I barely heard her as I sat staring at the wall. To me she was just another nameless monster bent on making my life as miserable as possible. I have learned well how to harden myself from such treatment. Kapitan has been an excellent teacher, and although he has never beat me, he has never showed me any respect, either, taking what he wants and leaving me to rot in what's left behind.

Now Mutti looks to Maria who nods in silence. They both look to the door where there's a flurry of movement, S.S. men and women barking orders and carrying on as if their work is of supreme importance. No time is wasted, no person's slack tolerated.

A woman with broad shoulders and hips stomps into the room. She wears the same drab uniform with the tight belt and small cap perched on her neatly-styled hair. She walks among the lace makers, inspecting their work.

"Schneller! Schneller!" she yells.

*Faster! Faster!*

When the guard isn't looking, Mutti slips a folded piece of paper into my pocket and pulls the lace from my hands. She shoves her work onto my lap and whispers, "Pick it up, Karin...tell her it's yours."

I look at her in confusion.

"Do as I tell you," she insists.

I pick it up as Mutti unravels some of my mistakes, then quickly corrects them. The guard makes her way to our table, insulting and shouting and grumbling as she plods on.

Moments later, she stands with her hands on her hips, her feet planted wide apart. "Gib es!" she orders Maria who immediately hands over her work for examination.

Satisfied that it's good enough, she tosses it back on the table, then orders Simka to hand over hers as well. "Wenn dies geschehen ist, stellen drei weitere!" she orders.

*When this is done, make three more!*

Simka nods without looking up at her.

Next the guard demands to see my work, all the while telling me I'd better have improved or she'll have to fill her quota for the week...whatever that means. Stitch by stitch she examines Mutti's lace and finally slams it back on the table saying, "Bessere dieser Zeit...das ist eine gute, kleine Schwein."

*Better this time...that is a good, little pig.*

I hear Mutti's breath catch, and glancing at her, I see a hint of a satisfied smile. But when the guard yanks my lace from Mutti's hands, I realize what my mother has done.

"Zu viele Fehler!" the guards shouts. "Das ist es nicht wert zu halten...und du auch nicht!"

*Too many mistakes! It's not worth keeping...and neither are you!*

I want to confess that the lace is mine, the mistakes are mine, and so the punishment should also be mine. But Mutti squeezes my hand beneath the table as if to keep me mute, to not let my first words in three years lead to my death sentence.

The Aufseherin orders Mutti to stand and shouts for two other guards to come take her away. Calmly my mother touches me on the shoulder and whispers in my ear. "Das wird schon wieder, Karin. Ich werde nicht weit sein."

*It will be alright, Karin. I won't be far away.*

Early the next morning I silently lie in my bunk. The space next to me that had once belonged to my mother has now been replaced by a complete stranger. She's cold and steals the blanket so I'm left exposed and utterly stripped of any comfort. I've bravely endured everything because of Mutti, at first because I needed to keep her alive, then because of her dedication to my survival. Now, even in my confusion, I know that Mutti has gone to be with Vati and Jurgen and Bruno in a place I can only imagine.

Yet I will not imagine her death or the certainty that her ashes will soon float into the night sky, then fall like snow back to this desolate place of lost hope. I will only imagine the joy in her eyes when she sees Bruno again and kisses his ruby red cheeks. When she holds Jurgen in her arms and tells him how much she's missed him. When she smiles at Vati with love and adoration.

Once again, I pull the letter from my pocket and finger the sharp corners where Mutti had carefully folded it. Slipping out of the narrow bunk, I walk to the window where only a sliver of the moon shines in the west. As sunlight slowly fills the eastern horizon, I open Mutti's last gift to me and read once again her words of love, of wisdom...and of hope.

*My dearest Karin,*

*How I love you, my sweet child, my firstborn. How proud I am to be your mother. I know I wasn't always kind or happy or whatever you might have needed, but I tried. I did try and you did your best to accept me as I am.*

*You have lost your childhood during this long, horrible war, and for that I am terribly sorry. I'm sorry I didn't ask to be taken to Kapitan's room that first day. I'm sorry I didn't protect you. I'm sorry I didn't comfort you more whenever you returned from his room, crying and in pain. Most of all, I'm sorry that I encouraged your silence so that we both might survive.*

*I've come to learn that all of our lives are the result of the choices we make. Even when we cannot choose our lot in life, still we can choose how we respond to it. I would never have chosen to hide the Zweigs like your father did, but he could not do otherwise and still be the honorable man I had married. I would have never chosen for you to be Kapitan's mistress, but you have endured it so that I could have food, and you did so because you are courageous and steadfast just like your father.*

*I'm making this last choice for you. Please don't be sad, for I know I'm going to be with your father and your brothers before morning comes. But you can still speak to me in your dreams, in your mind, in your heart, and I will always answer if you can learn how to listen with different ears, for our human ones will no longer suffice.*

*Now you must be the keeper of my memories as I have been for yours, so that you will always know how much I love you. Be well, my darling, for this war will soon be over and you will live as your father told you. I will watch over you from wherever I am and make it so.*

*Love,*
*Mutti*


For months I lie in bed while the others fitfully sleep through the night, thinking of Mutti, wondering where she is, trying desperately to listen for her voice.

I hear nothing.

I barely eat anymore and slowly become the creature I most feared - a walking corpse. Kapitan grows angry when he can see my ribs, ordering me to swallow bits of bread in his presence until he's satisfied that I won't waste away into nothing. He says he means to keep me as his pretty songbird, that even when the war is over, he will take me back to Köln to live with him and be his wife.

I don't believe him.

Yet right before Christmas when Buchenwald begins to evacuate women prisoners, Kapitan is ordered to accompany a transport to Bergen Belsen. He makes sure that I am on the list...and Simka as well. When we're marched to the depot with hundreds of other women, she holds my hand as gray skies above us cast an ominous gloom over the wasteland this world has become.

Simka's baby grows in her belly, hidden from sight, just as Mutti's letter is hidden in a pocket that I have sewn into the lining of my coat. Both are treasures to be cherished, mine whenever I need to feel the presence of my mother's love and Simka's whenever God deems the time is right.

As we board the train, I feel something, a gentle pressure deep inside my heart. And then Mutti's voice speaks softly. "Wherever you are, Karin...I am with you."

***

Another wave of pain passes through Simka as she grits her teeth and moans loudly. She looks at me with glazed eyes and I hear Mutti whispering in my ear, "Give her your strength, Karin." Wrapping an arm around her shoulders, I lift Simka a little higher and hold her close.

Vitya tells me to roll her onto her side. "Lift her leg onto my shoulder." When I do, Vitya nods. "That's it, Simka...when you feel the next contraction, push as hard as you can."

Simka looks into my eyes as tears well up and slide down her cheeks. "You keep my baby if I die," she gasps.

I'm startled by her request.

"You will keep my baby," she says again, grimacing in pain.

I look to Vitya who kneels on the bed, ready to help Simka give birth.

"*Karin!*" Simka's voice startles me with its intensity. "Promise me!"

I nod and squeeze her hand.

215

Borne away on a wave of pain, Simka cries out and tries to push.

"That's it!" Vitya encourages.  "Just like that.  You're doing wonderfully, Simka.  I can see the head!"

# Sapphire

The sun rising up 'hind the big house where Missus and me be setting with Pearl and Opal. Through the window in the dining room I see yellow light peeking through the tall pine trees, making 'em look like shadows a theyselves. Birds is twittering and singing in the magnolia jest like it be any other springtime day in Lincoln County.

But it ain't.

Missus say she gots to talk to us girls, so we been waiting on her a long while 'cause she ain't said nothing yet. They's the stack a papers Massa done brought from town yesterday setting on the table and Missus keep touching the corners, like they be sharp or something and gone cut her if she ain't careful. I cain't read all a them words, but Massa's name be on the top: "Samuel Wilson Settler," then the word *life* and a word I cain't make out.

While us set inside and wait for morning to come, Hale and Isaac be shoveling ashes where the barn used to be, making sure the fire be out. Keen and Old Albert be digging graves. One for Mama. One for Massa. And one for Mabel who was in the barn trying to save her babies 'cause she ain't know they was already safe. Hale found her little body in the corner where she done made a little bed for the kittens when they was born, and it like to cut me deep when he brung Mabel out and laid her on the lawn. Ain't she jest like my mama who sacrifice her own life to try and save her babies?

Now I understand a little more who Mama really be. She more than jest the person who give life to me and my sisters. She more than the slave who cook and clean and make lace. Mama be brave and true. To do what she done, she musta love Massa Sam jest like she love any one a her chil'ren.

Missus clear her throat and turn up the kerosene lamp so it glow a little brighter. Her eyes be red and swole up, but she stop crying long enough to put Marybelle and Little Sam to bed in her room, both a them in shock to know what they daddy done. She give 'em a spoonful a medicine that make 'em sleep, but I don't want to sleep no more 'cause all I gone get is more bad dreams.

Pearl and Opal and me done sat with Mama 'til Hale say it time to put her in a sheet and take her to over to the place where baby Amber be waiting on her. My sisters tie one a my rag ribbons on her finger so a little bit a me can ride up to heaven with her. I tell them to tie one more for Daddy and they do. I kiss them ribbons 'fore they swaddle her real special with the quilt from our bed. It feel good to know she gone be warm wrapped in something her mama done made.

And ever since then, we's setting here waiting on Missus to start talking. Fin'lly she do.

"I'm so sorry about what happened," she say, her voice full a pain. "I'm sure Samuel never meant for you to find him, Sapphire...or for your mother to do what she did." She take a deep breath. "He's been upset for quite a while about the plantation and the end of the war and what that would mean for you and for the men."

Pearl rub her tummy and I 'magine her little baby be hungry for his breakfast. She press her lips together like she got something to say, but she jest keep still and listen. Opal stare at the wall like she listening, but only half way.

I don't say nothing either. Feel like all a my words got burnt up in the fire with Mama and if'n she ain't here to talk to, I's jest gone stay quiet.

Missus shuffle some a them papers. "When Samuel went into town yesterday, he made some changes in his will and made sure that his life insurance was up to date."

*What life insurance be?* I want to ask, but I don't.

"He told me what he wanted in the event of his death, but...I never thought...I never thought he'd take his own life." Missus stop for a moment and keep moving that stack a pages 'round 'til she find what she looking for. "I think that's why he started the fire...to make it look like an accident so we...so we wouldn't know that he... so we wouldn't know what he did."

*I know what he done,* I think. *I ain't need to 'magine nothing 'bout that...not like you do.*

Missus clear her throat 'gain. "Before I tell you what Samuel wanted me to do with the plantation, you need to know something about him and your mother. He made me promise never to tell you girls...that it was something Ruby would tell you if she thought you needed to know." Then she stop like them words jest cain't come out a her mouth.

My heart hurt. It feel like someone standing on my chest and ain't gone get off. I wish Missus jest get on with it and say what she got to say 'fore I bust open.

Her eyes fill up with tears. "Samuel and Ruby were brother and sister...they had the same father."

I look to Pearl and Opal, but they be staring at Missus, they faces confused, they eyebrows knitted up.

"Massa Sam's daddy be *Mama's* daddy?" Opal ask.

"Yes."

"You know this the whole time?"

"Yes."

"And you ain't told nobody?"

Missus shake her head.

Opal look to me. "You understand what she mean, Sapphire?"

I nod.

Opal turn back to Missus. "So Massa be our *uncle*?"

"Yes."

"Well, that 'splain Sapphire's green eyes," Opal say, real smart-like. She ain't mean it to shame me. It jest be her way.

Still, I dart my eyes to the tablecloth where I see my favorite dish with the Queen Anne's Lace pattern on it that Mama done set there last night so's it'd be ready for breakfast. It make me think how she in heaven right now talking to God 'bout how He make the most perfect lace on earth...all by Hisself.

Missus look at me directly now. "Sapphire...your mother loved Samuel very much...and I know he loved her, too. They grew up together, just like you and Little Sam. He watched over her when she was little and she took good care of him when he grew up and became a man." Then Missus look at Pearl and Opal. "When his father died and he took over the plantation, Samuel did his best to keep it running, but his heart just wasn't in it. He didn't want to own slaves, but he couldn't sell Ruby or any of you girls because that would be like selling his family. So he kept trying...and failing...and in the end, I think that's why he did what he did."

Missus reach over and pat my hand. "He always wanted to take care of you and your sisters, Sapphire. That's why he didn't sell your Mama to Mister Birch and gave him your daddy instead. And I don't think he ever got over it...knowing how he hurt you all."

She set back and move more a them papers 'round. "So when Samuel settled his estate yesterday, he made some important changes. I'm to receive the benefits from his life insurance and will keep whatever possessions are mine here in the house." Then she look from Pearl to Opal to me. "But the house itself and the plantation are yours...to keep or to sell as you see fit. Samuel had intended to pass it on to Ruby as she's his sister, but now...well, now it all belongs to you."

It like to knock me over to think that I's setting in a place that be Opal's and Pearl's and mines. It don't feel real, like this whole night be some strange tale Old Albert tell while we's setting 'round the fire pit.

"Now that the war is over, you're free to do as you wish," Missus say. "From what I understand, coloreds will be allowed to own property in the south and I'd prefer if you'd stay on until the children and I can make our way back to Cleveland. I think Keen and Albert might want a place to live and work until things settle down."

"Where we gone go?" Pearl ask, looking like she cain't believe what she hearing. "I ain't never lived nowhere but here my whole life. I ain't know nothing different."

"I'm not sure what will happen in the future," Missus tell us. "But the land will be worth something...not a lot, but enough to get you north if that's what you want to do."

*How we know what we want?* I think. *I ain't even know what to do with myself, but I sure ain't gone leave my Mama.* Tears come to my eyes and spill over onto my cheeks.

Missus hand me a folded paper and say real quiet, "Sapphire...can you read this?"

*Ruby Settler* be written in black ink and it be in Massa's handwriting. I's holding a letter he done wrote to my mama that she ain't never gone see.

"You keep that for now," Missus tell me. "When you're ready, you can read it."

I don't say nothing, jest set there swiping at my eyes 'cause them tears won't stop.

"I'm going upstairs to lie down," Missus say. Seem like she take a bit a that medicine herself and it be making her sleepy, too. She get up and leave all a them papers on the table, a bunch a words scratched on paper that mean ain't no mans running Settler's place no more.

Opal and Pearl and me be the owners now.

But what that mean? I don't have no idea how to be nothing but a little girl. Pearl and Opal ain't much older than me and they cain't even read. What we gone do now?

So many questions make my head hurt, so I lays it on the table, covering my face with my arms. Them tears spill onto Massa's letter and make Mama's name blur up a bit. I don't care and I don't 'magine she'd mind neither.

"Sapphire...go on back to the shack and get some rest," Opal tell me. "We come and get you when it time to send Mama off to glory."

I stand up, then take both the letter and the dish with me, but I don't stop in the kitchen to put the dish in the cupboard. 'Stead I tote it with me as I walk out the door and go by Missus' little garden, then what left of the smoky barn that now jest a pile of burnt up wood and ash, and finally walk into the shack where Mama's pillow still hold the shape a her head.

Lying on the bed, I put the letter on the plate and set it where I sleep, then curl up on Mama's side and put my head on her pillow. I smell her smell. I feel the sag in the straw mattress where she been lying night after night, keeping me warm, keeping me safe.

Massa's letter set there looking at me...Mama's name in black 'gainst the white paper. It then I decide I ain't gone open it 'cause it be Mama's and not mine. Them words is 'tween her and Massa Sam, and I 'spect they in heaven right now and he be telling her all a things she need to know. Reading her letter be eavesdropping and Mama done taught me to be a good girl and mind my own business.

So I do.

'Stead I get up and cross the shack to the shelf where Mama put the pattern pieces for my Easter dress. They be pinned together real neat-like, jest like Mama always do. I pull her sewing basket from 'neath the bed and slip Mama's thimble on my finger. It be a might big, but no matter.

I's gone grow up fast anyhow.

Then I thread the needle and get to work. I think on Mama and wonder what she doing now...what she'd tell me if'n she was setting right here, knowing this whole place be hers. I 'spect she'd say ain't nothing really belong to nobody, that we's all jest here for a little while and everthing we has gone belong to somebody else some day.

Mama told me once, "It don't matter what you got...it matter who you *is*, baby girl."

I wonder who I is now 'cause I ain't Massa's slave no more, and I ain't nobody's chile...least not here on earth. Now I get to be jest Sapphire...but it ain't at all the way I thought it would be.

222

As I stitch on the work Mama done start and I gone finish, I wonder what it be like in heaven. Even though my tears is still falling, I smile a little, too, 'magining Mama be trying on a pair a lace wings an angel done give her 'cause I ain't had no time to knit her some myself.

# Karin

Simka lies moaning in the darkness as Vitya wraps the tiny baby in a bright red sweater I've been keeping in the basket beneath our bunk. It once belonged to one of the Aufseherin, but Herman said I could keep it if I wore it to his room once in a while. I've never worn it for Herman, as I would surely risk being beaten for being too bold, for having a rare and precious item of clothing that could be traded for food. Instead I've kept it hidden for the baby. Now that she's finally here, Vitya swaddles her in the sweater, then hands her to Simka.

"A lovely little girl," Vitya smiles. "You should be proud."

Simka traces the baby's nose and mouth, still covered with blood and mucous. "My precious angel," she murmurs, barely able to form the words. Simka's skin is ashen, her lips nearly blue. She's lost too much blood and there's nothing that can be done to save her.

Tears fall down Simka's face as she looks into my eyes. "You will keep your promise, Karin."

I nod, then hand Vitya the scissors so she can cut the cord. When our eyes meet, I know that it won't be long. She waits for the placenta to be delivered while Esfir and I peer over Simka's shoulders, gazing at her newborn daughter.

"She's lovely, yes?" Esfir asks.

She is a beautiful baby with small, rosebud lips and a perfect little nose. Her eyes are shut tight as if she doesn't want to witness the dreadful place in which she's been born and I can hardly blame her.

The barrack overflows with women rotting in their own filth. Many have died that day, their bodies taken by prisoners to be thrown on top of countless others in mass graves. Those that remain are listless and sullen; only a few are aware that not ten feet from where they lie, a new life has been born.

Still I'm startled by what I see.

Simka's daughter doesn't look like her or Alexi, at least not how she had described him to Mutti and me. Studying the baby's face, I realize she looks exactly like Herman and the expression on my face must reveal to Simka that I know the truth.

"He took me only twice...after Appell that first week," Simka cries. "Only twice, but it was enough."

A long silence falls between us.

"You promised," she whispers, caressing the baby's cheek. "You will care for her, Karin. No matter what Kapitan has done, she is innocent...she is *innocent*."

I nod, my eyes wide and filled with tears.

Esfir looks at me. "Innocent of what?"

I don't answer.

Simka tries to speak, but no words will come as the baby lets out a keening cry, then wails loudly.

"Can you feed her?" Vitya asks her. "Try and put her to your breast."

Simka isn't strong enough to move on her own, so I guide the baby into the crook of her arm where she latches on and suckles hungrily. Gently, I trace the crown of her head where her tiny soft spot throbs with the strength of her beating heart.

Simka looks at me with longing, with shame, with sadness. "Tell her I love her," she says softly. "Tell her..."

I reach out to hold her hand.

"Skazhi yey, chto budet sledit' za ney," Simka says, the words slurring.

Vitya whispers, "She asks you to tell the baby that she will watch over her."

I nod, tears falling down my face.

"Vy mozhete idti," Vitya gently tells Simka. "Idite s Bogom...vash rebenok budet lyubit.'" Then she looks up at

225

me. "I told her she can go be with God...that the baby will be loved."

Simka blinks slowly, then closes her eyes. Her daughter nuzzles closer to her breast, then sighs deeply. They both seem as if they've fallen asleep, but moments later, Simka's arms are lifeless and I tenderly reach out to gather the baby into my own.

Her soft, peachy skin reminds me of Jurgen, and her red cheeks of Bruno. Kissing her forehead I breathe in the warm, earthy scent of her brand new life and silently name her Ruby.

As dawn comes, I hold Ruby close to my heart while she restlessly dozes in my arms. We're able to make it across the compound, the baby hidden beneath my shawl, as I hurry to Herman's room, praying to God that he won't be there or that anyone who stops me will simply think I've been summoned to do my duty. Corpses litter the camp, prisoners who walked to the doorways of their barracks to see the sunlight before they collapsed to their death. The smell is unbearable and yet I move quickly, desperate to do whatever I can to keep my promise to Simka.

Nothing is as it has been. Most of the officers have deserted the camp and only a handful are left to wait for the British to come. Kommandant Kramer sits in his office, prepared to surrender while I quickly make my way to the only place where there is milk for Simka's baby.

No one is in Kapitan Dieter's building...at least not now. When I enter Herman's room, Ruby awakens with a loud howl. Fumbling with the latch on the wooden frame of the cabinet, finally I'm able to open it. Cans of sweetened condensed milk and stacks of chocolate bars tempt me to forget the child and gorge myself. But I know better than to do that. I am Henry Vogel's daughter. I am Josephine Vogel's child. They have taught me how to live a life that's worthy of heaven...and how to die if I must to save another's life.

Gently I put Ruby on Herman's bed, then sift through the cupboard drawers, searching for something I can use to open a can. The baby cries at the top of her lungs and I'm frantic as I pull out boxes of cigarettes, pens, and a host of junk Herman has collected over the years. A photograph of a stout woman with two small children is framed and stashed in the bottom of one drawer. I toss it in the pile with the other things I've unearthed and dig deeper.

I find a rusty bottle opener and quickly use it to cut two holes on either side of the lid. Cradling Ruby in one arm, I then dip my finger into the milk. When I hold it to her lips, she stops screaming and startles for a moment. What I'm offering her isn't Simka's milk, but she doesn't seem to mind, and I'm relieved when Ruby sucks eagerly at the thick, creamy liquid. Kissing her soft crown, I dip my finger more deeply into the milk and offer it to her.

Without stopping to think about the consequences of being heard, I sing *Im stiller Nacht*, Vati's favorite song. Every note calms her, encourages her to keep eating...to keep living. When I reach the end of the first verse, I understand in part why I'm still alive.

*In the quiet night, at the first watch,*
*a voice began to lament; sweetly, gently,*
*the night wind carried to me its sound.*
*And from such bitter sorrow and grief*
*my heart has melted.*
*The little flowers - with my pure tears -*
*I have watered them all.*

I need to try and save this child as an atonement for Bruno...and for Jurgen and my parents. For the Zweigs and Frau Daiga and Simka. Their memories are flowers in the garden of my heart and I have watered them all with my tears.

All of a sudden I hear the S.S. shouting to each other to make way for something I cannot see. And yet I hear the

227

rumble of tanks and the sound of British voices announcing on a loudspeaker:

Ruhig...ruhig sein. Bleiben Sie wo Sie sind!
Hilfe ist auf dem Weg!
*Be calm...be calm. Stay where you are!*
*Help is on the way!*

Then I make out the words I have been longing to hear:

Ihr seid frei! Ihr seid **frei**!
*You are free! You are **free**!*

Tears fill my eyes as I offer Ruby more milk...as much milk as she wants...as much as she will need.

Suddenly a man stomps up the stairs and bursts through the doorway, his footfalls thunderous and frightening. Herman stands before me wearing tattered civilian clothing and carrying a knapsack. I've never seen him dressed like this and it startles me.

"What are you doing?" Herman demands. "Whose baby is that?"

Without thinking, I angrily shout, "She's *mine*! Don't you touch her!"

These are the first words Herman has ever heard me speak beyond the songs he makes me sing. He's heard my soft soprano, but never my callused contralto.

Holding Ruby closer, I tell him plainly, "You will *not* take this child away from me."

Herman's eyes darken as he notices I've broken into the cabinet. He sees the pile of his belongings on the bed and steps toward me.

I move back, cautious and vigilant.

"What is this?" he yells, pulling his pistol from its holster. "What did you steal from me?"

"Nothing...I swear it," I reply quickly. "Just some milk for the baby."

"Whose is it?" Herman asks again, pointing the gun at my head.

"Mine...she's *mine*," I tell him, my voice sounding odd and unfamiliar.

"She is *not* yours."

"She *is*!"

"Then she's mine, too, *Little Bird*," Herman smirks, mocking me.

He cocks the gun, but before he can shoot, voices fill the hallway, British soldiers tramping through the building. Herman looks over his shoulder. Without thinking, I reach out and grab his wrist, twisting it as hard as I can. Startled, Herman drops the gun and I kick it beneath the bed as a soldier appears in the doorway.

In an instant Herman has me by the throat. "I'll kill you," he growls.

Ruby cries at the top of her lungs as I gasp for breath, struggling to hold on to her.

The soldier crosses the room quickly, then aims his rifle between Herman's shoulder blades. "Let her go!"

Herman's fingers loosen their grip, but as he releases me, his eyes bore into mine. "Sag ihm, ich bin ein Gefangener...oder ich werde sicherstellen dass du hangen."

*Tell him I'm a prisoner...or I'll make sure you hang.*

I'm shaking uncontrollably as the soldier shouts his order once more.

Herman turns to face him, his expression stubborn and stoic.

The soldier looks at me, then the baby and his face softens. "Sprechen Sie English, gnadige Frau?"

I nod, tears filling my eyes because of the kindness and respect in his voice. It's been years since I've been treated as a young woman, not a possession or a slave. "Yes...I speak English...a bit."

"I'm Corporal Frederick of the Allied twenty-first division," he tells me. "You're free...the camp has been liberated."

Tears spill onto my cheeks as I nod, so he'll know that I understand.

"Are you alright? Did this man hurt you?"

I look to Herman and he glowers at me. "Sag ihm!"

*Tell him!*

I don't know what to say...or how to say it. Do I tell all of the unspeakable things he has done to me and to others or do I tell of his kindnesses, his generosity, his confessions of love? Herman was caught with his hands around my throat, and I can still feel the constriction warning me to keep silent about his many crimes and only reveal that which will absolve him of any wrongdoing.

Corporal Frederick levels his gun at Herman. "Who are you? What are you doing here?"

"I'm a prisoner," he replies staunchly. "Just like her...we've been waiting for you."

Corporal Frederick then looks at me in disbelief. "Who is he, miss?"

I say nothing, holding Ruby tightly in my arms. She's finally stopped crying and is suckling on one of her fists.

"Who is he?" the corporal asks once more.

I know that I must speak, but I cannot find the words to tell of my shame and grief, of what I have endured and survived. And so I say the only words that will rise up from my throat. "He is S.S. Kapitan Herman Dieter."

"She lies!" Herman shouts.

Corporal Frederick looks from him back to me.

"He is S.S. Kapitan Herman Dieter," I say again, louder this time.

"I thought as much," Corporal Frederick replies. "He looks too clean and healthy to be a prisoner."

I nod. "He is S.S. Kapitan Herman Dieter."

Herman loudly protests as the soldier orders him to raise his hands and put them on his head.

"He is S.S. Kapitan Herman Dieter," I say once more, clearly identifying him so that there can be no question.

Corporal Frederick calls for assistance. "I've found one in here!" Soon three other soldiers enter the room and wrestle Herman into the hallway. Then the corporal turns to me. "Are you alright?" he asks. "Is your baby alright?"

"She needs milk," I tell him. "And water for a bath."

Corporal Frederick nods, inviting me to sit on the bed. "We're working on that...I've never seen a place such as this."

Ruby gurgles, making little kitten sounds in her sleep. For the first time I allow myself to believe that we may just survive this unholy place. But where will we go? And what will I do?

Corporal Frederick sits next to me and opens up his kit. Offering me a chocolate bar, he says, "Take this...it's not much." He offers to hold Ruby, but I shake my head, unwilling to give her up. So instead, he unwraps the bar and breaks off a piece, handing it to me.

As the chocolate melts on my tongue, memories of my mother come rushing back to me...the hot cocoa she would make in the winter; the warm, wonderful kuchen she would make for our birthdays. Tasting such a wonderful treat makes me feel human again, as does Corporal Frederick's kind smile.

"I have a little one at home myself," he smiles. "Just a little over a year."

I nod.

"A little girl...what is yours?"

"Ein Madchen....a girl."

The corporal pulls his wallet from his kit and shows me a photograph of a sweet, little baby wearing a long, white gown. "This was the day Claire was christened."

"She's beautiful."

"So is your little one," he smiles, fingering the picture of his child. "We have help on the way...doctors who can make sure she'll be well."

"Can I keep her...I mean, can I stay with her?" I ask, fear bubbling up inside of me.

"I think so," Corporal Frederick answers. "I don't know for sure, but I'll do everything I can to help you."

A soldier steps into the doorway. "You alright in here, sir?"

The corporal nods. "We're just fine...did Dieter give you any trouble?"

"Some...but we'll let the prisoners take care of him."

I can only imagine what that means. Then I think of the words emblazoned on the gate at Buchenwald: "Jedem das Seine," *to each his own*, and I know that whatever happens to Herman, it will be what he deserves. I will play no more part in it.

And I will never speak his name again.

Corporal Frederick sits with me, offering chocolate, telling me stories from his life in Surrey, tales of his wife and his children and his dog, Yancy. He spins amusing yarns that only a soldier can tell when he's away from home and much of it I don't understand. I try to listen, for he's being so kind and gracious, but I'm beyond needing his words of hope and freedom.

For now, as I cradle the baby in my arms and trace my finger along the soft slope of her precious little face, all I can hear is Mutti's voice whispering in the quiet corners of my mind. Ruby yawns, then folds her hands beneath her chin as if she's about to pray. I kiss her cheek and softly repeat Mutti's words in her ear...

"Ich bin so stolz auf dich, mein tapferes und schones Tochter."

*I am so proud of you, my brave and lovely daughter.*

# Epilogue

It's a sunny Saturday afternoon in Shaker Heights as Sapphire sits in the window of her granddaughter's yarn shop, warming her wrinkled face and hands. A small pile of lace sits on her lap, a little handkerchief for her best friend, Alma, who turns ninety next week. Sapphire now lives with her daughter in a small, but tidy apartment off of Fairfax Road where she's content to grow old surrounded by her loved ones.

She moved to northeastern Ohio at the turn of the century, having married Earnest Bates, a former slave who had seen her at the mercantile selling her lace to Mrs. Snow, the same woman who years before had supplied Ruby with yarn and material. Earnest and Sapphire had three children -- two sons, Timothy and Samuel, and a daughter, Jewel, who Earnest once said encompasses all of the strength from Ruby, Pearl, Opal, and Sapphire herself.

Earnest has been gone for over a decade, gone to be with Sapphire's Mama and Daddy and Timothy, who died of scarlet fever when he was just a boy, and Samuel, who was killed in action during World War I. Now it's only Jewel and Sapphire and Jewel's daughter, Esther, who remember stories from the old days, stories of slavery and freedom, of hard work and dedication to their families.

Every afternoon, Jewel walks Sapphire to Esther's store, *Spin a Yarn*, where she can knit and enjoy the company of the neighborhood ladies who love to listen to her tales of Tennessee. She's been transplanted up north for the better part of fifty years, and yet these days, it seems Sapphire can remember life in Lincoln County with greater clarity than life in Shaker Heights.

*Spin a Yarn* has been in business for almost five years now. After World War II, it seemed every single woman on the block was eager to get married and start a family. Since then, the baby boom has kept Jewel and Esther busy ordering delicate silk yarn for trousseaus, and sturdy, yet soft yarns for layettes.

Before Sapphire developed cataracts, she taught little ones how to knit, gently guiding their hands while they sat on her lap, holding the needles. "In through the front door...then once around the back," she'd say, teaching them the knit stitch. "Peek through the window and off jumps Jack!"

The children would giggle with delight to learn a new skill accompanied by such a jaunty rhyme. But Sapphire's favorite was teaching the purl stitch. "Under the gate...catch some sheep...back you go....off you leap!" she'd chant while their tiny fingers manipulated the needles and yarn.

Oh, what a joy to watch those children make simple scarves, then hats, then mittens and even socks! Even though she no longer teaches, Sapphire is delighted whenever a former student drops by to share their latest creation.

"My Mama be proud to see all them things you done made," she often says. Then Sapphire might point to the framed lace placemat that hangs near the cash register, saying, "My Mama, Ruby, made that way back in 1864! Can you believe it?"

Every once in a while, a child will exclaim, "That's almost a hundred years ago! How old *are* you, Miss Sapphire?"

When she smiles, Sapphire's green eyes sparkle, nearly disappearing into the folds of her mahogany skin. "I cain't 'member when my birthday is, but I's ninety-three years old. How about them chickens?"

Another long winter has passed. A new year and a brand new decade has begun. The spring of 1950 is unfurling its wings, and with it, another lovely day in early May. Robins chirp in the cherry blossom outside *Spin a Yarn* and bouquets of lily of the valley delicately scent the air.

As Sapphire looks out the window, she sees a young woman and her daughter admiring a lace shawl on display. The little girl points to Sapphire and waves. Sapphire waves back, squinting. *Do I know you, chile?* she wonders.

Moments later the bell over the front door tinkles softly as the woman enters, then carefully guides her child into the store. "Vorsicht jetzt, Liebling," she whispers in German, then again in English. "Careful, darling."

"Mutter, kann ich etwas Garn für meine Puppe?" the girl asks, holding up a porcelain doll with long, auburn curls. "Konnt du ihr ein Kleid zu machen?"

"Ya, meine Liebling," the mother nods. "I promised."

Esther finishes with a customer at the cash register, then attends to the woman and her child. "May I help you, ma'am?"

The woman smiles shyly. "Ja...yes, thank you. I am looking for some yarn to make a dress for my daughter's doll."

The little girl proudly holds up her prize. "It was my birthday last month," she says, her voice thick with a German accent. "I'm five!"

"You're a big girl!" Esther beams. "Is this dolly your birthday present?"

"Ya," the girl nods. "From my Cousin Helga!"

Esther winks. "How nice."

Sapphire studies the woman carefully. Her dark blonde hair is pulled pack into a tidy snood and she's dressed smartly in a light blue skirt and blouse. She carries a small, red purse and holds her daughter's hand in her white-gloved palm. Sapphire has seen the woman walk past the shop many times before, but she's never come in...not until now. Before she was always alone, carrying a bag of groceries or a small satchel filled with books. Even though Sapphire couldn't see the woman's features clearly then, she recognizes the sad smile on her face.

"Liebling, go sit and look at the pattern books," the woman says to her child. "Choose a dress you like while I select some knitting needles."

"Ja, Mutti...werde ich."

*Yes, Mother...I will.*

"Do you knit often?" Esther asks, guiding the woman toward a shelf filled with needles.

She shakes her head. "It's been a long while."

"Are you from overseas?"

"Germany...but after the war my daughter and I moved here to live with our cousin. Helga sent me to your store as she says your yarn is the best in Shaker Heights."

"Oh, that's nice," Esther smiles. "What's her last name?"

"Oppenheimer," the woman replies. "She's a cook for Mr. Croswell, and helps take care of his child...a girl named Annie."

"I don't know them," Esther says. "But I bet I remember her even if she came in here just once. What's she look like?"

"Tall...thin...brown hair," the woman says quietly. "She makes her own clothes...very bright colors."

"Yes!" Esther's face shines. "I know her! She likes to knit socks with fancy stripes for her daughter, right?"

"Ja...yes, that's her."

"How nice...tell her we're getting in a new shipment of sock yarn next week."

"I will."

"Pleased to meet you...?"

"Karin...Karin Vogel."

"I'm Esther Sanders and it's so nice to have you here." She gestures toward the shelf. "These are our best needles...please feel free to open the packages and try them out."

Karin nods. "Vielen Dank," she whispers timidly. "Thank you."

Sapphires picks up her lace and slowly begins another row. Her fingers are so adept with the pattern, she no longer needs to watch her hands. Instead she watches Karin and the way she slowly touches the wooden needles, selecting a set of rosewood double points.

Carefully opening the package, Karin then runs her fingertips over the smooth surface. Sapphire wonders what she's thinking as she presses the tips to her cheek, inhaling deeply.

"Them's the best needles we got," Sapphire smiles, gesturing to the work in her hands. "I don't work with nothing else but rosewood."

Karin turns and nods. "My first needles were rosewood...my mother's." Sliding the needles into the package, she then turns to check on her daughter before joining Esther near the cotton yarn display.

Moments later the little girl wanders over to Sapphire. "See my dolly?" she beams, holding the toy in front of Sapphire's milky white eyes.

Sapphire squints. "She nice, honey."

"Mutti is making her a dress," the child says. "She promised me."

Sapphire points a shaky finger to the ancient corn cob doll sitting on a high shelf over the cash register. It still wears the calico wrap Ruby had sewn the day before she tried to save Samuel's life. The material is yellowed and tattered, but still it remains, a solitary reminder of a mother's gift of love.

Sapphire nods. "That be my dolly when I was your age."

"What's her name?" the girl asks.

Sapphire chuckles. "She had one a long time ago, but I don't 'member it now."

The girl laughs.

"What be *your* dolly's name?" Sapphire asks.

"Josephine," the girl replies brightly. "After my Grossmutter, my *grandmother*. But I never met her. She died before I was born."

"Hmm," Sapphire says, shaking her head. "I's sorry to hear of it...that be too bad she ain't got to know a nice little lady like you."

"Who're you?" the girl asks, tilting her head.

"I's Sapphire."

"I never heard that name before."

"It be a blue stone...like a jewel."

The girl's eyes brighten. "I'm a jewel, too!"

"You are?" Sapphire asks, the lines around her eyes deepening as she smiles.

"My name's *Ruby*," the girl beams, pointing at herself.

"My land," Sapphire replies, pressing a hand to her heart. "That be my Mama's name."

"Truly?"

Sapphire nods. "Truly."

The girl points to the bright red satin shoes that grace her little feet. "Cousine Helga says I'm a precious jewel just like the ones on those ruby red slippers Dorothy wore in *The Wizard of Oz*...the ones that helped her get back home." Ruby looks at Sapphire. "I wanted the sparkly shoes like in the movie, but Helga says maybe when I'm older."

*Ain't it a miracle?* Sapphire wonders. *Here be this little chile with my mama's name and I hear my daddy's words come right out a her mouth.*

"Is Ruby bothering you?" Karin asks, gently taking her daughter's hand.

"No, ma'am," Sapphire smiles. "We's talking like old friends."

Karin admires Sapphire's work. "That is lovely."

"You a lace maker, too?" Sapphire asks.

Karin nods.

"I's Sapphire."

"I'm Karin," she replies, offering her small hand.

238

Instead of shaking it, Sapphire places the lace in her cool palm.

Tears bead in Karin's eyes. "I don't know if I can...it's been years," she whispers, sitting next to Sapphire. "But I want to keep my promise to Ruby."

As Karin's sleeve slides up her arm, Sapphire sees the tattooed numbers on her skin. *I know what they is*, she thinks. *Yes, suh...I know what this sweet lady done been through.*

"Esther!" Sapphire calls to great-granddaughter. "Why don't you show Miss Ruby 'round to where the kids set and color. Her mama and I's gone have a knitting lesson."

Karin bites her lip and pulls her sleeve to cover the tattoo. "I don't want to be a bother."

"No bother at all," Sapphire says, patting her hand. "You can watch your little one while she color and have a tea party with my Esther."

Sapphire pulls a ball of light yellow yarn from her bag and hands it to Karin. "You want to practice with this?'"

"Yes, thank you," Karin nods. She slowly pulls the needles from their package and makes a slip knot. Then she carefully casts on a few dozen stitches.

"What stitch you gone try today?" Sapphire asks. "I's working feather and fan. It be the only one I can 'member these days."

Karin smiles. "I don't know...maybe I'll try a chevron."

"Girl, you starting out with a tough one all right!" Sapphire exclaims. "You need my help, you jest ask."

For long minutes the only sound in the quiet store is the clicking of Sapphire and Karin's knitting needles. Sapphire moves at a snail's pace while Karin's hands quickly remember the cadence of the yarn overs and slip stitches.

Sapphire watches her work with a strange fascination, as if Karin's hands are working separately from her thoughts. She recognizes her own mother's determination in Karin's rhythmic movements, the way her hands create the fabric while her mind wanders elsewhere...as if making lace is saving her from having to speak, to listen, or to remember.

*Maybe making lace save me, too,* Sapphire wonders to herself. *All the things I done made has saved me from smacking Mr. Rotten when he take my daddy when I was jest a bitty thing. It save me all them years when I done near gone crazy raising my kids.* She rests her hands in her lap and gazes at Ruby, giggling over a coloring book with Esther. *But truly I think it save me from myself when I's so tired a my life, when I cain't take missing my husband and my boys...when I misses 'em so much, it make my heart like to break.*

Karin's needles stop. "Are you alright, Miss Sapphire?"

"Yes'm...I's fine," she smiles. "I's jest thinking 'bout all the things I seen in my life, and all the things I done lived through." Sapphire pauses for a moment before she nods toward Karin's arm, the tattoo covered with her gauzy blouse. "I know what it like to want to be free and you cain't...I 'magine you know all about that, too."

Karin lowers her eyes and nods.

Sapphire sighs deeply. "And even when you is free, there still a part a you that ain't...not really."

Karin's hands drop into her lap, the tiny piece of lace falling from the needles.

"You lost lots a peoples you love?" Sapphire asks gently.

"Everyone."

"Hmm...," Sapphire murmurs. "But you's still here. And your baby girl...she here, too."

Karin smiles sadly, thinking about Bruno and how he would be almost ten years old now. Then she smiles at Ruby, at the miracle of how she was born, how she survived.

Sapphire watches Karin's face and wonders what she's thinking. "You got your mem'ries, too...at least you got them."

Karin presses her lips together as she carefully places the dropped stitches back on the needle.

"It ain't the same, though, is it?" Sapphire asks. "Some a them mem'ries ain't worth holding on to. That why I still be knitting after all a these years. I make lace to 'member my Mama and my sisters and all a them things we done together. Then sometime I pick up my needles so I can forget...so that my mind can jest relax into the rhythm and I don't gotta think about nothing."

Sapphire nods at Karin's hands, which keep working as if separate from her awareness. "I can see you got the gift like I do and my mama and her mama before her. My Jewel got it, too, and I 'magine your baby girl gone have it one day...when you teach her."

Sapphire suddenly remembers Ruby's quiet lesson about the Queen Anne's Lace...how they live and die and then live again. She thinks to herself, *My mem'ries be living and dying and then living once more, too. All the while I set here for years knitting and thinking about all the things I'd rather forget, maybe I need to be like God's lace. Maybe it be a good thing my mem'ries rise and fall jest like the sun. Maybe I's lucky to keep Mama and Daddy and my husband and my sons alive in ever stitch I make. They be something new in God's heaven even though I cain't see 'em yet...jest like ever seed in a Queen Anne's Lace gone be something new someday.*

Karin watches Ruby eagerly choose a new crayon to color the flower she's drawn.

"You ain't got much to say, do you?" Sapphire says sweetly. "I don't mind none...some folks talk jest to hear theyselves." She nods to the delicate lace on Karin's needles. "When our work speak for itself, words ain't nothing."

*Arbeit macht frei*, Karin thinks, remembering the words on the iron clad doors that slammed shut behind her at Auschwitz. *Work makes you free.* Her work there eventually gave her the chance to be sent to Buchenwald instead of the gas chamber. The long, silent hours sitting making lace with Maria and Renatta and Simka gave her the opportunity to live one more day.

And another.

And yet another.

Since Ruby was born, Karin's hands have sewn clothes and baked bread. They've washed dishes and swept the rug. They've typed letters for Helga and smoothed Ruby's forehead when she was sick. They've worked conscientiously in countless ways, but they've not made lace for five long years. Now as Karin watches her fingers manipulate the needles, effortlessly weaving the yarn into a pattern that Mutti had taught her when she was a little girl, for the first time since her mother died, it doesn't feel like work.

It feels like a choice to keep living.

*Mutti...du fehlst mir*, she whispers.

"What you say, honey?" Sapphire asks.

"I was telling my Mutti that I miss her."

Sapphire nods, gently patting Karin's arm. "Ever morning I wake up and watch the sun peeping over the evergreen trees in my backyard. Seem like sunrise be the time I miss my mama most of all. She surely did love the beginning of a new day."

"My Mutti liked sunset," Karin says quietly. "*Dämmerung*. That means twilight."

"Ain't it funny how we all different?" Sapphire asks. "Ain't no two peoples alike, and that be a miracle even though some folks don't want it that way." She nods to the lace in Karin's hands. "You making an original piece of art, jest like you is." She nods at Ruby. "Jest like she be, too. Jest like my Jewel and my boys and all a them folks that done pass in and out a here ever day."

Karin's face softens.

"Some a them ain't never gone know how precious they is...how precious life can be. But we do. We knows how long it take to create something beautiful out a something so ugly, most folks don't want to know nothing about it."

242

Ruby brings her picture to Karin. "Schaust du, Mutti! Schaue auf meine Blume!" She glances at Sapphire and remembers to speak English. "Mother, look at my flower!"

"It's beautiful, Liebling," Karin replies, softly touching the purple tulips. "Is this for Cousin Helga?"

Ruby eagerly shakes her head. "Nein...das ist fur dich!"

"For me?" Karin smiles.

"Yes! To thank you for the pretty dress you're making for my doll."

Karin pats her leg. "Sit here, sweet Ruby. It's time I taught you what Grossmutter taught me when I was a little girl."

Ruby climbs into her mother's lap and awkwardly takes the needles in her tiny hands. Several of the stitches pull free and unravel. "Oh, Mutti," she cries. "Ich brach es."

*Oh, Mother...I broke it.*

"Nein, meine Liebling," Karin says as she gently manipulates Ruby's hands to pick up the lost stitches and place them safely on the needle. "When you're making lace, you might make a mistake sometimes, but you can never break it."

"That sure is true," Sapphire says, winking. "I always tell folks that the best knitters make a lot a mistakes."

"Why's that?" Karin asks.

"'Cause mistakes show us what we need to learn...what we can change and what we cain't," Sapphire smiles. "Ain't none a us ever gone be perfect, but we can always go back, undo what we done, and try one more time."

## Author's Note

While <u>The Lace Makers</u> is a work of fiction, I spent the better part of a year researching the real lives of Civil War era slaves and Holocaust victims. It was a harrowing and life-changing experience, just as writing this novel has been. There are countless names and faces I've encountered who have given me the determination to finish a book that revealed itself to me over time and in a manner unlike anything I have ever experienced.

Along the way, I discovered the work of a heroic photographer, Mendel Grossman, who risked his life to take pictures of the Lodz ghetto in 1940. Eventually he was sent to a prison camp and later died during a forced march, days before the Germans surrendered.

He still had his camera with him.

Grossman's images are haunting. One in particular sat on my desk as I wrote <u>The Lace Makers</u>. The photograph shows a brother sharing food with his little sister...such a simple, yet incredibly profound image. I imagine that neither of the children survived the purging of the Lodz ghetto, so in many ways, I wrote this novel for them and for all of the children who did not survive slavery or the Holocaust.

They have no living legacy, but the stories that remain help keep their memories alive in our hearts.

# Suggested Resources

## Books

<u>To Be a Slave</u> by Julius Lester

<u>Uncle Tom's Cabin</u> by Harriet Beecher Stowe

<u>Growing Up in Slavery: Stories of Young Slaves as Told by Themselves</u> edited by Yuval Taylor

<u>Incidents in the Life of a Slave Girl</u> by Harriet Ann Jacobs

<u>Roots</u> by Alex Haley

<u>Up From Slavery</u> by Booker T. Washington

<u>Slavery and the Making of America</u> by Jimmy Oliver Horton

<u>Remembering: Voices of the Holocaust</u> by Lyn Smith

<u>My Secret Camera: Life in the Lodz Ghetto</u> photographs by Mendel Grossman, text by Frank Dabba Smith

<u>The Auschwitz Report</u> by Premo Levi

<u>The Liberators: America's Witnesses to the Holocaust</u> by Michael Hirsh

<u>Auschwitz: A New History</u> by Laurence Rees

<u>I Never Saw Another Butterfly</u> by Celestre Raspanti and Hana Volavkova

<u>Man's Search for Meaning</u> by Viktor Frankl

# Films

"The Civil War" documentary by Ken Burns

"Twelve Years a Slave"

"Roots"

"Up From Slavery"

"The Color Purple"

"Slavery and the Making of America"

"The War" documentary by Ken Burns

"Schindler's List"

"Night Will Fall" documentary by HBO

"Hitler's Children"

"The Book Thief"

"The Reader"

# Websites

Slavery and the Making of America
http://www.pbs.org/wnet/slavery/resources/index.html

The Civil War
http://www.pbs.org/civilwar

American Slave Narratives
http://xroads.virginia.edu/~HYPER/wpa/wpahome.html

The War
http://www.pbs.org/thewar

Five Million Forgotten
http://remember.org/forgotten

The Shoah Foundation
http://sfi.usc.edu

# Author Biography

Kate Ingersoll has been an award-winning educator for over twenty-five years, first as an elementary school teacher, and now as a hatha yoga instructor for adults and children of all ages.  She also teaches self-awareness and creative knitting workshops.

In addition to The Lace Makers, Kate has also written a memoir, four novels in a literary series, and two compilations of essays from her blog, *Open Road*.  She has also written articles for The Examiner website.

Currently, in-between yoga classes and knitting projects, Kate writes about living and learning in the Heartland at www.katiesopenroad.blogspot.com.

You can learn more about Kate and her work on:
Facebook:  Kate Ingersoll, Writer and Novelist
LinkedIn:   Kate Ingersoll, Spirit to Spirit Consulting Services
Amazon.com:  Kate Ingersoll
Goodreads:  Kate Ingersoll
Pinterest:  Kate Ingersoll

Novels by Kate Ingersoll
Surfacing
Seven Generations
A Tapestry of Truth
Common Threads

Non-fiction by Kate Ingersoll
Open Road:  a life worth waiting for
Open Road:  Year One - The Journey Begins
Open Road:  Year Two - Where My Heart Is

Made in the USA
Charleston, SC
09 March 2016